The Garden of Earthly Delights

long stories

Tasha Haas

February 2020

Editor: Kevin Rabas

Woodley Press
Department of English
Washburn University
1700 SW College Avenue
Topeka, Kansas 66621

ISBN: 978-0-9987003-0-4
Library of Congress Control Number: 2020906531

Cover art: Detail from *Sedation* by Kris Kuksi
Cover design: Eric Sonnakolb
Author photo: Dr. Kat Williams
Text design and layout: Pam LeRow
Graphics: pngtree.com – https://pngtree.com/

"Il Maestro!" was published in *Enduring Puberty Press, Issue 1, Privacy Invades Back,* Fall 2017

Author contact: www.tashahaas.com

"For a while, she wasn't sure her husband was her husband, much as, when you're dozing, you're not sure whether you're thinking or dreaming, whether you're actually in charge of your own thoughts or have completely lost track of them out of sheer exhaustion. Sometimes she thought he was, sometimes not, and at other times, she decided to believe nothing and simply continue living her life with him, or with that man so similar to him . . ."

—Javier Marías, *Berta Isla*

The Garden of Earthly Delights

The First Day

"When are we going to come to the point in our relationship, darling," she said, rolling onto her back and out of my arms, "when we start to hate each other? Not that I'm looking forward to it, don't get me wrong—but, you know, every couple arrives there sooner or later, depressing as it may be. That point when the jealousy and mistrust kick in, the defenses and attacks, the blame and accusations. Until every little thing the other person does is like fingernails on a chalkboard." She sighed and crossed her arms behind her head. "It's probably only a short distance from where we are now to there, let's be realistic—not that I'm not having a great time with you, I am, these last four months have been . . . well, they've been romantic and fun and even beautiful, really. It's just that I can't stop wondering when we're going to go from thinking the other walks on water to scrutinizing each other's faults—and we're both bound to have them—with a magnifying glass."

She had been lying on her back while she spoke, leaving me with only her profile to try to read her emotions on, a one-dimensional cardboard cutout from a stage set, strangely fitting since her words sounded to me like a parody, scripted, something she'd drawn up as a practical joke while I was in the shower. Now she rolled over to face me on the hard-as-concrete hotel bed, her bare breasts squeezing together, making them appear bigger than they were, not that I had any complaints, I was perfectly happy with Tara's breasts, in fact I was perfectly happy with all of her and also with the way our relationship had been going. Naturally, then, her words took me by surprise.

She threw the sheet off. It was hot in the room, the late afternoon light amber on her damp skin. I ran my hand over her belly and down between her soft thighs, holding on.

1

She turned her large, liquid brown eyes on me and added, apologetically, "I don't mean to sound gloomy, darling, it's just that that's what always happens. Right?"

The French doors were open, and outside our room spring had claimed Madrid. The row of potted red geraniums the hotel had put out in a box along the scrolled iron railing in an attempt to distract from its ramshackle (though historically charming) facade glowed in the slanted sunlight. It was an absurdly beautiful day and it was absurd for us to be lounging in bed on our first day in the city but that's what you do when you're in love. It was our first romantic getaway together, five days of nothing but each other. And it's taking a disastrous turn, I thought with a surge of panic.

I met her eyes briefly, then rolled onto my own back. I'd give her a taste of her own medicine, let her try to read my mind with only my profile to inspect. I sighed. "What are you trying to say, Tara?"

She sighed back. "I'm not *trying* to say anything. I'm *saying* it's bound to happen sooner or later and I think we'd better be prepared for it."

"Prepared for it? How do we prepare to start hating each other?"

"I don't know. We talk about it. Which is what I'm trying to do right now."

I pulled the sheet up over my waist. "For god's sake, we just got here."

It was her turn to lean over me, to put her hands on my body, to placate me. I let her. "I know, that's why I wanted to talk about this. We're about to spend five days together, just us. No distractions. No work, no email, no calls to return. No friends, no one but us. It's bound to put some pressure on our relationship."

We'd agreed we'd put our cell phones on vibrate and we wouldn't check our emails. We'd let our clients know they'd have to wait, any urgent business could not be as urgent as love. We'd agreed, too, to eschew the myriad of tourist attractions Madrid has to offer, we'd both been there before and neither of us had any burning interest in Spanish history, Spanish architecture, or Spanish culture unless you counted the food, for food we would make an exception, after all, even lovers have to eat. Nor did either of us speak the language (Tara had studied Japanese for her PhD language and I German for mine), a fact Tara saw as working for us but I saw as working against us since it would make it that much harder to accomplish the mundane daily tasks such as finding our way on the subway or rooting out those hole-in-the-wall restaurants that are the best in any foreign city. Tara insisted the language barrier gave us an advantage—that's how she put it, as if there were some force against us, some unseen enemy or unknown antagonist that had come along with us in our bags—since the purpose of the trip was to shut out the rest of the world and absorb ourselves entirely in one another. The only reason we'd chosen Madrid (other than the discount tickets on Travelocity) was Tara's passion for that weird painting by Hieronymous Bosch, *The Garden of Earthly Delights*, which hangs in the Prado. I'd seen it before but I didn't remember it that well, it hadn't made much of an impression when I was twenty-two and backpacking around Europe the summer after college graduation with my girlfriend, I only remembered it because Carrie had pointed it out as a painting we'd studied in Art History together. She'd made flash cards to study for our final exam and it was the one painting I consistently failed to name on those homemade cards. But Tara had never seen it. When she was backpacking around Europe the summer after college graduation they'd been doing some work on it, they'd been doing some preservation or restoration or whatever it is they do to polish up great masterworks of art and make them appear as vital as the day they were painted. Five summers after I stood before that painting, she planted her own feet there, but she found herself staring at a blank wall instead of a remarkable but not, to me, particularly memorable painting and now she would not let me hear the end of it. "You seriously don't even remember it?" "It's hardly the only masterpiece in the Prado," I defended myself. "That may be, but it's the most fascinating."

Back in New York, she'd shown me *The Garden of Earthly Delights* in the art history coffeetable book she'd finally replaced her college art history textbook with when she started, not that long ago, to make decent money. I had to agree it was an interesting painting. "It stands apart from all those other medieval Christian paintings because it seems to celebrate the pleasures of the flesh. Does this not look like a good time?" She pointed out the naked bodies twisting around each other, fondling and feeding among giant fruits, floating in transparent spheres, sprouting flowers from their heads or asses. "And yet at the same time it condemns them, look at this gruesome scene." It appeared it was so: in the third panel (the painting is a triptych, oil on oak panels, circa 1500, Dutch) the bodies' bare flesh was lanced with elaborate spears and arrows and daggers and fishhook-looking things, inventive instruments of torture. Tara pointed out the gambler impaled on his poker table, playing cards flying, the enormous pair of ears with a knife thrust between them, the sinner being crucified on a harp or the woman eaten by a hairless blue bird with human legs. "It's an enigma," she said, "and a very controversial painting, no one can agree on its true meaning. I find it both beautiful and repulsive, don't you?" I said I did.

We'd go see it, and decide for ourselves what Bosch had intended. The painting would give us a goal, one and only one thing to accomplish in our five days in Madrid. "The rest will all be fun. Fun and sex," Tara had said. "Fun *and* sex." I leaned across the book to kiss her, running my hand up her thigh. "They do go well together."

That's how it had been with us, lots of fun and lots of sex, the last four months since I met Tara at a friend's book signing had been a euphoric blur, that's how it is when you're falling in love, which we were, even though the words—those honeyed or poisoned words that have blessed and ruined so many lives, that is, the words "I love you"—had never been spoken, love—it was obvious—is what it was. I was falling in love with her and I had every reason to think she was falling in love with me, no one does the things Tara did unless they're falling in love, such as taking my hand as we walked down the street without speaking, stroking the back of my neck in the dark in the cinema, getting up early to make coffee and bring it to me in bed, still wearing her negligee, then slipping under the sheets with me and slipping it off. Touching my hair and landing little kisses on my neck, resting her head on my chest, whether clothed or unclothed. Or we'd be sitting at a restaurant having a glass of wine or a coffee and out of the blue she'd say, You know what I like about you? I really like this, or I really like that . . . and you could see she meant it by the shine in her doe eyes. We'd had long evenings sitting on the rooftop terrace of my apartment building watching the sun set and the moon rise through the skyscrapers and the veil of smog, sitting close in metal garden chairs after cooking a gourmet meal together—Thai peanut curry, chicken marsala, softshell clams—and the week before our trip, Spanish dishes we found online. Tara was a fantastic cook and she was educating me in the kitchen, since my divorce and before Tara, I'd lived off frozen Indian curry dinners and bottled pasta sauces. We turned the music up loud—Coltrane, Johnny Cash, The Black Keys, Tara liked all my music—in my apartment and opened all the windows so the music would float up to the rooftop (I live on the top floor, luckily, I like my music loud and I don't like anyone complaining about it) and laughed and talked deep into the night, telling each other about our days and then, as her wine or my Guinness went to work, treading into deeper waters and relating the histories of our dysfunctional families, the devastating moments of our childhoods, the flaws and shortcomings of former lovers and the unjustified and outrageous mistreatment inflicted on us by them. We sat side-by-side looking over the buildings trying to glimpse the stars, fingertips stroking the other's hand absentmindedly or, rather, with feigned absentmindedness when truly our hearts were beating wildly behind the fragile bars of our rib cages, our minds spinning with the thought, I love him, I love her, at last I've found her, this is the woman I'm meant to be with, this is the man I've been waiting for. No, neither one of us had yet mustered the courage to say those holy or terrible words, that is, we hadn't said them aloud yet but our touches and long looks and all the other words we'd spoken added up to them, we were both thinking them while I was waiting for her and she was waiting for me to say them, that's how it goes but it was only a matter of time before one of us couldn't hold back and gave our tidal waves of feeling voice. Probably, I'd thought, it would happen on this trip.

And now things were taking a disastrous turn. "Are you saying you want to break up?"

She emitted a bark of laughter. "Do you think I'd have come on this trip with you if I wanted to break up?"

"Well, you make it sound like it's inevitable."

Neither of us spoke for a few minutes. We lay staring up at the plaster of Paris ceiling with its crown molding of grape leaves rather than at each other (what about all those long nights of foregoing sleep just to gaze into each other's eyes in the near-dark?). The baroque chandelier rocked slightly as footsteps sounded in the room overhead, another couple had checked in and we could hear them chattering happily as they set up house, with each movement the floor creaked and the chandelier jiggled in the plaster, it looked like it could drop at any moment, impaling us with its brass talons as if we were a couple of those sinners in *The Garden of Earthly Delights*. The chandelier had the semblance of one of those centuries-old gold-plated chandeliers complete with ceramic candleholders (now light bulb sockets). If it was the real thing it was a charming touch to the room, if it was a mass-produced replica made in China a few years ago, I didn't want to look too closely at it.

"I'm just being realistic," Tara said at last.

When I said nothing, she went on, striking a diplomatic tone. "Right? I mean, at our age we've both been around the block enough to know no relationship is a walk in the park." Mixing her metaphors, well done. How smart is this woman, really? I thought for the first time, a thought that seemed to come from a voice outside myself and that startled and horrified me. Tara's intelligence was one of the things I liked most about her, she was witty, creative, and well-educated, we both had PhDs and I'd never dated a woman with a degree equal to mine (even if she didn't use hers—Tara had her own business as a portrait photographer and as far as I could tell, it was doing well), it was one of the facts I was constantly citing to myself in support of the idea that this time, this one had a chance at lasting. "Darling, I don't want to break up. But knowing what we know, it's better to be ready for it when it starts."

"When *what* starts? You're going to make it start just by expecting it."

"That's the whole problem—expectations. In the beginning, you build the other person up into an ideal, and even though you tell yourself you want to know everything there is to know about them, really you only want to bury your head in the sand and keep seeing them up there on their pedestal and keep feeling that woozy, buzzy feeling the first stage of any romance is famous for"—was it just my imagination, or was she avoiding the word "love" like the plague?—"and then the infatuation wears off and you start to see who your lover *really* is—with all their flaws and insecurities, their addictions and bad habits, their annoying little gestures like picking their toenails or sucking their teeth, farting or snoring, well, you know, the things that give us away as human, and that shatter all your expectations in the meantime."

I rubbed my hands over my face. "I see. Are there things about me that don't live up to your expectations? Are you starting to see them, is that it?"

"I'm speaking theoretically, dear."

"Do I snore? Is that it?"

"You don't snore."

I tried to keep the irritation out of my voice, at least I think I did. "All right. So what do you want me to do?"

She didn't bother keeping it out of hers. "If it's that much trouble you can start by fucking off."

I threw the sheet off and sat up, unsticking my skin from hers in the process. "Tara, listen, I'm sorry. Don't get upset. I'm serious—what do you want me to do?" I looked over my shoulder at her, met her eyes. Were those tears welling up, or was it just my imagination? She turned her face away.

I moved closer, put my hand on her bare belly, leaned over her. "Tell me what to do and I'll do it. I really want this to work, you know . . . I really . . . like you."

She rolled her head back and met my eyes. No. It was just my imagination. "I like you too."

A little curl of a smile starting on her lips. She trailed her fingers down my arm. "I don't want you to do anything. I just needed to talk about it. I'm just afraid of things changing between us."

I came down beside her and drew her to me, enclosing her in my arms. Her hair in my face. The smell of her lotion on her neck. Her soft breath coming and going on my skin. "Things *are* going to change between us. They're going to get even better."

We lay there a few minutes, breathing together, the room too warm to be so close. Then Tara rolled away, laughing. As suddenly as that doom and gloom mood had struck her, it lifted. "God, what about that—what was it—Fernando? What was his problem? I mean, did we really deserve that?"

The loony old man who had insulted us at the café that morning. Of course! I thought. That's what brought all this on, women are so sensitive, they can't stand to have their feelings hurt and maybe she's getting ready to have her period on top of it, I hope not, that could put a dent in our trip.

We'd been sitting innocently enough (at least, in our eyes we were innocent) in a café, starving after being on the plane all night but not so much for food as for coffee or rather, decent coffee—what the airline served was a step above brown water—and after checking into our room, we'd gone straight out to the first café. Which, to our delight, was a little hole-in-the-wall full of locals, free-flowing Spanish, and cigar smoke (which I can't stand but put up with for the nostalgic quality of the place) and only a tourist or two in the shadows and even more to our delight, served unbelievably strong espresso, even for professional coffee drinkers like us. Tara and I were the type of people who drank our coffee black and drank it throughout the day—and we weren't about to have it con leche (though in Spain that meant constantly befuddling the waiters), we had this in common too and I considered it one of the cornerstones of our relationship. Now, looking back, that's laughable, it's hardly enough to base a relationship on and, honestly, there are thousands of women in New York with PhDs.

We were sitting inside at a rickety wooden table by the window sipping the motor-oil coffee and talking about whether we should go straight to the Prado today, to get it out of the way so it wasn't hanging over our heads all week, *The Garden of Earthly Delights* hanging in the Prado and hanging over our heads, that single simple duty we'd set for ourselves had the potential to preoccupy us and ruin our undiluted devotion to each other this week and so we agreed to get it over with on the first day. As soon as we'd had our second cup.

He was sitting alone at the bar with his back to us, seats empty on either side of him. That should have been our first clue. Fernando—not that we knew his name at that point. I noticed him right away because of his red coat which stood out among the blacks and browns and grays the other men wore, bland hues which matched their hair and faces. The place held mostly old men, sitting alone or clustered at tables reading the newspaper (it was charming to see old-fashioned newspapers, all you see in New York is phones) and drinking coffee and smoking cigars and talking. Fernando was a bulky man, his shoulders hunched up around his ears, curly hair under a black wool cap, nothing or no one out of the ordinary but for the faded red coat he wore over his shoulders without, I saw when he rotated on his stool, bothering to poke his arms through the sleeves, the end result being it resembled a cape. Not only was it weird to wear a wool coat in that weather—it was seventy degrees at mid-morning and warming up— the threadbare coat was covered in military medals, so many there was hardly a bare spot left. He was talking to the barista or perhaps to himself, grumbling, in such a low voice I suspected that even if I'd spoken Spanish, I wouldn't have been able to make out what he was saying.

At one point I looked up from my coffee to find him glaring at me. He'd pivoted on the barstool and looked about ready to spring off it.

As soon as my eyes met his, it was like something clicked into gear in him.

"*Americanos!*" he spat as if the word were the vilest filth—raw sewage, a pus-filled boil, beer vomit. And then he lurched off the stool.

All eyes turned on us.

Beneath the clanking medals his shirt was unbuttoned, showing a tangled forest of black chest hair. While his clothes appeared well-made, even, once upon a time, expensive, now the dark trousers were shiny on the knees and the hems bedraggled. A bum, I thought, loco as the day is long. I rolled my eyes at Tara, murmured, "Ignore him. He'll go away."

Tara's eyes expanded. The large man with a jet-black coiled bullfighter's mustache and matching bushy eyebrows that were jumping up and down as if not quite attached to his face rocked between the little tables, which were already precarious on their uneven wooden legs, clattering an aban- doned cup and saucer on one table as he passed it, dangerously close to shattering another to pieces on the tile—he didn't care, the man had a singular mission and he was possessed by it. The barista said something to him from behind the bar but he kept coming. Then stopped, blessedly, six feet from us. As if he couldn't bear to be within range of our Americano stench.

He stood looking down on us, ranting in Spanish. We couldn't understand anything, of course—he didn't seem to realize this or he didn't care, his words weren't for our ears but for his own or those of the men in the bar watching coolly, bemusedly, putting down their newspapers and leaning back in their chairs, lighting up fresh cigars to go with the show. Really, it wasn't fair—since we had no idea what he was saying, we couldn't defend ourselves. Well, we had some idea . . . naturally we were aware there was plenty of anti-American sentiment going around, not just in the Middle East but across the globe and intensifying since the Bush administration and the Iraq disaster, Obama hadn't helped much, not to mention our relationships with Afghanistan and North Korea, Syria and Sudan, Russia and Iran, and most of the rest of the world but we didn't expect it to be that vehement or that, well . . . personal.

Spanish spit flew. His extravagant mustache caught some of it, not all, the rest arced out over the tables and sent a delicate spray onto the surface of our coffees. Tara had her head down under the onslaught, his words pelting her.

"Oh god," she said. "What should we do?" Now he was shouting something, then pausing, as if awaiting an answer. "I think he's asking if we speak Spanish."

I stared into my coffee, said, "Tell him no. Tell him we're Canadian."

She narrowed her eyes, a look that said 'you're an idiot,' I knew how to read it. She took a breath and raised her head, opened her mouth to say something to him but before she could the barista spoke.

"He wants to know what you're doing in his country." He said it in perfect English, factually and not apologetically, then went back to wiping glasses with his apron. Silence. The crazy guy glared at us, fingers stroking the tails of his mustache as if sharpening a weapon. Every ear in the bar awaited our reply.

Our eyes locked, Tara's and mine, looking for an answer in each other's gaze. What *were* we doing in his country? Fucking, eating, sleeping, none of which were a good reason to be there . . . Our immediate reaction— we both had the same one, we later admitted—was to shrink into our chairs, apparently so guilt-riddled about our unfortunate nationality it took a minute or five minutes for it to occur to us we hadn't done anything wrong, the man was being incredibly rude and we had a perfect right to be in his country, in fact we were doing it a favor, contributing to the economy as well as doing our part as global citizens, educating ourselves on another culture . . . at least, as far as he knew we were.

I glanced uncertainly at the barista. He raised his eyebrows and smiled. He'd put his glasses away and was leaning against the bar drinking his own coffee.

Tara kicked me under the table. She hissed, "Do something."

"We're, uh, we're admiring your beautiful country." I gestured feebly around the café as if it represented the whole of Spain.

The barista translated, which drew an irreverent snort. Then, Fernando said something we could understand. A single word in heavily accented English: "Selfish!" And again and again: "Selfish! Selfish! Selfish! Selfish! Selfish! Selfish! Selfish! Selfish!"

Did he even know what the word meant? Where had he picked it up? And why was he attacking us?

"*Tranquilo,*" the barista interrupted finally, if half-heartedly. And kicked him out, he went out wringing his large knuckles in the air, fingers heavy with large silver rings. He stopped in the window and shook the flap of his coat at us, the medals flashing, communicating something through the glass that wouldn't have been any more effective without the glass. A war veteran, I thought, schizophrenic, delusional, don't take it personally, don't let it get to you, even though the whole bar had now turned hostile gazes on us.

"It is Fernando," the barista said when he approached to clear a nearby table, meaning "he" rather than "it." "He does not love America." How observant, I thought, though at least he'd said America and not Americans. The young man had clearly gotten a kick out of the incident, he could have kicked him out a lot sooner. He could have been Fernando's son, with his identical handlebar mustache and coils of chest hair springing from his rounded, feminine collar.

A man at the end of the bar said in a clipped English accent, "The eternal Fernando, purging Madrid of tourists. Let's hope his efforts don't hurt the economy, God knows we can't afford it."

The man next to him, also British, chuckled. "Of Americans, you mean. I say let him, we've got more than enough. They're a bloody plague." He looked over his shoulder at us, not in a friendly way. Even the ex-pats hated us.

Indeed, at that moment a flock of elderly Americans—a bus tour, probably, organized by a travel agency—trotted by in bright windbreakers, the men in knit trousers and white tennis shoes, the women gripping rhinestoned handbags for dear life, fanny packs and digital cameras general across the group. They squawked Midwestern English loud enough to disturb the whole block. But . . . we weren't like that!

The men switched to Spanish, no doubt so they, too, could insult us freely. A café-wide discussion of our revolting persons or our country's abominable behavior or some combination of both was in full swing when we left. The barista called after us—ironically or not, I couldn't be sure, was that a mocking twinkle in his eye?—"Welcome to Madrid!"

On the sidewalk we didn't discuss what to do and we didn't talk about what had just happened. Our steps simply turned in the direction of the hotel, we weren't in the mood for *The Garden of Earthly Delights,* not now, not any more. We hurried along, not touching as we walked, feeling like open targets. Back at the hotel, we did what distressed lovers do, we comforted ourselves with sex.

"No," I told Tara now. "We didn't deserve that."

She drew in a deep breath, her breasts rising as she did so, breasts that were still new to me and still drew my eyes like magnets. Suddenly self-conscious as if she were reading my mind, she brought her arms across her chest, covering them. The humid May heat made the air hang heavily and seem to clutch at the walls, the furniture, that ambiguous chandelier.

"I hope not." Her dark hair was damp and tousled from our romp. "The last thing I want to be when I travel is the ugly American."

"How did he even know? It's not like we're wearing fluorescent jogging suits." In fact, I thought Tara and I looked more European than American with our black jeans and leather jackets, her French-style wraparound scarf and my Gucci sunglasses. "The guy was obviously loco—see, I know some Spanish. That coat, in this weather."

Tara considered this, putting a finger to her lips. "I don't know . . . he seemed pretty lucid to me. I think he was just mean. Not that there aren't plenty of reasons to despise Americans. I despise them myself. But to personally attack them when they're guests in your own country. What an asshole. I don't want to talk about it."

"Come on, he was schizophrenic or something. Didn't you see all those military pins? And those missing teeth? He's probably a vet who went crazy in the revolution."

"You mean the civil war? Wasn't that in the forties? The guy would have been a babe, if he was even born yet."

"Well, I mean, around then—" I said, trying to conceal my poor grasp of Spanish history.

But Tara said, "Or was it the fifties? I'm not very good with history . . ."

"Err . . ." I tried to think, men are supposed to know something about history or at least be interested in it, neither applies to me.

She swatted a ringless hand at the air. "Whatever. And what did he mean by 'selfish'? Why did he keep saying that?"

I rolled my eyes. "I have no idea. We clearly didn't deserve that. He doesn't even know us."

"I know. So rude. I don't get why you're defending him."

"I'm not defending him! I'm just saying it's obvious he has mental problems."

She half-rose on her elbows. "He knew what he was saying! Ever since Bush, Americans have a shit reputation—"

I guffawed. "It hardly started with Bush. I thought you didn't want to talk about it."

"You always have to be right, don't you? You always have to have the last word." Her voice had hardened.

"What? No." I gave a nervous laugh. Probably it was true, it was something women had accused me of before.

She flopped back down on her back, smiling. Tara can change moods like the weather, it's something most women do but her shifts could be particularly sudden, it put me on edge. "Oh well, I don't mind. It's kind of sweet, in a childish way."

I shrugged, not taking the bait.

"So tomorrow we'll go to the Prado. First thing."

"Si si, first thing."

"Tonight let's stay in bed and order tapas from room service and watch old black-and-white movies on television."

"Okay. But first kiss me and tell me you're sorry for before."

She kissed me, but she didn't say she was sorry, I let it go, pleased with myself for doing so. It turned out to be a perfect night, neither our little discussion nor the loco or simply cruel Fernando put a dent in it after all. The hotel, we discovered, didn't have a restaurant so I had to go out in the spring rain in my athletic pants (yes, nylon but not fluorescent) to fetch tapas from the bistro around the corner, passing the café where we'd been insulted that morning, its windows now dark. The tapas were microscopic and greasy and left us hungry and the movies were all in Spanish but it didn't matter. We weren't paying much attention anyway, nothing else mattered: we were in love.

The Second Day

To wake in a foreign city—it doesn't matter which city—your body pressed against your lover's, the parallel lines of the pink dawn seeping through the shutters, the sounds of morning greetings in a language you don't understand, of car doors slamming and metal grates being rolled up as the shops below open for the day—it's romantic, and I'm a romantic guy at heart. That's what none of the women in my past have ever given me credit for, the women I've dated, loved and liked and slept with have all been (until now, until Tara) so cynical and embittered they couldn't believe I am who I say I am: a sensitive guy who likes moonlight and candles and who all he wants to do is fall in love and settle down with the right woman. Maybe even have a kid. That, I always thought, wasn't fair. But Tara didn't do that to me, Tara liked my romantic side.

It had rained all night and the morning was cloudy and misty. This fact conspired with our own laziness to keep us rolling around in bed alternating sex and snoozing, telling ourselves we were waiting for the sun to come out, what was the point in getting out of bed when it could start pouring down again at any minute. Finally hunger drove us from the sheets and into showers (lukewarm, the fixtures coated with a mixture of mold and rust). We moved about the room laughing and joking, still shy about flossing and dressing in front of each other, it's one thing to slip back into your clothes after sex in front of your lover and another to pull your pants on over your socks in the morning like an old man. On our way out we met the couple in the room above us in the hallway, we were trading places—they'd already had their cappuccinos and croissants and were on the way back to bed while we were just on our way out. They were American or perhaps Canadian, and they were still chattering as happily as they had been the day before, holding hands and walking close together, we exchanged smiles with a secret knowledge as we grazed Gore-tex in passing. It was good to be in love.

We left the hotel and walked in the opposite direction as we had the day before, not wanting to run the risk of being spotted by Fernando, particularly since we were wearing our rain jackets, Tara's a bright pink Patagonia and mine a yellow and black North Face, brutally American—we couldn't help it, even if it wasn't raining, the skies were dim and threatening and it could start at any time. We had to find some breakfast or rather, lunch, we were both starving and after that it would be straight to the Prado, after that, we agreed, nothing could keep us from *The Garden of Earthly Delights*.

The cracked sidewalks were full of oily puddles and stinking mounds of trash were piled head-high on the curbs, some so large they threatened to block our way and we had to jump across the filth in the streaming gutters to get around them, we'd caught Madrid during a garbage collectors' strike, it happens all the time in Europe and I couldn't say I blamed them, I've always thought garbage collectors should be paid more than lawyers.

It was a damp and chilly May day but when you're in love every minor inconvenience and even the monstrous chronic impossible curses of your life seem irrelevant, even these eclipsed by the sheer amazing fact of the existence of the beloved and the obsessive rejoicing in the incredible good luck you've had to find this singular miraculous person who is, in fact, better than anyone you could ever have imagined and what's even more amazing is that they want you too.

We ended up in the famous Plaza Mayor, where we had potato omelettes and cold chorizo and dry pastries and very strong black café Americano at a touristy, overpriced restaurant (the least likely place for Fernando in his jangling red coat and the likes of him, if there were more of him, that is, American-hating Spaniards, no doubt there were), sitting outside on the stone patio because inside was full, huddled against the wall with the rain dripping from the plastic awning and landing inches from our plates and sometimes in them. The coffee was good and hot and we had one cup, two cups, three and it was nice to sit there talking, nice that the rain had started again and gave us an excuse to linger. We talked not about the impressive architecture or the frescoes or the monuments or the people surrounding us, but about things we could just as well have talked about back in New York as in Madrid: our pasts, our wild college days and my first marriage and Tara's last relationship, then we got on the subject of books, and from there films, those we liked and those that never should have been made. Tara and I got along so well and there was never any shortage of things to talk about. She would toy with her camera when some poor beggar child would come by, or a man with only one arm or paperbag-faced old women selling vegetables or wooden rosaries from carts, taking it out of her bag and then putting it back, resisting the urge to snap a photo, to *consume* the images and with them, the people, because we weren't the typical Americans and we could appreciate something without having to own it. Caffeine puts me in a wonderful mood and I sat there admiring her more and more with each sip. Tara had huge brown eyes, eyes like the Disney rendition of Bambi (had I ever seen a real deer? I wasn't sure), framed by magnificent dark brows, brows like an opera singer that curve over her entire eye and frame her lush black lashes. Tara had a wide, innocent face, a small mouth but full lips and sometimes, if she smiled just the right sort of smile, dimples appeared in her cheeks. She wore her chin-length dark hair in a flipped-out bob, countering her dollish face with the sexy cut. It swayed around her face as she dug in her bag (Tara was no different than every woman I know when it came to digging in her bag, which is to say she was always furtively doing so, like an OCD mole or groundhog). I've always told myself when I find a woman whose face I could never get tired of looking at (and it wasn't Amanda, what a disaster, I don't even find her attractive anymore), I'll stay with her forever and watching Tara then I thought, it's her, I'll never grow weary of that face, that hair, those eyes, those lips, it's her, it's her, it's her.

Still, I couldn't help but notice . . . Madrid was teeming with beautiful women. As the skies cleared and the sun came out they too seemed to come out of the woodwork. The word "sexy" must have been created for Spanish women, I thought stupidly, of course, there are some dumpy ones just as there are, no doubt, in every country, but the vast majority, my god . . . Women in flared skirts stepped into the square, perfectly balanced on heels a mile high, their glossy hair loose on their shoulders or flowing down their backs. They walked elegantly, swaying their hips and chatting and laughing as if they hadn't a care in the world—and certainly the young girls wouldn't have, other than their infinite boredom, they didn't care that twenty percent of the population was unemployed—their glittering black mascaraed eyes flitting the square looking for something to do or rather, someone, a man to spend the afternoon with, I fantasized, for a romantic interlude with a foreigner like myself in a cool darkened hotel room, not unlike our own of the day before. They didn't look like prostitutes but they could have been, in America they would have been thought for hire, not so much for the way they were dressed but the way they were letting it all hang out—their breasts, their red-lipsticked lips, their shapely legs and the seductive looks on their faces, they weren't hiding their sexuality like American women tended to and they didn't look away when you locked eyes with them. Not that I was interested in locking eyes with anyone but Tara.

She finally extracted what she'd been looking for in her bag, a map of Madrid she'd gotten at the airport, and unfolded it on the table. "It doesn't look that far," she said. "Should we walk? We have our jackets."

"Huh? Where?"

She stared at me. "To the Prado. What are you doing? Are you gawking at other women?"

"You're crazy. I was just . . ." *How do women know?*

"Whatever. Let's walk, okay? That way we can see more of the city. And we can always hop on a bus if we run short on time. It closes at four, remember."

I pushed my chair back. "Let's do it."

She looked at her watch. "Anyway we just need a few minutes at the Prado. *The Garden of Earthly Delights* is the only thing I give a fig about seeing."

She had stood and was digging in her bag again. She suddenly looked adorable. I reached for her. "You don't give a fig about much, do you? You're a fig-less quirky girl and I . . ."

The three words were tottering on the tip of my tongue, about to escape. I gulped them down. That's how it will be, I thought, when I or she says them, unrehearsed, an impromptu, natural moment when our feelings for each other refuse to be held back any longer. I thought she'd sense this, what had been about to come out of my mouth, and press me: "What? What were you about to say? Go on." But instead she said, murmuring, still rooting in the jumbled chaos of her handbag, "Woman."

"What? Oh, right. A quirky *woman*," I corrected. "And I do like quirky women."

"Good boy." Tara preferred to be called a woman rather than a girl, she'd let me know it before, though she reserved the right to call me a boy.

"*What* are you looking for?"

"I'm looking for the map. Oh, I want to buy a Spanish-English dictionary. It will help us get around."

"You're also very practical," I said appraisingly. "You're *pragmatic.*" I stressed the word, surprising myself, it came out with a bite.

"What's wrong with being practical?" she said without looking up from the black hole of a bag.

"Nothing. A lot of people are. Hey, it's right here." The map was in her chair, where she'd put it less than a minute ago. I handed it to her without folding it. I could have folded it, that's true. She didn't take it, she just looked at me.

"Don't you want to navigate?" I said.

"Fine." She snatched the map and walked off, bag swinging, map flapping. I grabbed my rain jacket and ran to catch up.

"Sorry. Here, let me fold it."

She raised her extravagant eyebrows. "I'm pragmatic, am I?"

Not about the folding.

"Well, I mean . . . all that stuff yesterday about 'when are we going to come to the point in our relationship.' All that 'let's be ready when we start to hate each other' and such." I really didn't mean it to come out as snarky as it did. But once words make their way out you can't stuff them back in. I tried to change the subject, in vain, of course—women never let the subject be changed unless they do it themselves. "Are we going in the right direction?"

She let out an enormous sigh, she was a master or rather, mistress, of the dramatic sigh. "I told you, dear," she said in just the sort of tone my mother used with me when I was five years old, "I just wanted to talk about it. It's a preventive strategy, that's all. Why are you making such a big deal out of it?"

"Preventive? Preventive or preemptive? It seems to me like a fantastic way to sabotage our relationship. Over-analyzing things, expecting the worst."

"I think it's you who's expecting the worst. It's like you're terrified I'm going to break up with you. Jesus, calm down."

Just then she stopped and looked up at the clock tower, checking the time, and for an instant her profile was silhouetted against the blue sky with the spires behind it, and I saw how her upper lip protruded slightly beyond her bottom lip, that is, her bottom lip receded and her chin continued the line, just a bit but, yes, Tara had an overbite. I'd never noticed it before and it was, frankly, not that attractive.

I smiled cruelly. "Don't worry, Tara. I'm calm. I really am. I'm *fine*."

To prove it, I started walking back to the hotel alone.

We didn't make it to *The Garden of Earthly Delights* that day. Nor did I walk all the way back to the hotel, I only wandered up the street a bit, wolfed down a packet of greasy churros and downed a piss-colored and flavorless bottle of beer from a kiosk, then turned around and went after her. By the time I found her standing in front of an old-fashioned dress-maker's shop—the mannequins in the windows were being changed, clad in tailored cotton dresses that looked like something June Cleaver would wear—it was well after four and the doors of the Prado shut tight. Tara said she wanted to wear a dress like that but I couldn't imagine anything less sexy and I told her so, too. We walked back unspeaking to the hotel and had a quiet—no, sullen is a better word—dinner of fish and rice from a street cart sitting on a bench outside our hotel and then went inside and made up by listlessly making love and apologizing sleepily afterward. Then Tara turned on the tv and watched a black-and-white movie in Spanish and I fell asleep.

The Third Day

We were out early the following morning, feeling industrious as we approached the grand facade of the museum that housed one of the world's finest collections of art. This time it wasn't our fault we didn't manage to see the Bosch. The doors were tightly sealed and the surrounding gardens deserted. We were mystified. It said very clearly in the guidebook and at the ticket office that the Museo del Prado was open on Fridays. We counted the days on our fingers, laughing about how lost we were without our smartphones, which we had not turned on since we left the airport, and it really hadn't been that hard.

It turned out to be Friday indeed, but it was also May 1st, Workers' Day in Spain and a national holiday, equivalent to the United States' Labor Day. This we learned by consulting an elegantly dressed elderly couple who were strolling arm-in-arm down the avenue near the museum and who explained the holiday to us in strongly—and charmingly—accented but grammatically perfect English. The man wore a silk suit and tie and the woman a fur collar and pearls and heels, next to them we looked like slobs.

We went off scowling, feeling ugly and terribly inconvenienced. In the Plaza Mayor, I stopped before a bakery window. "Let's have a pastry," I said, pointing at some sugar-crusted buttery tubes. The shopgirl told us—also in flawless English—they were "saints' bones," a traditional pastry unique to Spain, she even translated it for us, that is, *huesos de santo*, guessing we would find the Spanish quaint, which, honestly, we did and then bought a box of them to take home to our friends, to whom we would repeat the Spanish name, butchering it in our clumsy accents. We dipped our bones in hot chocolate in tiny porcelain gold-rimmed cups that looked two hundred years old (but probably were not, probably were made in China by children last year) standing at the bar on the cobblestoned patio. Watching her lick her small fingers like a girl, a beautiful girl, her pink mouth on French-manicured nails, I thought, I can live with that overbite, and the moodiness, too.

"We're in danger of becoming tourists," I said, looking about the posh bakery full of neon jackets and tennis shoes. It was eleven-thirty already. I caught Tara's eye, smiled. "We should go back to the hotel."

She smiled back. "We *are* workers. Don't we deserve a holiday too?"

"We do. Let's declare today Global Workers' Day."

"Let's do." Outside, I rotated Tara by the shoulders in the direction of the hotel, and whispered in her ear, "Get a bottle of wine, pull the shutters. We haven't taken a bath together yet, we could take a bath together."

She started to smile—I know it, I saw her—then she stopped herself, turned to face me. "Seriously, D—, we can't avoid all our problems with sex."

(I don't want to reveal my name, it's a personal enough story as it is, I hope you understand.)

"Why not?"

"Seriously."

I took her hands. "Seriously. We have problems now, do we?"

She shrugged, looked down the street, avoiding my eyes. A woman on heels walking a standard poodle, a man—at first I thought it was Fernando—picking through an enormous garbage pile. "I was so pissed at you yesterday."

"Why? What did I do?"

"You were being an asshole. 'Oh, you're so pragmatic, blah blah blah,' like I'm a stuffy old spinster. When you were sitting there drooling over Spanish teenagers!"

I put my arms around her. "Hey, I wasn't. You're the only woman I drool over. I'm sorry. You're right. I was being an asshole. I'm sorry."

One thing men learn early on, from their mothers, their sisters, their first girlfriends, I guess, is just to say it. Whatever they want to hear. Even if no part of you believes it, just say it. I said it and pulled her close, loving the way we fit—her chin in my collarbone, her nose in the curve of my neck, her heart inside her body beneath her clothes beneath my hands.

Despite our intentions not to be tourists, we wandered into a little museum on the walk back. It was in our way—Madrid, like most European cities, is full of museums great and small and anyway I didn't want Tara to think I was too eager to get back and try to solve all our problems with sex, so I suggested we have pity on the little furniture museum and check it out, after all it was probably desperate for visitors since it had stayed open on the holiday, perhaps that was the only way it could get any patrons in a city it shared with the Museo del Prado. Sure enough, it wasn't much—seventeenth-century furniture, rugs and flowered tea sets and vases. We didn't stay long, long enough for Tara to use the baño and for us to get lost from each other briefly, perhaps intentionally, naturally we needed a break from each other, it's hard to be with anyone twenty-four hours a day and even harder when you're trying to be your most charming and funny and interesting and desirable self under the unrelenting scrutiny of the other.

I ambled down the long marble hallways, stopping before roped-off exhibits but not really seeing them, the image of Tara was in the way. There's nothing like making up after an argument to make the heart grow fonder, to shore up the waves of passion, when you get through an argument together you feel like you've accomplished something and you have, you've mended something broken and made it stronger and it bodes well for the rest of the relationship and that's what I was feeling now, it gave me hope. Around every corner I kept anticipating running into Tara, how her face would change when she saw me, how it would light up.

Tara dresses more like a European woman than an American one (that is, cargo shorts or blue jeans, baggy sweatshirts that do nothing for the figure), today she was wearing black skinny jeans and a low-cut red silk tank top. Though she wasn't wearing heels, she wore them at home when we went out and I couldn't blame her for not wanting to click around the cracked sidewalks in them, she had brought one pair, she'd shown them to me and these she was reserving for going out to dinner (which we hadn't managed to do yet, not once). Today she was wearing flat sandals, not as sexy as heels but suitable for all the walking we were doing and better than the glaring white Nikes with neon laces or enormous hiking boots worn by the tourists and backpacking students who had also opted for that second-tier museum and whose singular aim was to stuff every piece of art in every museum in Madrid into their eyes, there are a lot of people like that and while I wasn't one of them when I was a backpacking student, my girlfriend was and forced me to stand with her before every piece of art in western Europe for at least three minutes in order, she said, to fully appreciate it. This was before cell phones and I still remember staring at her inclined profile while she stared at her watch, the second hand of which she spent more time looking at than the art. Tara's beautiful, she has style, I thought, watching the other, dumpy American women ambling about, she has class, unlike them and it really isn't fair how Fernando treated us, I wonder how he knew we were American, I wonder what tipped him off, is there some greedy or egotistical or over-advertised look on our faces we're not aware of and that we can't escape despite our efforts to rise above and beyond the vulgar, no-holds-barred consumer-capitalist culture our country so delights in? I cruised through a gallery of ceramics at the other end of which was Tara examining a teacup, though I didn't see her at first or rather, I saw her but I didn't recognize her at first glance since at first glance she looked just like any other American woman, that is, she didn't line up with the image in my head, the fantasy in my head. There was nothing unusual or interesting about Tara when my eyes first skipped over her at the end of the gallery nor anything particularly attractive about her in her flat shoes and too-tight jeans and awkwardly fitting bright top through which you could see the lines of her bra when my eyes returned to rest on her and for a split second, I thought, Why am I so crazy about this woman? Just then she looked up as if sensing my thoughts of betrayal, and her old face, the pretty face I knew, slipped back into place. She smiled and came toward me.

Madrid, like most European cities, is made up of winding and unpredictable streets, a maze of curves and forks that spiral into each other only to end in dead-ends or cul-de-sacs or to turn into other streets with no warning or identifying street sign until you're well down the other street and then it's too late, you can't recall what the last street was and it's even harder in a foreign language. As well as plenty of streets that have no names at all, that no one's bothered or been inspired enough to name, having run out of revolutionary heroes and military generals and botanical subjects to name them after. That would never happen in the States, where it would be an unforgivable laziness to let a street go unnamed, and where someone, no doubt, would be fined for such laziness. Which is all to say that after leaving the museum we headed back to the hotel or what we thought was back to the hotel but after we'd walked for a long time, who knows how long, I wasn't really paying attention since Tara was navigating or supposed to be navigating with her old-fashioned paper map and I was telling her stories of the stupid things I'd done in college, we found ourselves on one of those nameless calles, utterly lost. Unconcerned, we walked a few more blocks in the sunshine, holding hands and looking at the red and pink and purple blooms spilling from vines over iron balconies, the tall stone buildings, laundry hung on lines high in the air between them, the sounds and smells of dinner being cooked behind open windows. It wasn't unpleasant being lost, the sidewalks were deserted and it was as if the city had given them over to us, perhaps everyone was at home in front of the tv with their feet up, taking the holiday to heart. Somehow we got on the subject of our exes again, Tara and I enjoyed talking about our exes and how horribly they'd treated us, how they didn't hold a candle to each other. I found the following coming out of my mouth:

"But Amanda was really sensitive"—I silently wished back that "but," which made the quality sound like a good thing and you *never* point out your ex's good qualities to your current lover. "She called it 'intuitive.' Like, she could tell what kind of mood I was in as soon as I walked in the door, it was crazy."

"Interesting." This I was pretty sure was sarcastic, but I couldn't pin her on it. "And was that a good thing?"

I shrugged. "No, no. It was a good thing in the beginning. Later it felt like an intrusion. The way she could read my feelings just by looking at my face." Tara looked worried. "Also sometimes she would accuse me of feeling things I wasn't feeling, that was annoying."

Really Amanda hadn't done much of that, but she could have, it would have been like her. I sensed I'd wandered into dangerous territory. All Tara said was, "Hmmm."

We walked along in silence. She stopped in the middle of the sidewalk and dropped my hand to look at the map (ostensibly).

Finally she looked up. "So what changed?"

"What do you mean?"

"What changed in your relationship that changed it from a good thing to a bad thing? I mean, you must have been pretty connected if she could sense what you were feeling like that. What made it become an intrusion?" She waited, watching me. It was like an exam question, to which there was only one right answer, and a number of wrong ones.

"It? The relationship or her sensitivity? What do you mean?" I was hedging, I really didn't want to get into it today, for one thing, I was starving. And my feet ached from all the walking.

But Tara was onto me. She, too, had razor insight, it's unnerving how women can see right through me, can pin me into a corner with their X-ray eyes, I always feel like there's no refuge, no private place to go when I'm in a relationship and the further along it goes, the more I feel that way.

She rolled her eyes.

"Whatever. Both. What changed between you two?"

I thought. What did she want to hear? Fuck it. What was the truth? But I didn't know. "I have no idea," I said helplessly. "It just . . . changed, you know, the way things do."

She pounced, grabbing me with both arms. "Aha! That's what I was trying to tell you the other day. *That's* what I was talking about, how love can suddenly morph into hate. You *do* know what I'm talking about, then. Don't try to deny it."

I considered this, trying to remain calm. I shook free of her hands, took off my sunglasses and cleaned them carefully on my shirt. "So every relationship that ends ends for the same reasons?"

"That's not what I'm saying. I'm saying that we all have issues that can wreak havoc on our relationships and we're not always aware of them."

"Oh *that's* what you're saying," I said sarcastically. "Well, that's not at all what you said the other day and it's like nothing you've said so far. You've said a lot of things on this trip, Tara, that you haven't actually said."

"What does it matter what I said before? What I'm trying to get you to see is that if we don't work on our issues, they'll come back to haunt us. It's the story of my relationships, and it's probably the story of yours, too, whether you know it or not."

She was sounding more and more like a therapist and it was rubbing me the wrong way. "So what *issues* have you decided I need to work on?"

She pressed my forearm. "Don't be so defensive. I haven't *decided* anything, I'm only saying—"

"No, come on. What issues do you think I have?"

She shook her head. "I can't say."

"Well, if you had to take a guess. Which I'm guessing you already have."

26

"Honestly, D—, we don't know each other that well yet. I can't know what your particular issues are." I crossed my arms and nodded for her to go on. She threw up her hands. "I don't know . . . maybe fear of intimacy. For most men that's a big one. Or fear of commitment, of responsibility, of growing up. Most men prefer to stay boys to having to grow up and become men, at least the ones I meet do."

Her generalization infuriated me. I hate it when women lump all men together, nailing our worst qualities with blunt accuracy. Also there was her hypocrisy. I'd rather not have, but I did—I exploded. "So *I'm* afraid of intimacy? I'm not the one who forecasted the doom of our relationship the other day!" I scowled down at her, my face twisting cruelly, I knew I must have looked hateful, a small voice somewhere inside regretted it, but it was too late. "If that's not fear of intimacy, I don't know what is."

She put her hands up, palms to me, laughed. A high, tinny, out-of-control laugh. "All right. That's enough. This is useless."

She started walking away and I called after her, "Oh sure, when *you've* had enough—you start these conversations, Tara, you get me to engage, then you end them on a whim. It's not fair."

Suddenly she stopped, spying something across the street. She clapped her hands together girlishly, playing it up, pretending delight. "Look! It's the dressmaker's shop we saw yesterday. I'm going in. I'm going to buy one of those dresses you hate."

She stepped into the street and I followed, reaching for her arm. I warned, "We're not done."

She shook me off and crossed the street, opened the glass door and went in the little shop. I started to follow but she turned and, seeing me, shut the door hard, catching my fingers in it. I cried out and she laughed—*laughed!*

"Open the door, goddammit!"

She opened the door to let my fingers out then slammed it again in my face. They were badly dented, turning purple before my eyes, though the skin wasn't broken. She mouthed a mock "sorry" through the glass and turned to greet the bespectacled, mustachioed dressmaker. I stood outside staring at her back through the glass. Only three days had passed and we had, I understood, arrived.

Madrid was heating up fast. Under the noisy drone of the old-fashioned air conditioner lodged roughly in the wall of our hotel room, Tara and I made love again later that afternoon. That's what you do at the beginning of a relationship when you have a fight, when you don't know what to do or say to each other to make up or when you've already tried saying everything and all roads into conversation, into understanding, into truce appear to be dead ends. There's always sex. That's what you do at the end, too, when you're trying to salvage or repair or resurrect what you had in the beginning although the sex at the end is nothing like that at the beginning. And this time it was terrible, the worst we'd had yet. I was still angry about my hurt fingers (even though she'd apologized profusely, claiming she thought I was joking, pretending to be hurt, when she laughed after slamming the door, I wasn't sure I believed her), and I couldn't shake the image of that ordinary woman I'd seen in the museum (nor her overbite) and on top of that, in the middle of it she made this sound, an otherworldly moan that startled me because until then she had been moving silently beneath me. Typically when a woman moans during sex, it turns me on, the thought that she's getting into it gives me a charge, but when Tara moaned it sounded like the mournful cry of an animal caught in a trap and dying slowly of a horrible wound, or that's the image that came to mind and that ruined the rest of it for me. Yet when we were done, I clung to her like a man lost at sea clings to driftwood.

That night at last we had dinner out. An attempt to cheer ourselves up by stuffing ourselves with fancy food and wine (when sex doesn't work . . .). It was a pricey Spanish restaurante, elegant and thoroughly touristy—traditional dishes elaborately described in raised lettering in leather menus, the place didn't bother translating them into English like the lesser restaurants. We started out with wine and cured meats and an array of cheeses, the names of which we clumsily repeated at the waiter's cheerful insistence (Manchego, Tetilla, Cabrales . . .), he was accustomed to dealing with tourists and even seemed to enjoy it. We had a glass of incredibly dry, house-made wine. Halfway through another, I was relieved to notice that across the table, in the room darkened by velvet drapes and flickering red candles, Tara looked anything but ordinary. In fact, she looked gorgeous. Her brown eyes luminous and jumping with the reflections of the candle flame, her hair swept up but for a few choice strands twisting around her face, gold earrings dangling and black high heels sculpting her legs into the perfect legs, the archetype of shapely female legs every man desires and which she held crossed, perhaps deliberately, directly in the line of my sight even though it meant sitting sideways in her chair in what looked like an awkward and uncomfortable position. She feels as desperate as I do, I thought in what might have been a moment of sanity, might have been a moment of delusion, she's terrified of this going south too, another relationship down the tubes, and she's doing her best to make me want her. For instance, I thought, she didn't buy one of those dowdy dresses after all, she said she didn't like the cheap, stiff fabric, which could be true (Tara is one of those women who won't sleep on sheets less than 700-thread count), or could be because she knows I don't find them sexy and so tonight she chose her American clothes that look to me European, a shimmery black top and equally shimmery skirt, both fit her well and the black matches her dark hair, making her appear mysterious and alluring, after three glasses of wine.

She bit mouselike into a wedge of Manchego, and I said, "You know what, Tara? You're right, what you said today. We don't know each other that well. I don't really know you at all."

She looked up, instantly suspicious—you can't blame her, I thought, the way things have been going. She probably thinks I'm launching a new attack or trying a fresh strategy fueled by revenge, she'll be pleased to discover I'm waving a white flag instead.

"It's not a bad thing. In fact, it's good. You're a complex gir—woman and there's a lot to know. And I want to know everything. All of it. Bring it on." I smiled and reached for her hand. "I'm not afraid of intimacy."

That last bit was a mistake. Talking to a woman is like scaling a glacier, one wrong move and you're plunged into deadly waters. Her face tensed and her bright eyes narrowed, I knew how she was taking it, she was taking it as a passive aggressive reference to our previous conversation, to her accusing me of being afraid of intimacy, she thinks I'm taking a dig at her for that. I backpedaled fast. "I mean, as far as I know, I'm not. Or I don't want to be with you. If I am, I want to change. I want to give us a chance."

She considered this or perhaps she was considering something else, I couldn't read her blank stare into her wineglass. The main course hadn't arrived yet, and we were already halfway through the eighty-dollar bottle of wine that was making my mouth pucker like I was sucking on a lemon, though Tara seemed to like it. She lifted her glass for a toast. "To second thoughts."

I clinked it but didn't drink with her, it was strong wine. And she was wearing a tight little smile, a smile I didn't like the look of at all. I let a few moments pass, debating whether to wander into the trap she was obviously setting. Finally I took the bait, there seemed no other option. "To second thoughts?"

She set her glass definitively on the table. "Darling, this hasn't been an easy trip. It hasn't been the trip we were expecting. But you know what?" She leaned forward, giving me an irresistible view of her cleavage. I dragged my eyes up to hers. "It's perfect. It's *good* to have second thoughts. Because it means we're growing. We're coming down to earth."

"We are?" My blood pressure dropped precipitously, I felt a rush of relief.

"Yes. This is what I was trying to say the other day, the day we got here, and that freaked you out so much: that you don't really know someone until the shit hits the fan. It's easy in the beginning when your head is in the clouds and it's all roses and you're both putting on your best selves, showing only what you want the other person to see or are willing to let the other person see. And what I was trying to say is simply that I think it's smart not to invest too much in a relationship before you really know who the other person is, that's all, not that I don't want to be with you."

"So we have to fight to find out who each other is? Do you really not trust me at all? What about all the time we've spent together in the last four months? All the long talks, all the deep conversations, the great sex, don't those count?"

Yikes, she's going to accuse me of thinking it's all about sex, I thought, women love to do that to men and it's a great tactic because, after all, it's mostly true. Instead she said, in a know-it-all tone: "It's true we've had a lot of fun. In fact, it's been amazing so far, it really has. Which is what makes me even more cautious, since the heart has a way of clouding the mind. Because if you think about it in all those deep talks, everything we learned about each other was what we wanted the other to hear—as well as, of course, what we noticed on our own without the other knowing it, the subtle cues, the telling gestures and so on, but that information, too, was tainted, filtered by our past hurts and disappointments, our secret hopes and unfulfilled desires and expectations for who we want each other to be—the ideal lover, the perfect mate, etcetera, which is to say someone who doesn't exist."

I'd shifted back in my chair, away from her, a put-out posture or a I'm-getting-fed-up-fast-and-you-might-want-to-notice-it posture, one of those subtle cues she didn't seem to be picking up on. "So all that stuff you told me about your exes, how badly they treated you, how they walked all over you, how they didn't respect your needs and wouldn't call when they said they would and chatted up other women right before your eyes. Really I just got your side of the story, didn't I?"

She shrugged, apparently unruffled. "Sure. Or what a bitch you say Amanda was, how she intruded on your personal space with her uncanny abilities. Maybe you drove her to it, the same way you'll drive me to it eventually. How am I supposed to know?"

She glanced down at her mauled jamón, she'd destroyed it with her dinner knife, that's one thing I'd noticed on my own about Tara on this trip, she can't just eat her food, she has to slice it and dice it, mish it and mash it, she has to *tear it up* until it's unrecognizable before putting it into her mouth. I looked down at my own. It was in roughly the same tatters. Of course, I thought, that's because the Spanish slice their ham tissue-thin, it's almost impossible not to maul it. In this case maybe it wasn't her, maybe it was the ham.

"All right. So tell me something about you I don't know yet," I said. She looked up, knife and fork poised mid-air. "Preferably some dark secret or shameful personal flaw you've hidden from me in an effort to put forth your best self."

One of her perfect eyebrows peaked in a boomerang shape. "Oh, you're asking for it now . . . okay, why not? Let's see . . . I don't have many dark secrets, at least none that are all that interesting or that you don't already know. Shameful flaws, on the other hand." I couldn't tell if she was serious or being passive aggressive. She thought into her wineglass, took a few sips. "Okay. I get outrageously angry when a client is late for a shoot."

I made a face of mock shock.

"I know, it doesn't sound that bad, but I mean really, really angry. Like I'll start throwing things. Once I deliberately smashed a vase made by some Indian in Peru that my mom got me on her trip there—I mean this is a valuable vase, or was, I should say, a sentimental vase, you know what kind of relationship I have with my mom—by throwing it against the wall because I was so pissed at this woman who was twenty minutes late for her kid's shoot. I mean I totally overreact. It's just that it throws my entire schedule off, you know, especially if it happens early in the day. I pack my schedule super tight, especially these days so I can take a lot of time off, so I can take off on crazy trips like this with you. For better or worse."

She smiled that particular smile and the dimples I was, honestly, on the fence about, made a brief appearance. I nodded. "Actually I've heard you say that before. Not about the vase, but didn't you break an expensive light or camera in the same way?" She sort of giggled yes. "You've told me before you can't stand people being late, whether it's at work or socially. Which is funny because do you know what I've noticed about you, entirely on my own?"

At that moment the waiter brought our entrées. Roast pheasant in grape juice for Tara and for me a cup of gazpacho (ice cold and disgusting, I'd never have ordered it had she not wanted to try it) and steak with raisins and pine nuts.

A timely arrival, I thought, I'd better drop it, why start up something again? We've got two more days and then we'll get back to the city and our normal routines and continue with the business of falling in love at a respectable distance. I tried to change the subject. "Look at us being reasonable tourists and trying the native fare."

Tara was pushing a morsel of pheasant around in an oily dark pool. "We're coming around," she said without looking up.

I raised my glass. "To Spain. To el bonita Madrid! I only hope Fernando doesn't get word we're here, I'm sure he'd find a way to attack us for trying 'his' food in 'his' country." I made those little quote marks in the air with my fingers, a gesture I find myself using a lot even though it annoys me when other people do it.

"Ha ha. Si, si . . . Well? What?"

"What what?" I knew what she meant, she knew I knew what she meant, too. At home we often completed each other's sentences, or we'd pick up a conversation from a few days before without precursor, a skill we prided ourselves on, complaining that other lovers had required exhausting explanations to bring themselves up to date. Now, however, I found it a nuisance, that ability of hers to read me like a book just as Amanda had.

"You know. Come on, out with it. What have you noticed about me that's 'funny'?" She made those little quote marks in the air herself except hers were giant ones, exaggerated hooks with her fingers way up by her head. "You like making those imaginary quote marks, don't you? That's one thing I've noticed about you."

"I hate them! I just find myself—"

She held up a hand. "No, no—let's stay focused on *my* flaws. We'll get to yours soon enough. Let me guess—I can't stand other people being late but I'm often late myself."

"No, no, that's not it," I lied, not wanting to be predictable. "You run late sometimes, but not as a rule. As a rule you're right on time or even early." That wasn't true, not even close, but people, especially women, I've noticed, are easily duped when you're flattering them, they forget the facts in their eagerness to hear something good about themselves.

"What then?"

"Oh, it's nothing . . ."

"*What* were you going to criticize me about?"

"What makes you think I was going to criticize you? You're so paranoid, Tara. I simply said I'd noticed something about you."

"*Then what is it?*" Her eyes were smoldering.

"Well . . ." I searched my brain frantically for what it was, for something other than her consistent and discourteous lateness, which had driven me to madness on more than one occasion (but not to the point of smashing my own high-dollar camera equipment on which my income depended), not to mention making us late for movies, plays, concerts, restaurant reservations and outings with friends. I searched for something mundane and harmless, some inoffensive quirk that she couldn't possibly be offended by.

"You're forgetful. You forget things. If we're going out, for instance, we'll leave the apartment and get halfway down the block and you have to go back for something."

"Once! Are you talking about that time we went to Gregory's and had to go back for the wine? Anyway what does that have to do with being late?"

I had a bite of steak. It was bloody inside, all but raw. "Nothing—I wasn't talking about you being late. You always think you know what I'm going to say. Anyway it's not that big of a deal, it's only happened a few times."

"Well, what's 'funny'"—those quote marks again, more like claws wanting to gouge my eyes out than virtual punctuation marks—"about me being forgetful? Which I'm not even."

"There's nothing funny about it, I'm just saying—"

"What are you saying, *darling?*"

"I'm saying . . .," I stalled for time, I had no idea what I was saying, ". . . if you kept that in mind when your clients are late, maybe you wouldn't get so irritated with them. If you kept your own eccentricities in mind. We're all only human, after all."

Her eyes had gone from smoldering to glassed-over. We ate for a few minutes in silence.

Finally I said, "So, what do I do? There must be something I do that drives you crazy."

Quietly: "No, not a thing."

I pretended not to notice the razor edge in her voice. "Come on, there must be something."

"Nope. Seriously, I can't think of a thing." She poured the last drops of wine from the bottle and tipped her glass at a passing waiter for a refill, this miserable meal was going to cost an arm and a leg and I, in good will, had offered to foot the bill this time (typically we split costs down the middle). She gave me a plastic, dimpleless smile. "You're perfect just as you are."

"You will. And when you do, you can let me have it."

"I will." She sawed away at her already shredded pheasant. "You can believe it."

That was a depressing night. Tara was quiet—no, sullen is a better word—the rest of the evening, which left me no choice but to be sullen myself which meant we hardly spoke the rest of the meal, nor afterwards, on the cab ride home nor lying in bed in the dark hotel room, where we discovered the hotel, with its paper-thin wallpapered walls, was full of sounds we hadn't noticed before when we'd been the ones making them—shower faucets creaking on and gurgling off, televisions murmuring busily, locks clicking and footsteps groaning down the hallway, always footsteps, nameless and bodiless, approaching or vanishing in the distance or pacing behind the walls we shared with those feet and the people attached to them, perhaps the American or Canadian couple we'd seen earlier, if so, they were still in love, they were getting along fine, judging from the congenial tone of the muffled words we couldn't quite make out behind those walls. But we weren't really listening to those sounds, at least I wasn't and judging by the faraway look on her face as she lay on her back staring up at the ceiling,

Tara wasn't either. Probably we were both absorbed in the voices that had broken loose and gained ground in our heads, the voice in mine repeating the same lines over and over like a CD stuck in a roughed-up spot: 'she's going to leave me, it's over, she's had it, another relationship down the drain, what's wrong with me, I can't seem to make a relationship work, I'll be alone forever, it must be because I'm fucked-up in some mysterious way that will never be revealed to me and that's why every woman I've ever loved has walked out on me, well, that's not entirely true, a few of them I've left and thank god I did but we'll overlook those for now in order to wallow in self-pity for a while.' I wondered what the voice in hers was saying, probably it was running in the opposite direction of the voice in mine, as in, 'how did I ever get involved with such a loser, why do I always pick men who are afraid of intimacy, men with issues, I can't wait to get back home and call up all those other men I was dating when I met him.' 'Then again,' another voice in me piped up, 'let's be honest, there's also my feelings for her to consider, which seem to be changing on this trip. Do I really want to put up with such *abuse?* She's treated me abysmally this entire trip. And I'm noticing these little things about her, things I never saw before, like I can't shake how *average* she looked yesterday in that museum, though she did look great tonight, and there's her overbite, and that double chin that's been making an appearance more and more often, think what it'll be like when she's in her fifties or sixties . . .' and then I immediately felt ashamed of myself for being so shallow and judgmental, I wouldn't be looking so good in my fifties or sixties either, no doubt, and it wasn't all about looks, I'm not that shallow of a man but 'then again,' I thought next, 'perhaps my noticing these petty physical flaws is a deeper indication of the shallowness of my feelings for her, of how my feelings for her don't really go that deep and never have. She's funny, talented, beautiful and smart but there's something missing. There's just something not *there,* I should just admit it to myself. But I was so happy before . . . why didn't I notice it until now?' I didn't know my own heart. Next to me, Tara sighed and closed her eyes. I wondered if the sigh was an invitation to talk, well I wasn't in the mood to try to pry her feelings out of her, it was simpler to stay silent and imagine what she was thinking, which, to my horror, came to me as along the lines of, 'I'm not even attracted to him anymore, if I'm honest with myself I never have been and I've never enjoyed sex with him, he doesn't even know what he's doing, at his age it's incredible how incompetent he is, if only he knew all my orgasms have been faked.' I rolled over and closed my eyes. Love was hell.

The Fourth Day

In the morning Tara did not roll over to face me before getting out of bed. Our habit was to always cuddle or at least kiss before getting up, but when I woke she was already dressed and standing at the window putting some glossy stuff on her hair. The shutters were open to the gray daylight, it was still early.

Without turning around, she said, "We *must* make the Prado today. I don't intend to miss that painting, not after all this." I didn't ask and didn't want to know what she meant by "all this."

When I said nothing, she said, "I'm going even if you aren't."

I sat up. "Of course I'm going."

"Good."

Then she disappeared into the bathroom for a good half an hour. She was already dressed and had her makeup on, what was she doing in there? Crying? Taking a long-awaited shit? Berating herself in the mirror for coming on this trip? I paced the room, badly needing to piss, pausing before the door and starting to knock or, rather, imagining knocking—'I was under the impression you wanted to get going, otherwise I'd have slept longer, what's the deal?'—but I didn't want to start the day with a fight and so I waited, I didn't want to stir the waters, rattle the cage, or upset the turnip bucket or however that old phrase goes. Today, I decided, I would make one last ditch effort to repair what we had, I would put my ego aside and do my best to make it work. I would forgive and forget, I would take the high road and she would admire me for it. It was a perfect day out, bright and still. The sun filled the smooth blue sky with light. I stood over the bougainvillea on the balcony, considering pissing into it. Below, a man was zigzagging back and forth in the street. I could see only the black top of his head, he wore a wool cap, many men of his generation in Spain favored the same cap, it seemed, and it looked like he had a mustache, though I couldn't be sure from that height. There was something familiar about him—his lanky, oddly graceful way of moving or his long jerking arms, I couldn't pin it down. A car came along and the man stepped in front of it and unfurled a red cape, no, it was a coat, he'd been holding it bunched up under one arm. He shouted and darted out of the way as the car swept past, he was toreadoring or whatever the verb form of that word would be the cars! It was Fernando. I'd been right! Fernando was a nutjob.

A feeling that can only be called smugness welled up in me. Well, everyone likes to be right, if only about the simplest things. I turned to get Tara but she was standing there in the French doors, as if unsure whether to come out onto the close balcony and wrap her arms around me from behind, murmur in my ear, plant those little kisses on my neck she used to plant, perhaps even apologize. But I'd already turned and seen her, it was too late for that.

"Ready?" she said lightly.

I pointed down at the street. "Tara, look! It's Fernando."

She came onto the balcony. She smelled like lotion and cigarettes. Tara doesn't smoke. I looked at her. So that's what she'd been doing in the bathroom. "Have you been smoking?"

"I don't see him."

The street was empty. "Shit—he's gone. He was—he *is* nuts. I saw him, he was doing this bullfighting thing with the cars." She looked at me like *I* was crazy. "His red coat, remember?"

"Weird," she said in a neutral tone. "Well, let's hope he's gone now. Ready?"

"I told you the man had mental problems. I was right!"

She didn't care. "So you were. Come on, *The Garden* is waiting."

I followed her out, past the bathroom, which reeked like a tavern, and down the hall to the rickety elevator, where I said, as pleasant and non-confrontationally as I could muster, "I didn't know you smoked."

I despise smoking, and I'd told Tara as much from the beginning, right before she told me she didn't smoke, apparently she'd been putting her best self forth, or rather, lying. She was digging in her bag, she didn't seem too concerned at being caught at it. "Every now and then I have one. When I'm stressed out, mostly."

"You told me you didn't smoke." To my shock, she leaned over and kissed me on the cheek.

"Sorry, darling." She didn't sound sorry. She didn't sound sorry at all. And I had to piss like a racehorse.

When you enter the Museo del Prado, whether, I imagine, for the first time or the hundredth, a feeling of reverence comes over you, a deadly seriousness or perhaps it's intimidation or melancholy or, even, a sense of your own insignificance and doomed temporality or some combination of all of these as you come into one of the greatest collections of art in the world. The thronging multi-national crowds are hushed and straight-faced, they speak in whispers even in the great hallways outside the galleries and there are guards both posted in every room and milling around, ready to pounce on the errant or overzealous finger about to touch the sacred slab of stone or brass or oil on canvas or, in the case of Mr. Bosch, oil on oakwood, and mar it forever. But we didn't get to experience any of this on that day, our fourth and next to last one in Madrid, since we still didn't make it through those legendary doors. This time, we didn't even make it to the gardens, though not for lack of trying.

Within a few blocks of the sprawling museum, we began to feel a buzz, people were coming our way, floods of people talking noisily and looking frenzied. 'Great,' I thought, 'it's full up due to being closed yesterday and they're turning people away.'

As we rounded a story-high ornamental shrub, it became clear something else was going on—police cars were parked on the lawn, flattening the perfectly trimmed green grass, lights flashing, and policemen wandered around waving their wands and shouting, redirecting the crowds and blocking them from entering.

"Shit." Tara put it simply. "We're cursed."

It seemed we were. There had been a bomb threat in the Prado, we found out later from two American students, college girls on exchange who we met on the sidewalk and ended up walking back to the plaza and getting drunk with. They had been inside when it happened, they had the scoop. We sat with them at a café, slunk down in our chairs for fear Fernando would spot us consorting with other Americans and accuse us of trying to bomb his country's national treasure.

They had been steadily making their way through the seventeenth century and were almost done with it, they told us dejectedly, when the police barged in. They'd already made great headway on the Prado's vast collection over the last two days, having taken in all of the Middle Ages and what seemed like hundreds of pietàs and resurrections and annunciations and visitations and crucifixions and ascensions, also they must have "done" half of Velásquez and some of Goya and quite a bit of El Greco, too, not to mention a lot of other pretty boring stuff. They had to look at every single painting, they explained, it was a pact between them, they'd convinced themselves that stuffing all that great art into their heads was a prerequisite for getting into graduate school at Cornell, which was where they were both headed or hoped they were headed after returning to "the States" for one more dull year at the University of Maryland, not a terrible school but by no means an Ivy League one and not too impressive on an Ivy League graduate school application. Which was why they needed all the kudos (they actually used that word—incorrectly—a word I've despised since the day I heard it, it sounds like a granola bar or breakfast cereal) they could get. What if the one painting they skipped turned out to be on the GRE?

"The last one I remember was a crucifixion." "No, no, it was a resurrection." "OMG, we'll never remember." "OMG, like, we'll have to do that wing all over again." OMG . . . I knew from my niece it was the universal shorthand for "oh my god," the girls used it without holding back, even though such a term would not be too impressive in a graduate school entrance interview, Ivy League or not. Oh my god, I thought, subversively using the unabbreviated words, are these the representatives of our country? Europe is teeming with such students. No wonder poor Fernando's had enough of us, or rather, them.

Now, they were in a panic, they explained between shots of vermouth, because tomorrow was their last day in Madrid—they were studying in

Salamanca—and they still hadn't managed to stuff half the art in the Prado into their heads and tomorrow—also our last day—the Prado would, no doubt, be closed.

"Oh my god," Tara moaned, also using the complete words for that ubiquitous expletive, whether ironically or sincerely I couldn't tell, I had no idea what she was thinking anymore. She put her head in her hands and her elbows rocked the table, spilling our drinks. "Why?"

The girls had been studying in Spain for the year and considered themselves experts in all things Spanish. They discussed the issue among themselves, a sort of comedy skit in code language: "At least—like—I think it will be closed. Don't you, Brits?" "Oh. Yeah. For sure. I mean." "Spain's such a fucking weird backwards but forwards in some ways country." "I mean OMG it was like a *bomb*. They'll have to defuse it and look for fingerprints and everything." "Yeah but like when we had one in our dorm, remember? I mean it was just a prank but OMG like nobody blinked." "Pia says it happens all the time over here, that's why." "She's a solid bitch." "She's not even Spanish, did you know she grew up in Portugal?" They got off the subject, onto the girls in their dorm.

Tara and I sat close at the little round wooden table but not out of choice, the table was tiny and the café full, bustling with museum refugees. We couldn't help but graze knees or bump elbows now and then, but we didn't talk. We avoided each other's eyes, downing our beers silently. When her beer was gone the one who was Britney but went by "Brits" pushed her chair back. At the bar she spoke to the barista in what sounded to me like beautiful Spanish (though it may have been terrible). "He says it will be open," she reported on return to our table. "Like in Spain nothing is that big of a deal. Not like in the States. Here they're all like, aah, whatever, let's have a siesta." She tossed a hand wildly in the air, the gesture knocking her off balance and nearly out of her chair. From the bar the young barista who looked to my foreign eyes exactly like the one from Fernando's café laughed out loud. He raised his own glass, toasting the crazy Americans, and drank it down.

That was a strange day. Our final full day in Madrid (our flight was at one the next day) was murky and disjointed, as is any day you start drinking before noon. The two girls who had glommed onto us or who we had glommed on to in order to escape one another ('anything is better than being alone with him, alone with her, alone with the dawning realization that this is not working, anything is better than admitting she's not the woman I thought she was or he's not the man I hoped he was') tossed back beers with the vigor of matadoras and smoked Gauloises like it was the end of the world (of which Tara bummed three, though she did step outside to smoke them). At one point they even tried to initiate a sing-along with the whole bar, a Castile folk song they'd only half-learned, it didn't go over that well, the Spanish don't have anything against drinking early in the day nor group singing but the bar was mostly tourists, elderly Americans, Germans, Scandinavians and Asians, repressed people who cast a scornful eye at our table and turned back to soothing themselves with café con leches. The incident had, naturally, changed the atmosphere of the city. The streets were full of people standing in tight circles and chatting animatedly, there was a charge in the air, an excitement or apprehension or perhaps a feeling of foreboding, shops were closing while bars stayed open, it seemed the bomb threat was an excellent excuse to extend yesterday's holiday. It turned out to be only a prank, but we didn't know that at the time and everyone was shaken up by it, rumors flying about terrorists and radical political groups, ISIS was suspected. All this we absorbed from our surroundings—at our table the talk centered instead on the college girls' adventures in their year abroad (most involved partying). We listened, we heard about their travels and classes and friends, their hopes to achieve the perfect tan on the famous white sand beaches before leaving in June, but most of all about their love interests, the European and the American ones, ill-fated romances doomed to end tragically due to timing and geography. Tara was getting sloshing drunk, I noticed, she appeared to be having a great time, laughing and giving motherly advice and even joining in the sing-along, the message to me being, 'Nothing's wrong, I'm in a perfectly good mood even though our relationship has gone to shit, see what a friendly and fun-loving person I am, how reasonable and laid-back and how well people like me, it's you who's the problem, not me.'

At last the girls stumbled off with a couple of lecherous-looking Spaniards well in their thirties, leaving us to sober up alone. We ordered hot sandwiches and espresso and one more beer each. The drinking had loosened us up and we talked, finally, Tara's eyes joggling drunkenly, landing only now and then on mine, as we spoke about mundane details, the barista's too-tight red button-down, the Clint Eastwood poster from the seventies on the wall behind us. The conversation circled around to the girls and their obsession with seeing every painting in the Prado.

"I remember that kind of zeal," Tara said nostalgically, her words slurring.

I set my beer down and wiped my lips on my sleeve. "Zeal? Is that what you call it?"

"Yeah, you know, that obsessive consumption of culture. I was the same way when I did my semester in London. I couldn't get enough of the Tate, I'd skip classes and go there and just wander around, I loved it—"

"Consumption," I cut in, "is exactly what it is. It's about checking off the masterpieces on your art history syllabus so you can pad your transcript. Didn't you hear all their talk about GREs and graduate school applications? Those girls couldn't care less about culture. They're consumers is what they are." I reached instinctively for my empty beer glass, surprised by my own bitterness even though I knew I was right.

"Wow." She was chewing her ham and cheese sandwich with an absent look in her cowlike brown eyes.

"Wow what?"

She swallowed and cleared her throat. "Wow, I think I just got one."

"Got what?"

"You said when I think of something about you I don't like I can let you have it. Some 'shameful personal flaw' I think is how you put it." Those parodic quote marks again.

I sat back and folded my arms over my chest. "Bring it on."

"You're judgmental. You're a very judgmental person." Her words slid into each other drunkenly. "You're totally intolerant of anyone or anything outside your comfort zone." She shook her head. "It's so obvious. I can't believe I never saw that in you before."

I cleared my own throat. It was my turn. I focused on enunciating my words as I drove a final nail in the coffin of our relationship. "I never saw a lot of things in you, too, Tara, before this trip. I guess you've accomplished what you set out to do. You've made sure your prophecy came true."

She narrowed her eyes to gleaming slivers between her smeared mascara and gave me a look of such hatred it was unnerving.

I smiled and raised my glass. "To surprises, in love and war."

The Fifth Day

I ended up seeing a lot more of the Prado's collection than I'd ever wanted to. I was in no mood to look at art that morning, but it turned out to be less painful than I'd anticipated, in fact, I saw some good stuff (once I cruised past all the pietàs and resurrections and crucifixions and ascensions), though nothing as interesting as Bosch's piece. Desperate to escape each other and the closeness of that tiny, shabby hotel room, we'd gotten up early and arrived at the doors twenty minutes before opening time, relieved to see the Prado was, indeed, open. Contrary to what we'd said all along, we decided to spend a few hours in the Prado and to put off seeing *The Garden of Earthly Delights* until the very end, perhaps as an unconscious punishment of ourselves for our childish behavior of the past few days or perhaps we wanted to keep ourselves in suspense a bit longer or simply to push our luck.

The painting hangs conveniently on the first floor not far from the main entrance. By mutual agreement, Tara and I went our separate ways and meandered around the museum alone until it was time to go. I didn't run into her again, to my relief. I didn't want to see her across a museum gallery again, since, in my mind, that was the painful moment when my feelings for her began to change. Instead, my visual hallucinations took a different turn this time: rounding a marble pillar, I glimpsed a flash of red at the end of the corridor. Fernando. He'd followed us, he was stalking us, it was all his fault, he'd poisoned our relationship with his insane accusations. But the red turned out to be the purse of an elderly woman. And I knew we'd poisoned it ourselves.

We met up at the Bosch twenty minutes before it was time to leave for the airport.

I have to admit, it's an impressive painting. It's a haunting painting, creepy and visceral, incredibly detailed and weird, though I don't find it that mysterious. Scholars do. Particularly the central panel, which is titled *Imaginary Paradise* and positioned between *Paradise* and *Hell*. Some see in this panel a condemnation of sin and the lusts of the flesh, while others say it's a celebration of them, an affront to the stuffy, repressive church of the time. Others view it as satirical, suggesting Bosch is pointing out the greed and corruption bred by institutionalized religion, or that's what the audio tour provided by the museum informed me in crisp British English through my headphones. In the end, the guide surmised, no one really knows nor will anyone ever know what message Hieronymous Bosch intended by all those bare, bone-color bodies fondling and sucking and bathing, riding razor-backed pigs and spike-horned unicorns, hoisting headless fish and gorging on gigantic fruits. One was being devoured by a bird with a blue-skinned human body, another kissed by a pig in a nun's habit. It's a weird painting, to be sure, but to me its message is clear enough: Paradise is a dream, Hell is real, and for every pleasure there's a punishment.

It's beautiful, too, in a perverse way—just as Tara had said. I could see why she loved it. Though I didn't tell her this, that would have been too much like taking her hand. We stood before it, silent and untouching, wearing our audio tour headphones, our mouths slightly open and eyes fixed on the sprawling painting. We'd hardly spoken and hadn't touched at all since the day before, not even in the night, in bed, not even accidentally, she didn't want to be contaminated by me and I didn't want to be contaminated by her, or that's what we were pretending now that we were pretending to hate each other and we would go on pretending it even to ourselves until we stepped off the plane in New York and said goodbye at the gate and on into our loveless futures, until we forgot each other and until we remembered.

Il Maestro!

She had fire poker eyes, that's right, eyes like the pricked black end of a fire poker, the charred iron star you stick in the fire to stir the coals and a flaring mass of wiry, probably permed black hair that gave the impression a wild, slightly hysterical animal were clinging to the top of her head. She was leaning up against the brick wall of the army surplus store in her scarecrow body, one bony knee bent and her stiletto heel stuck between the bricks in a half-hearted attempt to hold herself up. 'What a caricature,' I thought when I first laid eyes on her. 'What a cliché of a burnt-out city hooker,' and yet, I could not take my eyes away.

She was beautiful, I guess, in a mauled and damaged way, those dully burning eyes, the strong features, a straight nose and jawline and something peculiar about the region around her eyes that gave her an . . . *unusual* look if not quite exotic, that made you look twice at that face to see if you were getting it right, that is, if it had a peculiar beauty or if it were just odd. From a distance she would have been striking but up close you couldn't escape her ravaged skin indented with little marks, probably the leftover scars of a bad case of adolescent acne but they looked like teeth marks, tiny compulsive bites made by a rat or by the repeated sinking of the tip of a knife—not too deep, just deep enough—into the skin on those high cheeks. Though that skin wasn't sagging yet—she was still young, in her twenties, I guessed, not much younger than myself, it would sag soon enough given the life she was leading. Nor had she done herself any favors with the dark lipstick the color of dried blood that made her look fresh from the grave, other than that she hadn't bothered to put on any makeup, not to cover those scars or enlarge those pitted eyes, she hadn't gone to any trouble to make herself attractive to her clients, she hadn't taken the time or had the energy, that is, she hadn't 'given a fuck' and the fact that she hadn't and didn't 'give a fuck' (as no doubt she would have put it) was written all over her face, she was not in the mood for it tonight: 'tonight I'd rather not, tonight I'm not in the mood for being fucked in two by strangers, I've shown up, I've clocked in but that's all I can bring myself to do tonight . . . ' I couldn't say I blamed her for not wanting to make herself up for that kind of work like a teenager getting ready for the prom, still, her shabby self-presentation was a poor business move, it had to be costing her money, I wondered if she ever thought about that. She might at least have made the effort to smile or put on a coat of mascara, a single coat of mascara can transform a woman's entire face and I thought the least I could do was stop and tell her this.

Of course, she had those legs. Perhaps she was counting on those mile-long matchstick legs (which made her look rather like a marionette) to draw them in. At least she'd dressed appropriately, her skirt was so short it couldn't really be called a skirt, it was more like one of those old-fashioned swimsuit bottoms women wore in the fifties to cover their hips but reveal their thighs, a square of red lycra that had to give a lot to make it over her wide but mannishly straight hips but that's what lycra is good for. She was leaning up against the brick wall well away from the street, too, she couldn't bring herself to go out to the curb as she should have done were she serious about making a decent living and as her competition was—which, if it wasn't stiff, it was abundant: the street was lined with a motley crowd of hookers, ten or fifteen of them paraded boredly up and down the block, their goods squeezing out of brightly colored miniskirts and bikini tops. On stilted heels they pranced out onto the furthest reaches of the curb like the most laissez-faire of tightrope walkers, balancing on the concrete, half an inch between their heels and the gutter and calling out catcalls and hoots at the rolled-down windows of the passing by cars or twisting adeptly on their stilettos in concentric circles that spiraled in and closed down on themselves until there was nowhere to go and the hookers stopped and just stood there, lost, suspended, until they lit fresh cigarettes and shifted back into motion amid the swirling green and red and yellow lights of the city streets and the steady flow of their nightly offices.

I pass through that sleazy zone every night on my walk home from the theater. Typically I keep my eyes drilled ahead of me and don't even register the ladies of the night holding rank along that two- or three-block stretch in the otherwise pleasant walk to my apartment. It's not like I'm passing judgment on them. I'm a well-educated person and I'm well aware of the shoddy state of the economy these days, I know that even a job in a discount store or gas station or selling cigarettes in a kiosk or cleaning toilets in the subway must be hard to come by these days and that a woman could get to such a place where her only recourse is to submit herself to the clammy hands and hard-ons of strangers in order just to make the rent and buy the groceries, and yet, I could never do so myself, I could never bring myself to *that*. I know that compared to them, those out-of-luck ladies, I was born lucky, even though I grew up in the stinking industrial suburbs of Boston with a crazy mother and no father and have had to scrape and claw and fight my way to get where I am. Nothing in my life has been handed to me on a silver platter or a bronze one—not my full-ride scholarship to Juilliard and not my lead roles in two off-Broadway plays and thirteen off-off-Broadway plays (I won't play anything but the lead, taking minor roles is the fastest way to ensure you don't become a star). I'm not one of the stuck-up privileged that come from old money New York and the theater crowd is full of, unlike them, every rung I've mounted up the silver ladder to success I've done so by my own sheer will and determination—of course, my raw natural talent hasn't hurt, although my voice isn't that strong. My voice really could be stronger.

Nor am I one of those sexually uptight or morally constipated women, I've slept with lots of men but I'm not promiscuous. I'm not averse to going to bed on the first date if I'm having a good time or simply feel like having sex but I don't take stupid risks, I always use protection and I don't sleep with toads or men without graduate degrees, and when it comes to dating, I only allow myself to be seen with stylishly dressed men with respectable professions (and *never* with wives). At this point in my career a nasty rumor (or nasty disease) could ruin everything. Also I'm well aware that these days the vast majority of prostitutes are liberated women who don't do that many drugs and don't have that many kids. They don't leave their crack babies on the apartment floor for days, they take them to free day care, and they don't put up with physical or verbal abuse from their pimps—they leave, they find themselves a new john who respects them or get rid of the john altogether and strike out free-lance. They have resources. Even though they're still depicted the old way in Hollywood movies, I know that the vast majority of prostitutes these days are nothing less than professionals serious about making ends meet and establishing themselves in their field.

Even though I'm *not* passing judgment on women like her, I'm aware I might look like it as I go *click click clicking* by in my Jimmy Choo heels and wool overcoat, clutching my tan Chanel handbag with my salon-coiffed blond hair bouncing on my shoulders, my Japanese-print silk scarf and oversized ethnic jewelry distinguishing me as a woman of the arts and not one of those stuffed-ass power-suit-sporting corporate bitches—surely, I thought, the hookers would hate those women more, everyone admires artists.

It was ten or ten-thirty and I was on my way home after a brief, irritating rehearsal. It had ended at eight or eight-thirty but I'd fretted around the theater afterwards pretending to check on this or that detail for tomorrow night's opening when in reality I was hoping to catch the thief who'd been making off with my makeup sponges—I was sure it was my understudy and I hung around the shadows watching my dressing room door waiting for her to show up and try to sneak in. She never did, perhaps she'd noticed I hadn't left yet and was going to outwait me, finally I scooped all the sponges in a plastic bag and put them in my purse, that was one way to foil her if not as satisfying as catching her red-handed. It wasn't the director's fault I was getting home late on the night before opening night, it was my own. This director is known for his short, to-the-point final rehearsals and he hadn't kept us long, in fact he'd let us go so early the cast decided to go out and were at that very moment getting drunk at the Irish pub around the corner, they'd be in no shape to match me onstage tomorrow night. They had, to their credit—though I could see it pained them—asked me to come along. I declined, it's of no importance whatsoever to me to 'bond with' my supporting cast, which they claimed was their professional motive for going out the night before our pathetic little historical whodunnit penned by a drop-out Columbia graduate student with stars in his eyes opened. I let them know it, too, hinting that I had something better to do, someone rich and handsome to meet, ha ha, they'll never know otherwise.

Anyway I like to go over rehearsals in my head afterwards, a sort of rehearsal of rehearsal in reverse, there are always plenty of off-key lines and missed beats and botched gestures to cringe over and I like to do this on my walk home. I take a perverse pleasure in torturing myself with mine and the rest of the cast's infinite failures and shortcomings and this is what I was thinking about while at the same time looking forward to sliding into a hot bath with a glass of wine and my laminated script and going over my lines one more time before tomorrow night when my eyes landed on her.

As I approached I saw she was shivering. She was gripping herself by the elbows as if that would make up for all the skin she was showing to the frigid air.

"Hi," I said—simple, to-the-point—the click-clack of my stride breaking as I found myself stopping before her.

A smirk. "What do you want?"

"You look cold."

"Okay, I am cold. It's fucking December."

"Actually, today is the last day of November. Tomorrow is December the first."

"Yeah, I know," she said in a totally unnecessarily nasty way. "I have to make rent tonight."

"Of course. Well—that's something to work for."

She gave a bitter laugh but said nothing.

I started to dig in my Chanel handbag, expecting her to stop me, she didn't. I took out my pocketbook. I really didn't have that much to spare (off-off-Broadway plays do not as a rule pay well), also it's never a good idea to take your pocketbook out on the street and it's plain stupid at ten-thirty at night. I snapped it shut.

"I'm sorry, I can't help you out. I never carry cash." She re-crossed her arms and half-smiled as if she knew I was lying. She put a finger to her mouth and started gnawing on a ragged nail or hangnail, a bad habit either way.

"I don't ask, okay? Now fuck off."

She was from somewhere, Eastern Europe, Romania or somewhere, you could tell by her pale, oppressed face and she had a slight accent ("ok-eay"), though otherwise her English wasn't bad and just like an American she had a love of the F word. She looked off down the street at nothing and a wild idea occurred to me.

"You look like you could use a hot cup of coffee. In fact, I have an espresso maker, I'll make you a nice strong latte, that'll keep you going." The silver beast of my new espresso machine that had arrived last month from Italy—*Il Maestro!*—rose in my mind. Actually I hadn't used it yet, I was still walking the six blocks to Starbucks for my morning cappuccino, the thing intimidated me that much. Well, a guest would be the perfect motivation to face my fears and fire it up. I work best under pressure.

"Look, I just live up the street, why don't you come to my place for a few minutes? You can even take a shower if you want. I have a great shower. It has a stereo in the wall." I would play Beethoven for her—no, Tchaikovsky. She looked at me. "A little break to help you get through the rest of the night. I'm sure it can't be easy."

"Why would I?" she replied surlily—as if *I* were asking *her* a favor!—the finger going back to her mouth.

I opened my hands (the Chanel lodged tightly in my armpit, you never know with these types). "Suit yourself, I'm just trying to help. One woman to another, you know."

I held her gaze, those burnt black stars under bare lids. I thought she was going to turn me down, and it would have been for the best, it would have, for her, for me, but then with a great effort she pushed herself off the building, her angular body unfolding stiffly like an origami crane, and put both feet down on the concrete. She was taller than me and I'm a tall woman—of course, her heels were much higher than mine, much higher and much cheaper.

She took her finger down, she'd gnawed it to the quick, it was pink and raw. "Okay, I will take a coffee. No shower."

"Great. You're going to like my place. And I make fabulous lattes," I lied.

It was a cold, drizzly night, more typical of late December than November. The streets were slick with wet trash, fast food wrappers and cigarette butts and soggy condoms and near the theater district there had been a damp carpet of ticket stubs flattened by thousands or millions of pedestrian soles, tomorrow night the ticket stubs of my own play would be among them, tossed down in disgust if things did not go well and if they did, by a lack of sentimentality or inability to recognize a rising star (if you think somebody's going to be famous, you keep the ticket, you know). Though very few wet leaves since there's not a tree around for miles in this part of the city, these streets are nothing like the tree-lined avenues near the campus of Juilliard, where I was awarded my BFA in drama in three and a half years (most people it takes four) and whose November sidewalks would have been—were being, at this very moment, no doubt—pasted in yellow and red and orange leaves by the soles of passing students, their tense faces straining as they hurry along reciting lines or trilling triplets or scaling scales over and over and over again in their heads, even at this hour, the students at Juilliard never stop. Juilliard is an incredibly competitive school and there's no laughter or beer drinking for the students there, there's no time for that and that's why it turns out such great artists.

We *click click clicked* along in silence, her heels marking the off-beats of mine.

"I knew the date because tomorrow is the opening night of my play. I'm an actor, see."

She didn't look over.

"Not in the movies, on the stage."

"Okay." She used the word for all purposes, she was definitely from some-where else, Bulgaria or somewhere. A beat passed, wherein she must have taken in what I'd said because then she said, "You're an actress?"

"I'm an *actor*. No one says 'actress' anymore, it's sexist."

"In English it's actress, yes? For woman?"

"It is, but it's no longer used." She looked over sort of cross-eyed. Up close, her skin was like a Brillo pad. "It's an attempt to even things out. Women have always gotten less recognition in the arts—in everything, really—and language is power, you know, the very words we say shape how we . . ."

Just then the drizzle expanded into a full-on downpour. I snapped open my umbrella and held it out for my unlikely companion to join me under but she wasn't interested, too intimate, probably. Well, that was all right, it was too intimate for me, too, I was only trying to be nice but truth be told, I didn't want to get too close to her, who knew what she might be carrying even if the vast majority of hookers these days do use protection and get themselves tested regularly. They're very responsible, that's what I hear and read, though perhaps the foreign ones are less so, less well-connected to social services, you know. She trotted ahead through the rain, a silly-looking teeter-totter run in her tight red skirt and obnoxiously high stilettos. She wouldn't be getting away from any abusive pimps or homicidal clients with that run, I wondered if she ever thought about that.

When we came in my apartment it was awkward. It's always awkward having guests over, people striding into your personal space and casting their cold stares over the intimate details of your life, on top of which ours was an unusual situation and therefore doubly awkward, in a social way, I mean. I'm definitely going to regret this, I thought as I went around turning up all the dimmers on all the lights. I wanted to make it difficult or impossible for her to steal anything—really, I thought, I'm doing her a favor by helping her resist the temptation. I have a lot of nice things, little sculptures and vases, knickknacks and framed art, a pair of Egyptian striped cats made out of marble that would fit neatly into the pockets of the gray pleather jacket she'd produced from somewhere, apparently her little yellow plastic purse though I couldn't see how it fit in there, it had appeared over her shoulders as we ran through the rain and when we came in she tossed it—raindrops and all—on my couch like a lazy teenager. I asked if she wanted to come with me as I went from room to room, to check things out, see if anyone was hiding out but she just shrugged and stayed put and so I kept one foot in the living room (which she stood uncertainly in the middle of) and one eye on her while I went around turning up all the dimmers. She wasn't the smartest hooker, this could have been a set-up, anyone could have been hiding out in the closets or under the bed.

The second we walked in she lost the pleather, exposing bony shoulders in a black and white striped tube top that was as tacky or even tackier than her skirt (hers was an 80's hooker look, understandably, Eastern European fashion runs thirty years behind American, or maybe all hookers dress that way, maybe her outfit wasn't outdated, just cheap), as if she were in a hurry to get out of her clothes. It must have been what she always did with clients: expose the goods, bare the merchandise so they knew what they were getting and could decide if they were willing to pay for it or perhaps it was her way of hurrying things along, of getting it over with.

She stood swaying in the middle of the blazing living room. Her black eyes scanned my apartment, the white walls and black hardwood floor and glass table and mirrors and art deco light fixtures, those fire poker eyes poking into everything, poking into me as they probed the most intimate details of my life. They looked like jacks, too—those metallic toys of the child's game I used to play on the sidewalks of my Boston neighborhood growing up, scuffing my bare knees and dirtying the too-tight white dresses my mother was so fond of dressing me in, even on weekdays. My mother was an uptight woman, all about appearances and no substance. She sends me a birthday card every year, which I promptly tear into bits and burn. It's a ritual.

"Nice pad," she said finally, I couldn't tell if she was being sarcastic or not.

"Thank you. Please, have a seat." I have excellent manners for having grown up in a working class family. I have my mother to thank for that. My mother never had a penny and she never had a husband but she always had manners (to other people) and she always dressed well.

The hooker gave me a wary look but stepped tentatively toward the loveseat, her heels snagging in the hand-woven Turkish throw rug. She extricated them by shaking her ankles free and folded herself onto the low leather couch, white, from Marshall Fields, a nice couch but not that nice. And not something she could leave a stain on, I thought, being leather.

She held her hand over her eyes as if shielding them from the sun—honestly, the gesture was melodramatic.

"Oh, sorry, too bright for you?"

"Okay, lady, it's night," she said, as if I should know what that meant.

"Of course." I turned the dimmer for the living room chandelier down only slightly (not enough to tell). "You prefer the dark. I'm sure you're more accustomed—I mean, you work mostly in the dark, don't you? It's just that—well, you have to see things my way, I mean, I'm taking a risk inviting you in, aren't I? I have to take precautions, I'd be a fool if I didn't. I don't even know you, after all. And—well—you must know the reputation you . . . your . . . how some people must think of you—not me of course, but some people . . ." I trailed off pathetically, I was doing my best to be polite but it's not easy when you don't have much to work with.

She gave me a look and reached in the pleather. For a split second I thought she was going to bring out a miniature revolver and blow a miniature hole through my heart or, worse, my throat, leaving me alive but destroying my vocal cords so that my body would still walk around and my head still sport its flaxen, Greta Garbo hair and my face would still be beautiful on top of my body but my voice would be shot (ha ha). An actor's voice is her *pièce de résistance* and if she loses that, she's done for. My fingers fluttered over my throat. The Japanese scarf felt like it was strangling me.

Instead she produced an ordinary cigarette. Her nails were long but un-painted, or rather they had been painted days or weeks ago, all that re-mained was a scratched-up fluorescent—was that *really* fluorescent?—pink polish.

"What is it, lady?" I must have been staring. She put the cigarette between her dark lips. I shook my head.

"I'm sorry, I can't put my voice at risk tonight. My play opens tomorrow night and I have to handle my voice with kid gloves tonight. In fact, I shouldn't even be having this much conversation. I don't want to strain it, if my voice were to give out it'd be disastrous."

Her thin eyelids lowered, the black pinpricks barely visible beneath them.

I went on. I'm a chatterbox when I'm nervous. "I play the lead. I have over three hundred lines—well, all right, some of them are pretty short but still—and this is a very important play for me. Also we're expecting the critics tomorrow night, and I know it sounds cliché, but this one could be my big break. Sure, it's off-Broadway but it's just around the corner, ha ha . . ."

She wasn't following, she lifted her lighter to the cigarette.

"No!" I screeched. "No smoking. Secondhand smoke. My lungs can't tolerate it."

She took the cigarette down but set it on the glass coffee table along with the lighter, clearly indicating she intended to smoke it later, when I wasn't looking. All while keeping her eyes locked on mine—defiant, like a rebellious child.

"I'll just start on your latte. You do like milk with your espresso?"

"I like to smoke," she said, then added after a second, "Okay, milk. If that's how you like to do it."

She was a very ill-mannered hooker. She was surly, that was her way. I wondered if her attitude was surlier than most or if it was the norm, probably they were all kind of bitter but could you blame them. Fortunately the living room in my apartment is separated from the kitchen by a half-bar so I could keep an eye on her while I made her latte, at least, I could keep an eye on her long calf and foot, the skinny leg crossed on top, the toe bobbing—she appeared to be quite at ease, unlike myself.

I quickly decided to make a double batch. No, triple. I wasn't having any myself (even though I would be up half the night going over my lines, caffeine late at night makes me anxious) but I thought she would want more than one cup—if I were in her position, that is, if I still had five or six hours of fucking strangers ahead of me, I would.

I turned to the gleaming stainless steel machine. *Il Maestro!* had cost a pretty penny, but that's how I motivate myself, by overusing my credit cards and then I have to pick up more roles to pay them down, it works for me. The thing was incredibly complicated, all those lights and gauges and spigots and what was worse, the little one- or two-word descriptors on tiny brushed pewter placards next to each light or gauge or spigot were all in Italian, which I loved, but it wasn't very practical. Also the instruction booklet was in Italian and while I took two semesters of Italian in school, I merely memorized what I needed at the time to read for *Rigoletto* (a part I didn't even get), and there's nothing in that opera about how to work espresso machines. The instructions could be found in English on the internet, the company assured in a polite little note in childlike English but I hadn't gotten around to it and now I was going to pay for it.

The water went in all right—there was only one place for that, right? I scooped up the Fair Trade organic Brazilian grounds (gorgeous coffee far outclassing my guest), measuring—probably foolishly but we would see—intuitively. That's when I heard the unmistakable scrape of a cigarette lighter.

I came around the bar like a house afire. In a voice that could cut glass I said, "Perhaps you didn't hear me, I said I'd rather you not smoke in here."

"I heared you," she replied, sounding like an idiot. The pelt of that unidentifiable wild animal was rising off her forehead as if rearing back to fight. Under it, I saw her widow's peak, vampiric. Widow's peaks have always given me the creeps, they look like weapons but I'm superstitious about stuff like that.

She lowered the cigarette to her thigh. Its thread of curling gray smoke traveled up between our faces. "Look, I am not rude. But . . . okay? I have to smoke. It calms me."

"Well, you can go outside." I pointed to the balcony, where the rain was coming down in angled sheets.

She twisted her mouth to the side. Shrugged and stayed sunk in the couch. A direct affront, a power play.

"Put. It. Out."

She needed an ashtray, I saw that. No. She—outrageously!—ground the burning end into my glass coffee table.

I saw I had a choice: I could grab those skinny arms and try to pull her off the couch and throw her out, or I could be kind. Generous. Understanding of a woman less fortunate than myself, she was clearly a damaged soul.

"Why did you do that? Maybe you're upset. You don't seem like it. You don't have to worry, I'm not going to ask you to do anything weird or anything like that—" a high, tinkly laugh I hardly recognized came out of my throat—"I'm not into that kind of thing. I asked you here to give you a break, remember?" In the kitchen *Il Maestro!* let out an explosive belch in Italian. I added, perfunctorily, "But I'd rather you not smoke."

The hooker, whore, prostitute, or streetwalker—what am I supposed to call her? I'm not sure what the politically correct term is these days—"sex professional"?—took her time. She took her time making her point. In a slow motion movement, she drew her pack of cigarettes out of her purse, extracted a fresh one, brought it up deliberately as if her hand were attached to a pulley or to marionette strings, slipped it between her lips *and lit it.* All the while keeping those eyes like coals dug from the dregs of a dead fire fastened on mine. In a low voice—her voice was already low, almost masculine, it had a weight ill-matched to her skinny frame—in an even lower voice than her normal one, she said, "It calms me."

I saw what I was dealing with. She could be dangerous.

"Fine." I went to the balcony and flung open the French doors. The rain was pouring down, it would come in and ruin the floor and I'd have to pay thousands of dollars to repair it.

I fled to the kitchen, stopping at the wall to turn the dimmer up ever so slightly, even though it really was like broad daylight in the room. My feet were hurting. I slipped off my Jimmy Choos, feeling her eyes on me all the while, my throat already feeling scratchy from the poisonous smoke, feeling her watching me bend over, watching my skirt tighten around my hips as I did so, watching me place the lizard skin heels neatly side by side on the black hardwood floor. I'm an attractive woman and I know it (unlike most women who refuse to own their beauty). Suddenly I felt self-conscious, exposed, in my bare feet. But I left the heels by the doorway, they would come in handy if I needed them, those Jimmy Choo spikes are practically weapons.

In the kitchen I poured myself a glass of wine ("it calms me"). I really needed to get in the bath and go over my lines, bits of them drifted through my head—*good morning Miles and how did you sleep . . . but Sheriff we were all here in this very room . . . wait, don't answer the door!*

I didn't see any coffee in the charming little silver pitcher yet, no water seemed to be dripping into it but there was plenty of steam puffing out the stainless steel crevices, the machine was doing something.

Then from the other room I heard her say, "You are an actress?"

The tone was conversational, perhaps even friendly. Was she trying to make amends?

I cleared my throat. "I'm an actor. As I've already told you, no one says 'actress' any more, it's a pointless patriarchal distinction. What does gender have to do with acting ability?"

She ignored my question; that was okay, it was rhetorical anyway. "You are in the movies?"

"God, no, I wouldn't stoop to it. My love is the theater."

"You should do movies. Make lots of money, yeah?" I could see the toe of her foot bobbing in her shoe and the thread of her cigarette smoke meandering into the room, in no hurry to exit through the French doors.

I gave a deliberately fake laugh. "I didn't go into acting for the money. I'm an actor because I care about acting. I do it for the *art*."

Silence. Of course, she didn't understand such an idea, I'd probably made her uncomfortable. I came around the half-bar and perched awkwardly on the loveseat opposite her. I was about to tell her I'd unexpectedly run out of coffee—she should go—when she leaned forward and ground out her cigarette on the sole of her stiletto. For some reason it struck me as a very sexy gesture, something Lauren Bacall would do, something I have never done and would never do. Was she being gracious, putting it out in my presence, opting for her shoe and not my table this time? She set the butt on the table next to the other one and fixed her dead stare on me, appraisingly. "You have a man?"

"Just one? Why limit yourself?" I smiled, she didn't.

Of course, she didn't limit herself, did she. The string of disastrous dates I'd been on in recent weeks went through my mind—Godfrey, the stockbroker: dinner on the patio of a French restaurant throughout which he'd smoked cigars, ruining my *lapin á la moutarde* and then he'd never called back. Daniel, the Elizabethan poetry professor who had a mustache that *collected* food. He hadn't called back either, I was secretly glad, I'm not interested in men who are intimidated by me (or who repulse me). Ezra, the Jewish performance artist who had too many opinions. Where had he gone?

"I go out with lots of men. I'm not interested in settling down with one, though. My career's my highest priority right now."

The hooker nodded, perhaps thoughtfully, if so it was the first politeness she'd shown since I'd invited her into my home. She reached in her purse, took out another cigarette.

"Please don't light that," I said, shaking my head.

She actually put her hand down, though she kept holding the cigarette.

"Do you? Have a man. I mean, besides . . ."

"I don't like men."

"Oh. Really. That's ironic, isn't it?"

"Fuck off, lady."

"What? I only meant it's odd, right, considering the line of work you've chosen?"

She rolled her eyes but was silent and we sat there, listening to the rhythm of the rain on the balcony—*pitter patter pitter patter pitter patter*—and staring at our legs, hers bare, mine encased in old-fashioned panty hose which for some reason I continue to wear (probably my mother's influence, she insisted on them, day in and day out), though other than that they weren't that different, both legs were long, streamlined, muscular, the quintessential legs men want. Neither of us should have been in the situations we were in. Romantically, I mean.

"So, listen: I was thinking how you could increase your customer flow. Improve your act. It is like acting, isn't it? Well, it's not what I do, but I imagine you do have to act the part, right? Make them think you're into it."

She frowned.

"Or maybe they don't care."

"They don't care."

"Still, I imagine you would get more business if you put on a little make-up. You could cover up that acne."

Her hand went absentmindedly to her cheek, the ragged fingers running over the ragged skin. She looked at her reflection in the long mirror on the opposite wall, sadly, I thought. "I don't like makeup."

"But *they* like it. You ought to know that."

Her perpetual scowl deepened, drawing the pelt of frizzy hair over her widow's peak.

"At least smile then. I mean, you're attractive, but you look so unapproachable."

"I don't want to smile for these fucks." I couldn't tell if she was using the term—"these fucks"—to refer to the sex acts or the actors, the men themselves. It didn't matter. What mattered was *hearing* her, getting it. I did get it: women expected to smile in the most unsavory and unpleasant situations, to be friendly and good-natured at all costs, even when they are being stolen from off their very own dressing tables or sodomized by flabby old rich "fucks" (which is how I imagined most of her clients). It was just another way of repressing our pain and keeping the patriarchal thumb smashed down on women's collective heads.

"You're right. Don't then. We have to demand respect if we're ever going to get it."

She took this solidarity as permission and brought the cigarette to her lips.

"Don't light that fucking cigarette!"

A half-smile deliberated on her lips. She flicked her lighter once or twice, teasing me. Then she dropped it on the table and said, "Do you make coffee?"

"It's—I'm just waiting for it. I'll check on it." I jumped up, calling back over my shoulder in the most casual way as if she were a houseguest, an old college friend come to visit, this is what it would be like, I thought, if I had an old college friend come to visit but I didn't have any friends in college but if I had it would be like this, how nice it would be to call over my shoulder at someone as I called at her now: "Did you want to take a shower? You're welcome to. I have great water pressure, and there's the stereo . . ."

The stereo set into the marble wall was impressive, she'd probably never seen anything like it. But she merely snorted, she didn't seem inclined to move, that was a relief, really. Of course I didn't want her in my shower. I took the milk out of the fridge. The coffee wasn't ready, I saw with one glance. In fact, there was still nothing dripping down. In fact . . . I leaned in to inspect *Il Maestro!* . . . Alas! Tiny brown rivulets were trickling out the seams of the machine and down onto the countertop, where they spread into rivers dotted with black grounds streaming down the cabinets and over the tile floor, storming the kitchen like army ants.

Apparently the water was not going where it was supposed to go. Apparently I'd poured it into the wrong place, or perhaps I'd poured it in the right place but neglected to remove some plastic tab or microscopic piece of tape such as they put on new machines in order to protect their delicate parts during transit and which the directions, were one read to them, would have plainly explained in little languageless drawings must be removed before operation but *I had not read them.*

Or perhaps the machine was simply defective? Why did everything have to be my fault?

I threw some kitchen towels on the floor and unplugged the machine. I straightened my spine and drew myself up, breathing, centering myself as I do before stepping onto stage. I stepped onto stage.

"Look," I said, standing before the prostitute as if I were on trial, "I really need to go over my lines. It's getting late, and I always go over my lines the night before opening night. Over the whole play, really. You have no idea how tragic it is to forget a line, not that I ever have. And I'm afraid the coffee's taking longer than expected."

She didn't say anything, she wasn't very good at social cues. She sank further down in the couch (leather does that, it sucks you down like quicksand, that's the only thing I don't like about it). Suddenly she looked very young and very pathetic to me. There really wasn't much left in her eyes. Probably she really didn't want to go back out there. Who knew what she had been through, what kind of life she'd had and what had been done to her. I've never wanted children and the last thing people would describe me as is maternal, but looking at her there, slumped in my couch like a skeleton with the blood, the life, the spirit or whatever makes people give a fuck all drained out of her, I was touched. I was moved. I sat down on the edge of the loveseat and in a soothing voice like you'd use with a wounded animal, not that I've ever spoken to a wounded animal, I said, "You don't have to do this."

She kept staring at her foot in the stiletto, bobbing, bobbing.

My hand ventured forth, I watched it go like a thing detached from my body, it found her bare thigh. She jerked a little.

"Did you hear me?" I said very softly. "You don't have to keep doing this . . . I mean it. You can stay here, just for a little while, until you find a respectable job. There must be something else you could do. I don't mind. I have a guest room, do you want to see it? It has a queen-size bed. We have to stick together, after all, we women have to help each other out."

With an effort she sat up and took the cigarette she'd laid on the table and lit it. Then she brought those fire poker eyes to my eyes and puffed a huge cloud of smoke *right in my face*. "I like my job, okay? Where's the coffee?"

I bounced off the couch like a jack-in-the-box. "Unbelievable. You are—no wonder—you people!" She was staring at me, yes, she was smiling. Smiling! "No wonder you're so fucked up is what I was going to say. You're ungrateful, that's what you are. It turns out I'm out of coffee." I went for my purse. "I'll give you a couple bucks, you can go to Starbucks."

"Not my terr-tory. And the fucking rain. I don't want to walk in the rain."

A switch in me flipped.

"Get out!" I screeched. "*You need to get out of my apartment now.*"

The hooker stood, wobbly on her stilettoes. She opened her mouth to say something but I never found out what because at that moment *Il Maestro!* erupted.

A great cloud of hot steam drifted over the half bar into the living room.

I rushed into the kitchen. The machine was trembling, its delicate lights flashing, steam shooting out its top. Scalding water sprayed my hands as I punched at the still-lit red power button. Hadn't I unplugged it? It hadn't been enough, *Il Maestro!* was unstoppable. It kept puffing away, spraying my kitchen, my hair, my face in a gritty black mist. The power button appeared to be stuck on, the thing must have had a backup battery or built-in generator, the Italians weren't about to go without their coffee in a power outage or perhaps it was simply possessed. I scratched at the switch, a caper-size button inlaid in stainless. It wouldn't budge.

I heard her behind me. I turned. She was coming at me with the icepick heel of the Jimmy Choo held aloft, her face set. I wasn't about to be murdered in my own apartment by a prostitute the night before opening night, what an embarrassing obituary that would be. What a failure of a life, not even making it to Broadway. I wouldn't have it. I didn't have a weapon like she did, but I had my wits and my guts—I've always had plenty of both. Before she could stab me in the throat, I pounced on her face, scraping my sharp fingernails across the already mauled skin of her cheek, skin that was used to it. She threw me off, her skinny arms were stronger than they looked. My back met the refrigerator and I splayed there, wind knocked out. We stared at each other through the hot steam. She lifted the shoe again. My heart pounded. Was this the end? I cowered, raising my hands as a shield, but she charged past me. To *Il Maestro!* She was attacking my brand new Italian espresso machine now! But wait—no—in one gesture, she poked the heel at the power button of the machine—it fit precisely, as if made for it—and the red light went out. *Il Maestro!* gave one last puff and fell silent.

All right, maybe she was headed past me at the machine, all right, maybe she was going for it and not me but what would you have thought? And that's *maybe*. We don't really know her motives, do we, and we never will. It's like a badly scripted whodunnit. It's exactly like that.

She dropped the shoe and went into the living room. I heard her gathering her things, taking her time. Leaving the butts on the table of course, I would find them later, bare of lipstick but damp with saliva. She stopped in the kitchen doorway. Her face looked like a miniature garden rake had been dragged across it: four long red marks, swelling rapidly. The new look wouldn't help her make rent, well that was her own fault. The hysterical pelt was flattened now, damp and coated in coffee grounds, not that you could see them in her coal black hair but her temples were thick with them. I had an impulse to hand her a towel. I have a big heart, it's what gets me in trouble. I resisted. Of course she couldn't resist giving me a long smirk before slamming the door behind herself. Women like her have no self-control.

It's really not like I'm passing judgment on them (although I know you'll think I am anyway). Women like her: they are what they are, shaped irreparably by abusive childhoods and fucked-up parents, and in her case no doubt poverty, violence, the gamut of social problems—Bulgaria, Romania, those places are all war-torn and miserable—and you can try to help them but there's no point because you can't, not really. That was my mistake: I wanted to help. But women like her don't want help.

The good news is I didn't miss a single line. My performance was rotten, horrendous—but I didn't miss a single line, I had to stay up all night after she left but I made it through the entire play, twice. That kind of dedication is what makes me the actress—I mean, actor—I am. I earned those roses making their way down the aisle to me in the arms of my takeout delivery boy, one of the Chinese boys who brings me my kung pao or one of the Thai boys who brings my curry, they're more than eager to make an easy fifty bucks on their night off. The curtain draws behind me and I step out from the line of the cast and approach the glow at the edge of the stage. Yes, here he comes, right on cue, two dozen white roses land in my arms. Of course the audience thinks I don't deserve them. Their half-hearted pitter-patter applause gives them away, and out on the street ticket stubs are being flung down like hot potatoes.

Religion

"Something weird happened to me today. Do you mind if I tell you about it?" He didn't pause for my reply, that was understandable, it was a rhetorical question really. He stared down at his hands and grew more somber than two whiskeys should have had him. "So I found myself at church— no, they call it mass, don't they? It was this Catholic church downtown, one of the execs dragged me down there, he's super religious, and totally against my will, you can be sure of that—"

I couldn't, because I barely knew the man, I'd met him only minutes ago when he sidled up to me, reeking of cologne though not the cheapest kind, it didn't smell bad. I was standing at the bar trying to order a drink (a woman standing at the bar always gets waited on last, the men standing there have more pull, it's because most people including bartenders hold an unconscious or conscious belief that men have more money, which statistically is true, and so they think they'll leave bigger tips) when he came up and offered to buy me one. He had a full drink in his own hand—he had come to the bar, he explained, not for a third whiskey but because he was fleeing the enormous group of people he was with—he pointed them out—colleagues and co-workers from his conference who had practically taken over the bar and were drowning out the low-key jazz band with their riotous cavorting (not that I blamed them, I've been to those conferences and by the time you get out at the end of the day you're bolting to the first bar). He was in town for the week for a conference, he said—break-out sessions in the Santa Fe room, dry bagels and coffee in styrofoam cups and a shit-ton of PowerPoints, you know the drill—but today something unusual had happened to him.

"—well, when everyone went up to get the, what do they call it, the drinking-the-blood thing? The drink the blood of Jesus thing?"

"Communion," said a guy in a red tie who had walked up in hopes of squeezing between us without us noticing, he couldn't resist being a know-it-all (men love knowing it all) and so he blew his cover, now he'd have to wait.

"Communion," the businessman repeated. "Thanks."

"That term is more commonly used among Protestants, I think," I said, although in fact I didn't "think," I knew very well (I have a bad habit of trying not to appear smarter than men, it makes them very uncomfortable when I do which makes me uncomfortable and ultimately only results in a miserable interaction for both of us), having been raised Catholic and educated distinctly on such things, that is, on the critical difference between the terms each religion uses to describe the very same rituals. "Most Catholics call it the Eucharist."

The eavesdropper nodded, giving weight to my feminine opinion.

"Is that what they call it? That's interesting,"—the businessman added that phrase people add when something is not at all interesting to them—"anyway, so everybody got up and started filing down the aisle like sheep, I didn't know what was going on, I've hardly been to church a day in my life, except for weddings and funerals, you know, my parents were atheists and I always thought I was lucky that way though now I'm not so sure . . . anyway, to make a long story short, which I really am not, am I?" He chuckled self-deprecatingly in an almost endearing way and took a sip of his brandy, his eyes flickering—don't think I didn't notice—on my cleavage as he did so. "Anyway when everybody got up and started trailing down the aisle I ended up going with them without really knowing what I was doing or where that trail was leading, I found myself down in front, kneeling, even—because everybody else was—kneeling in front of this ginormous"—he used the trendy word I despised but which everybody, not just teenagers, seemed to be using these days—"golden altar like something out of an Indiana Jones movie, right? And I'm kneeling down in a row with the rest of them, they're playing this music that sounds like angels on a pipe organ up in the balcony—"

"Cloister," I corrected, he didn't seem to notice or didn't care what the proper architectural term was. That was all right, he was caught up in his story, after all.

"—and then the priest comes by, or one of the priest's helpers, I mean, the priest's assistant, and he slips this little styrofoam cookie"—"wafer," I couldn't restrain myself from saying, this time he took notice—"wafer, in my mouth, which was no big deal, except it tasted like paper, nasty, then the real priest, the main guy, right? comes along with a chalice—a goblet, like the Holy Grail, have you seen *Monty Python*?"

I nodded bleakly.

"This golden goblet, and I thought, it's straight out of *Monty Python!* I know, I know, I must sound like an idiot but you see I have like *zero* experience with religion, this is all crazy new stuff to me, and he lifts it to my lips like he's feeding a baby, a helpless little baby who can't even manage to hold his own head up, that's how I felt. It was real wine, red, of course, I know enough to know it represents Jesus's blood, but then he says—this is what got me, I'm telling you," he shook his head, stared into his glass, his hands cupped in front of him on the table between us, meaty pink fingers curling and uncurling involuntarily, "it really got me, I can't explain but I have to explain," again he paused, leveled his eyes at me, "I mean I want to tell somebody, I hope you don't mind me laying this on you, I know it's not your typical get-acquainted conversation—"

I started to shake my head, to reply that of course I didn't mind (I have a bad habit of hiding my feelings when it comes to men, of being too accommodating, I'm far from the only woman who does it but it's something about myself that really bugs me, to be honest, I find it a little pathetic when I do it, I started to do it again—fortunately, he cut me off before I could), but he wasn't interested in my reply, not really.

"—and then the priest says—in this booming, don't-fuck-with-me voice, 'Drink of this cup and ye shall have eternal life . . . ' And I'm like, holy shit! he really means it. This guy really believes that. He really believes that by me drinking this thimbleful of Merlot he's giving me eternal life and then just for an instant I thought: *what if it's true?*" He paused, longer this time, to let it sink in I guess, his round nut-brown eyes expanding to orbs, spheres, like marbles I could see the sides and depth of in their sockets, he was fat but he did have sort of nice eyes. "*Eternal life.* And you know what? For an instant I believed it, too."

He sat back, apparently this was the end of the story. Smoothed his tie and straightened his suit jacket. At last he spread his hands which had been curled on the table all this time like lizards, lizards sleeping or biding their time, waiting to pounce on their prey, now they stretched out, revealing themselves as not reptiles but the hairy limbs of his fingers, and he laughed the sort of inward laugh you laugh when the humor is shared with no one but yourself.

"I *did*." As if I was going to argue with him. "That was the thing—it was this feeling—I don't know where it came from or if it was real or even what it was, really, but *time stood still* when he said that and when I took a sip and swallowed time froze, the air in the place froze, it was like suddenly I was lifted out of time and—I don't know"—he shook his head again, desperate to be understood—"it's impossible to explain, a spiritual experience like that which is I guess what I had today. Something that blows your mind, I can't explain, it's changed everything, I can't stop thinking about it."

He looked at me appraisingly, searching my eyes. "I'm sorry."

"What?"

"I don't know, to lay all this heavy—"

"No, it's a great story. I've had experiences like that before."

He heartened. "You have?"

"Well." I shrugged. "I mean, I've had spiritual moments in my life, like when you see everything very clearly suddenly or you suddenly get this insight about some major problem in your life. Like the fact that you should leave your asshole boyfriend, not as if it hadn't been obvious for years, ha ha."

I glanced at him, he was all poker face.

"One time I lost my keys and I had to get on an airplane. I really had no idea what I'd done with them—like *no idea*. Then from nowhere this image flashed in my head of them lying at the bottom of my aquarium—my aquarium is right by the door and sometimes I put my keys on top of it when I come in, which is dumb because I have a bad habit of leaving part of the lid off the aquarium after I clean it, meaning the keys are vulnerable to falling in the water and I still do it—leave the keys there *and* leave the lid off, even after this, you'd think I'd learn my lesson. Anyway sure enough, when I got back from my trip and finally made it home—after an incredible mess with the locksmith and all—there they were, rusting on the fake coral in *exactly the spot and position* the image had shown me. The mystery is why I didn't hear the splash when they fell. I guess we'll never know."

He looked worried.

"The fish were fine."

"No, I don't think you understand . . . what I'm talking about, the *gravity* of—"

"The point is something larger than myself knew something my smaller self didn't. It probably happens all the time and maybe it's just a sixth sense or something, but I think of it as a spiritual thing."

"Okay, but what I felt was—"

I butt in, it wasn't like me but my cognac was kicking in. "You found the fountain of youth, great! You drank from the cup of eternal life, I'm all for it. As long as you share it with me." I was trying to be funny, he wasn't having it. On impulse I covered his lizard hand with mine, surprising myself. "I don't mean to make light of it. It sounds like a very profound thing for you. I think it's great that you can talk about stuff like this, most guys are afraid of such topics."

He sighed and looked away, over my shoulder at something, some image in his head (the golden altar? the golden chalice?) or some other woman or perhaps at his cavorting co-workers who would be wondering where he'd gone. "I don't expect anyone else to understand. It was a very private thing."

He drained his glass and slammed it on the bar like a cowboy. "So what was it you said you do?"

The next day, he calls. It's about twelve-thirty. I'm on the toilet when I hear my phone, so I don't pick up and he leaves a message asking me—he knows it's spur of the moment—but would I like to meet him for lunch, he's got a break between PowerPoints and there's something he wants to tell me. I've just had a crabmeat and avocado sandwich with sprouts, so I don't want lunch—healthy food is more filling than you think—but I have nothing else to do today (it's a Friday and I don't have to go in to my boring, pointless, but decent-paying low-level tech job) and, too, I'm not getting any younger.

I did give him my number, though I'm not sure why. I guess because I'm not getting any younger. He was the most ordinary corporate type you can imagine but then most of the men these days are: late thirties or early forties, budding potbelly, hair—hair! a decent head of it for a man his age, that was encouraging—and an average, wide-ish face pale from the blue light of the computer screen and slightly flabby from, no doubt, years of airport food, drinks over dinner with clients, and weekend beers.

I'd hoped for a little more "action" last night (to use a term a man would). But after we left the bar, after telling his big story, he'd seemed to slip into a melancholy or even cranky mood. He walked me straight home on the damp streets, I lived near enough to skip the cab. The sidewalks were pooled with rain that had fallen while we'd been inside and it was a cool summer evening, starry skies, romantic, perfect for meeting someone new, yet we walked along not holding hands or anything, the clicking of his shiny loafers freshly buffed, no doubt, in the airport on his way here (white businessmen love to get their loafers buffed by little black boys or Mexican boys in the airport when they travel) on the concrete the only sound. He was oddly silent for how effusive he'd been earlier, and then he merely nodded goodnight—no kiss, no light touch on my back or hip or arm and not a single hint that he wanted to come up and so I didn't suggest it. By morning I'd written him off. Then he calls.

I called him back.

"Let me guess," I said, referring to the teaser he'd left in his voicemail, "you've attained enlightenment."

"Ha ha. Thanks for listening last night. It was profound for me."

"I gathered that."

He wanted, disgustingly enough, to meet at the deli downtown next to Dunkin Donuts—I knew the place, it wasn't far from his conference center nor from my favorite shops—so he could have a Long John from the chain donut shop for dessert. "Those chocolate-frosted cream-filled ones? I know, they're terrible, it's my weakness, a couple of those and a steaming cup of black coffee—did you know Dunkin Donuts brews fantastic coffee? Personally I think it's better than Starbucks."

I admitted I did not know that, and we arranged to meet at the deli in half an hour, the mystery of what made up his potbelly solved. I put on a black bra and a black silk top that unbuttoned easily, thinking, a *couple* of those? half a Long John would put me in a diabetic coma. I added dark blue Gloria Vanderbilt jeans that clad me like a wet glove, reasonable heels (why overdo it?) and diamond studs in my ears, and a fire engine-red silk scarf for color. Everything in my closet is black, I wear my color in my accessories, my belts and bags and scarves and shoes, and I have plenty of all of these, but the red scarf turned out to be a mistake because it drew a cardinal to my shoulder in the park where we'd gone to have a walk after lunch, the birds in the park downtown are incredibly tame, as a matter of fact they're a nuisance, they're so used to people feeding them they've taken to harassing them for food and in this case the cardinal was essentially attacking me but my lunch date didn't notice. "Look how he matches your scarf!" he exclaimed, Long John frosting sticky on the fingers reaching for the scarf I'd bought in Paris, the only thing I had from Paris, I don't make a lot of money but I like nice things and I have a few. I jerked away just in time. He was so taken by "the beauty of the world" as he put it, he didn't notice the bird pecking and shrieking at me with true viciousness.

"You look different in the light of day," he said as I walked toward him on the sidewalk when we met. It was just what I was thinking about him, and I hoped he didn't mean it the way I did, that is, that in the cold cruel light of day his age as well as his general disheveledness was more apparent—the creases in his shirt where he bent his arms at the elbows and the creases in his tie as if both had been worn several times over and not dry-cleaned in between as well as the creases in the flesh of his face as if it, too, were a well-worn or well-broken-in garment, in a way it was, that's what life does to us, breaks us in and wears us down. On the other hand it was plain he'd once been a younger and better-looking man, which is enough when you're in your forties, the knowledge that a more attractive self once resided in your lover is good enough, in your forties you can't ask for more than that. He was about six feet tall or perhaps an inch or two under and he moved in an athletic way if you know what I'm talking about—it's subtle but it's something you can see in a man if you watch for it, a sort of grace in the movements that conjures a high-school football career. Now he had that puffy, blanched look akin to a fillet of whitefish on ice and brought on, no doubt, by too many long days in front of the computer and on the phone while buzzing down the freeway soothing clients and making money (making money these days requires an unhealthy lifestyle) as well as red-eye flights, too-tight shoes and airport hamburgers, after-dinner brandies and during-dinner martinis (to soften the annoying task of wining and dining whiny clients). Beneath this, however, the bone structure was good. I saw this. The eyes were a nice brown if not the dark mysterious Antonio Banderas-style brown I prefer in men, and they had nice long sun-faded eyelashes, feminine but not too feminine.

"I do?"

He smiled. "You look even better in the daylight."

He knew just what to say or maybe he meant it, who knew.

"I want to thank you for last night," he said. We were standing in the hot sun on the crowded sidewalk and I was about to step inside to the cool air-conditioned air of the deli, the flocks of people rushing by trying to make the most of their lunch breaks were getting on my nerves as no doubt having to dodge us was getting on theirs and here he was launching into conversation, the kind of opening statement that implicitly requests the listener stay put rather than listen while moving. "For listening to my story. I know it wasn't the usual first-conversation fare, but I have to tell you how nice it was to share all that with a willing ear"—that's how he put it, as if any willing ear would have done, which made me feel a little insecure but I set the feeling aside—"which helped me understand it myself—what that experience yesterday meant to me, it really helped a lot to put it into words."

He shifted onto the balls of his feet, looming toward me, and I smelled his breath, a faintly stale smell of food, it sounds disgusting but it wasn't that bad, a lot of people's breath smells like food, after all that's what we put in our mouths.

"Have you ever found yourself telling someone something and suddenly you realize what you're saying and you realize you didn't understand it yourself until the moment you said it?"

I nodded, actually I had had that experience but he didn't stop to notice, he was off and running at the mouth again.

"It was because you were such a good listener, you helped me get insight into my own experience and now I understand what happened to me— because that's how I've come to think of it, as something that happened *to* me from *outside* myself instead of something I made up or made happen myself—which makes it even more profound, naturally—but now I understand it so much better than I did before our dinner and I just wanted to thank you."

He wrapped it up. Was he really done? He stood there blinking in the sun at me.

"Really? I'm glad. You seemed so quiet on the walk home last night. To tell you the truth, I didn't know if I'd hear from you."

"No, no." He put his hand on my arm, almost tenderly. "I was lost in thought, that's all, I was in a very . . . err, contemplative mood." He laughed. "I don't think I've ever been in a contemplative mood in my life, ha. No, really, it had nothing to do with you. After I left you"—just then a woman in a suit and stilettos rammed into him, her briefcase swinging around and very nearly smashing into his groin, he gave a little hop to avoid the hit while the woman nearly teetered off her six-inch spikes and onto the pavement, she cursed, just managing to regain her balance. She turned and shrieked at my companion, eyes tiny daggers slitting her face, "*Move*, fucker!"

Watching her click away at lightning pace, he chuckled. "That's exactly what I'm talking about." Shook his head. "It's madness. Just madness, the way we live now."

"Yeah, it's pretty crazy. Do you want to go inside? I think we're in peoples' way."

"Sure—just one more thing: last night? After I left you. I took the long way back to my hotel, I actually walked, I don't know how long it's been since I walked anywhere unless you're counting airports, which you shouldn't because I always take the moving sidewalk, I mean, who can resist the moving sidewalk? I just walked around looking at everything, oh, I've spent plenty of time in this city but this time I saw it with new eyes, even the homeless bums and crack whores looked beautiful to me last night, all desperate and ragged and all, after all, I see now we're all the same, you and me and them and us, we're all *human*, see, we're all eternal souls walking around in human skins. Even the lights"—his voice pitched, he was getting worked up, he rocked back and forth on his feet and I grabbed his elbow to pull him out of the pedestrian flow—"the neon and the red and green and yellow traffic lights are all the same color when you get down to it, aren't they? They all come from the same single color, and they all looked so beautiful to me . . . when I finally got back to my hotel I sat there in the window staring down at the lights forever—I didn't even have a drink, you don't need one when you're in such a state of mind, and I thought about my life, I thought long and hard, it must have been four or five in the morning when I finally lay down."

We'd finally moved out of the sidewalk flow of eternal souls walking around in human skins and flattened ourselves against the glass of the deli windows, the people sitting at the table behind us must have had a fine view of our asses.

"I thought about my divorce, regretfully,"—he glanced at me—meaning-fully?—"not of the split but of all the mean words exchanged between us and the petty harassing by both sides over what is, in the end, a pet-ty amount of money, but then, everything seems petty in the context of eternity." He looked around, at the madness of the city or that's what I thought he was seeing which is to say that's what I was seeing, I did agree with him, it is crazy the way we live now, anybody can see that. "It all seems so pointless . . . And yet, so *right*, too. So real and full of beauty."

"I know what you mean. Yeah. It really does. So, do you still want to have lunch?" My stomach was rumbling like a thunderhead. It was nearly one-thirty and the sprouts were long digested, that's the problem with sprouts, they're super healthy but they don't last long.

"I do. Just one more thing: I thought about my daughter, too, and I saw how even though she refuses to speak to me—except to ask for money, of course, but that's how college kids are—we're still connected, we've never not been because we are *one and the same*. We're all connected in eternity, I saw that crystal clear last night and there's not a bone in my body that doubts it, I mean, I know it sounds woo-woo but our separateness really is an illusion, I'm part of you and you're part of me and what you think is what I think and what you feel is what I feel." His lips twitched and his fingers convulsed as if jolted by the urge to touch me, we were standing only inches apart, my bare arm touching his arm through the sleeve of his pale blue button-up, he wasn't wearing a suit jacket as he had been last night, really you couldn't see much of a potbelly. His eyes lingered on my bare neck, his voice when he spoke again was raspy and he cleared his throat self-consciously. "I'm you and you're me. Don't you think?"

"I do," I said, lying. "I know exactly what you mean."

"You do?" His eyes dropped, this time without trying to hide it, to my breasts, the cleavage of which my blouse was, I have to admit, exquisitely showing off.

"Hey," I breathed, leaning in, letting my fingers touch his chest through his shirt, then his skin between the buttons, hairy, damp. He was sweating a little, it was pretty hot out. "Do you want to—"

Skip lunch, go back to my place but he cut me off, as he was prone to do.

"Talk about it more over lunch? I do! I still have a lot to tell you."

Could there really be more? How enlightened could one man get? He flung open the door and swept his arm across it like Prince Charming himself.

The businessman gobbled down his Swiss-slathered corned beef on rye like a starving wolf. Spiritual illumination hadn't dented his appetite or perhaps it was all that consciousness expansion that made him so hungry, though apparently not for anything else if you know what I mean. I had a bowl of house-made sauerkraut and a slice of raspberry cheesecake (despite his scolding I'd have no room left for a Long John) and a Diet Coke and entertained myself by examining his eyebrows and the sun-faded tips of his reddish lashes, really, he was not bad-looking—while he talked. More musings on the nature of immortality and reality or not-reality. After that we went to the park where he wolfed down a couple of Long Johns, that's when the cardinal went at me. I had to fight it off with no help from Mr. Saint.

At the park, he turned to me and said, "What if they've had it right all this time?"

"They?"

"The religions. Religion. They've been trying to tell us, about eternal life, about how simple it is, how natural, how it's our birthright, how our very nature is eternal and yet we won't listen, we keep banging our heads against the wall and clawing our eyes out, agonizing over our apparently permanent deaths when in reality there is no death and we never die, not one of us." He paused, thinking. "I mean, I guess if you believe you have to be baptized or saved or whatever to live forever, some do die. Or go to Hell. That part doesn't really click for me. I mean, it's pretty medieval. Maybe it's true, but that's not how it feels to me. It feels to me like we all get it and we don't have to do anything for it."

I had put my hand on his arm at this point, I was stroking it absentmindedly (or feigning absentminded-ness) through his shirt sleeve, hoping to get something started. It's not that I'm only interested in sex but that's how I've always connected with men, at least initially. I paused and looked around at the varieties of people in the park, the in-shape and out-of-shape, the bent and unbent, lumpy and firm, pretty and repulsive, smiling and scowling. I was raised Catholic but college had drained it out of me and I had never looked back. I did have a friend who had given me Reiki once, with profound results (it made me tingle all over for hours after).

I said, "I don't see how you condemn some people to eternal damnation unless you're absolutely sure about it. That seems like the kind of thing you should be able to prove before you go swinging gavels."

"Exactly!"

I went back to stroking him, smoothing the hairs of his arm one direction and then the other through the thin cotton. Most men would have been going crazy by now. He was gazing at the sky with his jaw open a little, like someone not quite right in the head, as they say.

"Maybe it was God," he whispered.

"What?"

"What broke through to me yesterday. It must have been God." His color rose. "God himself!"

The way people—men and women and everyone in between—insist on referring to God as male has always irked me. The thing is, they don't even realize they're doing it, it's become so normalized, so blindly accepted, no one even notices they're using a pronoun that leaves out half the population, and also it's stupid because I find it very doubtful that if there is a god, it has genitals.

"Maybe it was something you ate. Like your body chemistry was just right and it kind of tripped you out. Or hormones. If you were a woman, they'd say it was your hormones."

He bristled, straightening his spine and slipping his arm from under mine, if not entirely—we were still touching or I was still touching him, rather, touch isn't always mutual even if someone allows their body to remain in contact with yours, their flesh on yours or their clothing grazing yours, that doesn't mean they're participating in the contact, they can be inwardly rejecting that touch and that's something that can easily be felt by the outreaching party.

"You're making fun of me."

"No, no, no"—I was, of course, but I'm not the type to come out and say what I mean, I never have been. "It's just that that's what they'd say, if you were a woman."

He was looking at me askance. "Who's 'they'?"

"You know, everybody. And by the way, God is not necessarily a '*he*,' you know," I went on, saying what I meant, he'd brought it out in me, "I get so tired of people calling God 'he' all day long, when we really have no idea if God has a penis or not. Let alone if it exists, but that's another issue." I took a breath. I was shaking. I had removed my hands from his body and put them in my lap, now I saw they were shaking. "And how convenient"—my voice pitched, becoming "shrill," I think is the word for the hysterical woman who lets her thoughts be known to the world—"*how convenient* for half the population—and I'm not talking about the better half—that the ultimate authority on all things happens to be male and not female."

"Calm down," he said, putting his hand on my arm now, it was his turn to reach out and mine to recoil. "I don't see what the big deal is, it's just a pronoun."

"Pronouns matter," I said, sitting back down—I had half-sprung off the park bench, people were staring. "If pronouns don't matter, nothing does."

He smiled at this rather nonsensical statement, though it made perfect sense to me and it was, after all, the kind of generalized profundity he had been spewing for the last twenty hours so he should have appreciated it. For a few moments we were silent as he considered me, happily, I thought. Then: "I like your passion."

I like your passion! I nearly slapped him. His phone rang just in time (I'm boasting, I don't have it in me, I've never hit a man, it's too bad because so many of them deserve it), a cheerful pop song I'd heard a hundred thousand times but couldn't name. He jumped up and dug it out of his pocket, cursing when he saw the screen, apparently he didn't want to talk to whoever was calling.

"Yeah? . . . Yeah. Yeah. Yeah. Okay." Long pause. "To be honest with you it completely slipped my mind. I know I know I know. I thought it was tomorrow . . . Okay. I can be there in fifteen."

He hung up and blew out his cheeks, looked at me with a "hangdog" face, that's the 1950s term that comes to mind, I have no idea where it comes from but it's the perfect descriptor for the long face he now pulled (to use an equally old-fashioned verb). "I'm in deep shit."

I was still seething. He must have noticed my gritted teeth, my tense face, then again, men aren't as detail-oriented as women and they often miss the little things. Then again, they miss the big things too. The little signs of discontent, the big signs of fury, the little signs of tenderness, the big signs of disgust and everything in between, they miss it, not because they don't care (some of them do, I realize that) but because they don't *want* to know what the woman standing right in front of them is feeling, it's simpler not to. It's true I don't like men, not all of them but most of them or just their general way of being, though that doesn't stop me being attracted to them and even falling in love with one now and then. That's natural, I guess.

"What now?"

"I was supposed to give a PowerPoint this afternoon. I completely forgot." He sighed deeply. "You know, none of this is even relevant anymore. My eyes have been opened to how utterly pointless everything I do is. *Power-*

Points. You know what my PowerPoint is over? The point one zero drop in sales last quarter and the fascinating forces in consumer behavior that account for it, such as that constipation rates were up so more of them were sitting on the toilet than buying our product. That's as plausible as what I argue, which is some bullshit—I mean, really, I can't help it, point one zero percent is anyone's guess!—I argue that it's the fall-out from the release of a competing company's new line last fall but I could be as full of shit as our constipated customers are. What a waste of my fucking life."

"So quit."

He raised his eyebrows, gave me a look.

"Quit if it's so meaningless. Walk your talk. If you're suddenly so spiritually enlightened, prove it. What have you got to lose, anyway? You're an eternal soul walking around in a human skin. Nothing can hurt you, right?"

Lamely, he said, "I just told my boss I'd be there in fifteen."

Surprising myself, I stood up. Flipped my red scarf over my shoulder in a Katharine Hepburn way. "I have to go."

"Wait!" He leaped up and grabbed my elbow. "You're right."

"I am?"

"Yes! I'll quit. I'm quitting my job."

"You're ridiculous. Don't quit your job."

"You're right, that would be stupid . . . Okay, look, I'll just call him and say I'll do my PowerPoint tomorrow morning. There'll be an open slot, there always is. He's not going to fire me for that."

I threw up my hands. "Whatever."

He put his hands on my arms and ran them down my silk sleeves. He locked his eyes with mine in a meaningful way, and in a husky, ridiculous voice said, "Let's spend the day together. I'm only in town for a few more days. I want to spend the day with you."

I made him wait. I pretended to look away, at something in the distance. "Okay but *you have got to stop talking about your religious experience*, okay?"

"Yes. I know. I'm going on too much. I'm sorry. I'm usually not like this." He put a finger over his lips in the universal sign for hush.

I waited on the park bench while he paced some steps away—just out of earshot, who knew what he was really telling his boss if indeed it were his boss, it could have been his wife, or his ex-wife with whom he still had a complicated relationship, I didn't really care. He returned smiling. "It's all good. Tomorrow morning. Constipation and Sales: The Unseen Market Force."

"Ha ha, I suppose it could be a factor."

We walked down the sidewalk through the park, arms linked, not speaking or him not speaking for once. It was a nice change. I noticed it was a beautiful day, not as hot as it had been the last several days, and the sky full of those puffy white clouds, archetypal clouds, the kind you would spend hours making into dragons and elephants lying on your back in the green green grass when you were a kid (at least I did). That sort of summer day—how had I not noticed this before? The park was filled with bright zinnias and I have always loved zinnias. The businessman reached for my hand. His felt warm and damp but not unpleasant. Without discussing it, we walked out of the park and up the street back into the busy city. The unspoken understanding was we were wandering, destinationless, that was fine with me. I had nothing but time.

We passed by a church with its doors open to the good weather. Inside we heard singing, one of those stuffy old hymns. *Shall we gather at the river? Where bright angel feet have trod . . .*

He stopped, motioned with his head, grinning. There was irony in his voice: "Religion."

I smiled, sent the irony back. "Religion."

"C'mon, let's check it out."

"No. It's really not my thing."

"Come on, it's all new to me, remember? I'm curious. I'm like a kid in a candy store."

I eyed the alphabet sign out front, one of those with the changeable plastic letters, it read IF YOU DON'T LOVE GOD GO TO HELL. It needed a comma, badly. Inside, bodies swayed in the pews, arms stretched above heads, fingers wiggling as if trying to tickle the underbelly of a sky god. Pentecostal. "It's not Catholic. It will be very different."

"Perfect. Broaden my range."

We went in but stood at the back behind the pews, I had no desire to sit in those hard-as-stone wooden pews religions favor, loving suffering as they do. No one seemed to notice us, their eyes were shut tight. Twenty or thirty people, most white-haired but some were young and there were even a few teenagers. The piano crescendoed, demanding action. A woman with waist-long undyed brown hair in a turquoise polyester-blend dress, mid-calf-length, capped sleeves, very 80s like something I wore in middle school, answered. She broke rank and approached the pulpit, eyes closed and arms raised like a zombie. Her mouth was moving and gibberish was coming out in a sort of musical way. The preacher, obviously the lead man, pulled her up on stage with him. They linked hands and started shouting indecipherable syllables at the sky—the whole congregation clearly thought God was up there somewhere, lurking in the ceiling beams or beyond them in the clouds, I wondered what their reasons were.

I looked at the businessman, who was staring unmoving, lips parted slightly as if he wanted to join in. No, I thought, cringing inwardly, he wouldn't, he won't. But I was misreading him. He turned, feeling my gaze. His eyes met mine and held them and I saw there bemusement, perhaps shock. This counts too, I wanted to point out—all the weird ways human beings try to connect with something bigger than themselves, if you're going in for any of them you have to count them all, I wanted to point this out but I didn't. We were standing close, our arms touching slightly through our clothing but I didn't feel a charge, not a sexual one. It was just contact, and maybe connection.

"I don't know if I want to be eternal," I said over the din.

"What?"

The rest of the church had found its tongues too, a cacophony of fragmented, wordless sounds rose and mingled in the rafters, driven by the piano. I leaned over to speak loudly in his ear, like you do in a night club. "I don't want to live forever. It's an excuse to behave however you want to in this life. To be an evil asshole, to rape the earth, whatever. It doesn't matter if you're eternal. Muck it up and you've got eternity to get it right."

"Come outside." He led me onto the front steps and closed the big wooden doors behind us. It seemed unnaturally quiet out there, the cars humming by at a distance. We faced each other in the sun. "That depends on the nature of that infinite energy you're connected to. If it's evil or even neutral, cold, indifferent, then yeah, I could see that might be the outcome. But if whatever it is that's eternal in you is benevolent—is love, light, sheer goodness—then that is what you would want to be too."

"Wait. Say that again, would you?" It suddenly struck me as profound, what he had said, it suddenly struck me as true. He said what he had said again, word for word, I thought. A wave of energy washed through me. A moment later, I lost the feeling.

"Put your hands on me," I told the businessman. His pudgy face smiled down, glowing, before I would have described it as smug, now I thought it simply kind. Who was he? He had been a stranger only twenty-four hours before—perhaps, I thought crazily, he wasn't real, perhaps he was my guardian angel, scenes from *It's a Wonderful Life* flashed in.

"Transmit that to me, what you just said. I almost got it." I faced him and he leaned to meet me, seeming to know what I wanted. I put my forehead on his and he put his hands on my shoulders.

"No," I said. "On my heart."

The Dead Wife

He wasn't wearing dark glasses, he wasn't crying, his eyes weren't swollen and red and they weren't staring blankly into space in stricken astonishment like someone who's just lost his beloved to an act of incomprehensible violence. Perhaps he was trying to forget that was who, indeed, he was, and was getting himself through by focusing his mind on the mundane details of death to be dealt with: the headstone designs to be mulled over, the phone calls from long-lost relatives and friends to be returned, the sympathy cards to be read and replied to, the flowers to be transferred to urns and vases and those that needed thrown out since they had already gone limp. Or perhaps he was trying to forget the bloodstains on his own hands.

I nudged Sven, who was standing too close to me. Sven had had a terrible crush on me all these years and we both knew it, it was something we let lie—besides, he had a wife and I always had a lover coming or going. Objectively considered, Sven is a very attractive man but personally I could never go for him since whenever I get too close to him, I'm overwhelmed by the scent of vinegar—perhaps he eats too much fish and chips or perhaps his body chemistry simply doesn't agree with mine. This along with the over-large pores on the end of his nose (which everyone has, honestly, if you look close enough) I inevitably find my attention drawn to during the hours-long conversations Sven and I like to have at middle-eastern cafés, hole-in-the-wall bars, mediocre Indian buffets and crowded cocktail joints (our rule is never the same place twice) make it impossible for me ever to sleep with him.

"Do you think he did it?" I whispered in time with the upsweep of the violins as they began a composition featuring a solo by Nicola (the dead wife). She'd been a world-class violinist before being found hacked to pieces on the floor of her bedroom last week.

"Of course not," Sven snapped, his long brows slanting like field darts. He was twiddling something obsessively in his suitcoat pocket, probably a Camel though last I knew he'd quit. It made him keep bumping my elbow, it was getting on my nerves. He leaned over: "Maybe. Do you?"

"It's possible. Look at the man."

Dean was standing with his hands in his wool trouser pockets. His pink lips made hooks in his large tan face as he frowned down at the coffin, sighed, looked up at the gray sky, back down. He looked perfectly content, even tranquil. No—he looked bored. Or perhaps it was just my imagination.

These days it's hard to tell what's your imagination and what's not. What's reality, what you didn't see in a dream or Netflix show and what you did. Especially when it comes to reading other people. I have no idea how other people, even those close to me, are feeling. People are so disconnected these days, from each other as well as from themselves, they're so busy staring into screens, worrying about the climate, trying to make another million or simply get by, they don't have time for such serious business as deciphering their own projections from who other people really are.

I didn't know Nicola that well, yet I considered her one of my best friends. That sounds odd, I know, but these days it's the best we can hope for. I met her when we played in the same orchestra, I won't go into how or why we became friends, it's not that interesting of a story and besides, it's embarrassing, it involves me having too much to drink, a forgotten item of clothing, and Nicola happening to be the only other woman in the dressing room. The details don't matter, what matters is there were certain things about Nicola I liked very much and I'm shocked and horrified at what's happened to her. Perhaps the thing I enjoyed most about her was her tendency to wear huge, overbearing (and very expensive) jewelry, jewelry I would never wear but wished I had the bravado to. Her favorite piece or the one she wore most frequently was a choker of enormous, unpolished pink pearls, pearls the size of sweet onions hung with a chunk of onyx the size of a child's fist. That piece provided for a lot of chit-chat party conversations, there are more boring things to talk about. I liked, too, the way she carried around her twenty-thousand-dollar violin upside down over her shoulder as if it were a plastic toy, moving in her black spaghetti-strapped dresses in an athletic, almost masculine way. At five-eleven, with her loose tawny hair and slanted, gray Romanian eyes, Nicola cut a stunning figure. Superficial things, I know, but it's the details that tell you who someone is, that are your best clue to what's inside. She was kind, too, sometimes funny. A musician with rare talent. I didn't see any reason her husband or anyone else would want to murder her. She did get a big mouth when she drank too much, but we all have our flaws.

I didn't play in Nicola's orchestra long. I moved on after six months, the conductor had a grudge against me and tried to drop me down to assistant concertmaster when clearly I'm a concertmaster. I found a new position with an orchestra (only a slightly less prestigious one) that recognized this, my only regret is it's in the suburbs and comes with a long commute, at least I can take the underground, so it doesn't wear me out that much. I thank god, as I have thanked god for twenty years, I'm not a cellist—toting a violin around is bad enough.

But we stayed in touch, loosely, and I saw Nicola at parties, art openings, or by chance in champagne bars and ritzy restaurants. We always greeted each other warmly and talked easily, we recommended books to each other and exchanged concerts and plays and films we wanted to see or had seen and that had changed us forever (for better or worse). She had good taste and I like women who have good taste. I complimented her outfits and she complimented mine—though hers were always glaringly more elegant (and that jewelry!). I would have liked a closer friendship but I never pushed it, she was obviously a busier, happier woman than I.

For one thing she was married to a *very* rich man. Nicola's husband Ramon Dean was a well-known businessman. He was a large, burly man, broad-chested and handsome, as for some reason so many rich men are. The few times I met him he struck me as something of an asshole—he didn't, for instance, seem to have the slightest appreciation for music, at least he never brought the subject up with me, which is something that always offends me, I mean, if people aren't interested in music, that's their loss but when you know someone's entire life is devoted to their art, an art that demands hundreds of hours of practice a week or it seems like that much (I may not make as much money as him, but I bet I work more), which how could he be married to Nicola and not know how much she had to practice—well, you could at least mention it, at least *feign* appreciation. The few times I spoke to Dean at parties or champagne bars all he talked about was the chalets, yachts, and racehorses he owned. Honestly,

I found him really boring. Men with money usually are, or men with too much money. People said he was worth billions, he'd invested in some microchip or something in the eighties that was raking it in for him. He was rumored to own several diamond mines in Africa, too. Disgusting. Still, I could see why Nicola was attracted to him, personally I never have been but most women are attracted to rich men and it's not the money, it's the power. Most women feel so helpless and lost and pathetic (even if they don't show it on the outside), they think they have to latch onto a powerful man to get anywhere in life, maybe they're right. But I'm glad I've never been like that.

Men—and I do mean men—as rich as Dean can do whatever they want. They can get away with anything and they know it, even murder. Bribing the police would have amounted to little more than pocket money for Dean, he'd probably even find a way to write it off. Perhaps he was the reason the police had closed the case so quickly, pronouncing it a random robbery only days later, even though the crime had all the signs of deliberation and personal vengeance.

Sven and I considered the evidence at a piano bar on Highberry Road. We'd ended up there after the funeral—against my better judgment, I had a matinee the next day. I could tell Sven felt like getting drunk—I did, too, it's only natural to want to get drunk after the funeral of a friend. I'd simply have to make it an early night, I really didn't want to be hungover again tomorrow.

"Such an awful death," I said. "Surely even if he wanted to get rid of her he wouldn't have had the balls to do it that way. Surely he's too civilized for that?"

Sven nodded and put a fingertip in the wasabi, touched it to his tongue, made a face. He hated sushi but the place served complementary and very mediocre sushi to go with its terrible piano jazz and we didn't turn it down. "You'd think. There's also the fact that whenever I saw them together they always seemed so happy. Even, I daresay, in love."

"You daresay?"

He didn't catch my rib. Sven's oblivious to subtext, he misses half my meanings, that's another reason.

"I daresay because God forbid two people be genuinely in love these days."
He regarded a California roll skeptically. "We've become so cynical, you
and I. We're so jaded and suspicious, don't you think? We act like it's impossible for two people to fall in love and stay in love anymore, like love
is a thing of the past, a nostalgic relic that's pleasant to recall but doesn't
really exist anymore, like drive-in movies or the idea smoking is good for
you."

"Sometimes I think it is, a thing of the past. In my experience it always
turns into one, ha ha . . . But what about his behavior today? He looked
bored to death—pardon the pun—like he was at one of those brain-numb-
ing corporate meetings he must have spent his life suffering through rather than his wife's funeral."

Sven was looking around. His eyes found the smokers gathered on the
patio. "I want a cigarette. Should I?"

"I thought you quit."

"I did. That's what I mean." I gave him a look.

He shrugged. "Maybe he was putting on a good face. Everyone reacts to
trauma differently." He stared at the tablecloth or his beer or both. "Then
again, if they really were in love that may be all the more reason to suspect
him of hacking her up. People in love do desperate, terrible things. Maybe
he found out she was cheating on him."

"Mmmm, it doesn't seem like her. But I know what you mean, whenever I
saw them together I got the impression they were crazy about each other.
That's why his behavior today makes me so suspicious. Whenever I saw
them they'd have their hands all over each other, they'd be all long looks
and private whispers. They hadn't been married that long—a few years? I'll
never forget—it's funny, now that she's dead, I remember her more clearly, she's more vivid in my mind or maybe I just see my memories of her
as more precious, knowing there won't be any more of them—I'll never
forget that time I saw them coming out of a play . . . I was outside fuming
over one of my many fights with Peter. Remember Peter?"

Sven smiled. "The short one?"

He loves, I thought, the thought of my many failed loves. His large fingers uncurled their death grip on his porter and inched toward mine, as if the thought of Peter's shortness stirred in him a sexual impulse. It probably did. Nothing turns people on more than the notion of their own attractiveness. Sven has a complex about his nose and he should (though he's got it wrong—it's not the size of the nose but the size of the pores), but he's very vain about his Scandinavian height.

I inched my hand back and casually put it in my lap. "He was as tall as me which is tall enough. Anyway, I don't remember what play it was but it must have been boring enough or our fight bad enough I didn't mind missing some of it, I was outside smoking and nursing my wounds—Peter was very cruel to me, I don't think you ever realized that. He hid it very well, he treated me like a queen in public but as soon as we were alone he turned into a monster. For an actor he really was a decent actor if you know what I mean. Anyway, I was out there smoking—that was back when I smoked, thank god I've quit, it's such a repulsive habit"—Sven rolled his eyes—"and feeling lonelier than I've ever felt in my life, in fact that was the moment I realized Peter and I weren't going to make it, yet another relationship down the tubes, on top of that I could hear the audience laughing through the theater walls, an audience laughing and clapping through theater walls when you're out on the cold street on your own has got to be the loneliest sound in the world . . ."

I paused to glare at the pianist, who had pushed her bench back and was bowing spastically like a jack-in-the-box stuck on repeat. She'd just finished butchering a jazz rendition of Satie, the very notion of Satie in jazz is butchery, sacrilege. I hoped she was done for the night.

". . . and no doubt my own wretched desolation at that moment influenced how I perceived Dean and Nicola as they came down the steps outside the theater toward me, I have to keep that in mind. But I'll never forget how they looked when they came down the steps, they looked like this fairytale couple to me, like the kind of relationship I've always wanted. They'd left the play early themselves—perhaps they were that eager to go home and get in bed—they came down the steps toward me, linked arm-in-arm and they weren't talking as people usually do when they leave a play, they weren't saying a word, as if they didn't have to, as if they were so in tune they could reach other's thoughts. Their faces leaned into each other touching slightly, and I remember her hand stroked his arm with such tenderness, as if he were as fragile to her as a China doll, which is the last thing you'd ever think of Dean as, fragile. Perhaps, it struck me then as it strikes me again now, love is simply not despising the other person for being what we all are deep down: totally vulnerable, frail, helpless and pathetic human beings. Perhaps that's what love really is, not the presence of some feeling but the absence of disdain and disgust . . ."

"I know what you mean. Like nothing repulses me more than a needy woman. So did they notice you?"

"What?"

"Did they notice—"

"No, the other thing."

"What?"

"Never mind," I said, making no effort to hide my loathing. Sven, like most men, can be a sexist pig though he's totally unaware of it (not that that's any excuse). "No, they did not see me. Of course not, they were absorbed in their own little world, you know how lovers are. Dean glanced at me but to him I was merely an object to avoid colliding with, as insignificant as a scrap of trash on the street." I'm well aware I'm not as beautiful as Nicola and I never will be, but I'm one up on her now—I'm alive. "I watched them walk this way all the way down the street to their car and then he opened the door for her and kissed her against the car. For some reason I couldn't keep my eyes off them."

"You saw in them what you desperately want but are afraid you'll never have."

"That's obvious," I said with more (or perhaps less) bitterness than I felt. "Or what I think I want or think I *should* want but do I really? From the outside love looks so good, but whenever I find myself in it, I end up more miserable than I am alone."

"Maybe you're just a miserable person. Maybe the problem is you, not your relationships."

"Fuck off, Sven."

"C'mon, it's because you pick the wrong men. I've been telling you that for years."

"Yeah, because you think I should pick men more like you."

Sven put his hands up. "No, no, no. This isn't about me. Well, maybe a bit but what I'm saying is you don't have the best radar for men, not for good ones or available ones. It's probably an unconscious commitment phobia. Most of us have one."

I watched the pianist absentmindedly. She lifted her fingers from the keys to flip her hot pink feather boa over her shoulder, I'd never seen a musician if she could be called that wear anything tackier. It had slipped down between her knees, drawing attention to her unladylike position, though it is, of course, a necessary one for playing the instrument, or playing it well which she was not.

Finally I said, "Maybe you're right. I'm not always the best judge of character."

Sven wiped the beer foam from his giant Swedish mouth with a paper napkin. Most women find Sven's plump, cherry red lips attractive but for me they're too fat, they remind me of the lips of those cherubs in Renaissance paintings. "You're not the only one. You know I can't stand Lydia."

His wife. She was an annoying woman. She was always quoting political opinions you knew she'd gotten off Facebook or NPR and trying to pass them off as her own and she spent her days getting manicures, her hair done, shopping for shoes or handbags, she was that sort of woman. She was also poisonously jealous of me, she'd always been but then, Sven and I's friendship pre-dated her by a few decades (we met in college), so that was understandable.

I couldn't help but laugh. Maybe it was the martini coming on already but my laugh came out sounding like a girlish giggle or a hyena. "You're the one who married her."

"I know. That's my point. When I married her, I didn't know I couldn't stand her! At the time I thought I was madly in love with her . . . maybe I was." He contemplated. "Or maybe the signs she was a superficial bitch were there all along and I turned a blind eye to them. I didn't want to see them, so I didn't see them."

He looked at me, I knew what he was waiting for. "They were."

He tilted his head, grimaced in agreement. I crossed my legs and looked at my drink. Honestly, I didn't feel much like drinking tonight and these were conversations Sven and I had had before. On my way to the funeral I'd stopped by the video store and rented Bergman's *The Seventh Seal* (Max von Sydow plays chess with Death, surely you know it, it's only a masterpiece) on Blu-ray, there are still some things you can't stream believe it or not. It'd been years since I'd seen it and the funeral, the rainy gig-less weekend, Nicola's murder, my own impending forty-ninth birthday, something had put me in the mood for it tonight. Also renting it had been a strategy to keep myself from going out tonight, now it was too late and I'd better have another one if I didn't want to face a deadly depression when I got home. I'd just have to drink a lot of water and load up on ibuprofen before I went to bed, I had that matinee on the other side of the city tomorrow.

I took a sip. It tasted cold, metallic, good. "And what about Nicola? Surely if her husband was a psychopath there would have been some signs. Did she turn a blind eye to them? She wasn't dumb."

"Right, she wasn't. Even though she was beautiful." He grinned, I didn't take the bait. "Did she not wonder about that axe that appeared suddenly in the back of the closet, the box of rope and three-inch screws?"

"God, Sven, please—"

He drained his beer and popped the final roll in his overlarge mouth. He lifted his finger for the waiter, who saw him and changed direction. "Just quoting the *Times*. They didn't leave anything to the imagination, did they? The bastards, they love a story like this . . . Another porter, please."

He turned to me.

"And a raspberry martini." Even though I was only halfway through the first one.

"A raspberry martini for the lady. And an order of fries, please."

"Fries?"

Sven arched his brows at the waiter. "French fries?"

"I'm sorry, sir, we don't serve French fries," said the young middle-eastern waiter with his hands behind his back.

Sven made an astonished face. "Surely you have potatoes?"

"I'm not certain, sir." The waiter looked unperturbed. "We have a limited menu. Our specialty as you may know is Japanese appetizers."

Sven scowled at me. "*As you may know.*" Back at the waiter. "How about oil?"

"Sir?"

"Don't tell me you don't have potatoes and oil to fry them in."

"He's drunk," I said.

"I'll see what I can do."

"Do that," Sven snarled.

The waiter left and he added, a half-assed defense, "I'm starving. Sushi never fills me up."

I watched the people hurrying past on the sidewalk, umbrellas coming out. The rain that had been misting down all day had finally unleashed full force. "Well. We don't know he did it. Speaking of misjudging character, maybe we're barking up the wrong tree altogether."

Sven sat back and crossed his legs. His movements were elegant even though—or perhaps because—he was well on his way. He was staring again at the smokers on the patio like a child wanting to go out to the playground. And as if with its own will, his hand was creeping across the center line again, toward mine. He pulled it back. I saw something occur to him. Shaking his head, he said, "No. He couldn't have done it."

"Well?"

"A conversation I had with him once at a party just came back to me. Well, it wasn't really the conversation but an incident that happened in the middle of it. Oh, I can count the number of conversations I had with Dean on one hand, and they were always brief, I'm not rich enough to warrant talking to for long, you know. Nor were Nicola and I that close, even though I've sat next to her now for, what, seven years? It's going to be strange going back next week . . . She and I never went much deeper than small talk, I don't know if you knew that."

I nodded. Nicola kept her guard up when it came to men, she was too gorgeous to let it down. I remember her telling me once how much energy it took to fend them off, what a relief it was to get married so she could simply hold up her ring finger. As opposed to the third finger? I'd said. Both, she replied with a half-smile, men are a pain in the ass.

"Anyway it's funny how a single incident can reveal so much about a person's character. Yes, recalling what I'm about to tell you—in light of this—I find it impossible to imagine him screwing those bolts into her long, lithe—"

"Sven! Please."

"Sorry. I'm just saying—Dean can't be that bad a guy. Did you know he's into sailing?"

I rolled my eyes. "*That's* why?"

He leaned up, widening his blue eyes. Sven does have lovely blue eyes. They suddenly looked childlike (if watery). "Yes, I love sailing and it just so happens Dean is into it too. Yes, that endears him to me to some extent but no, that's not why. In fact I don't think it's nearly the obsession for him it is for me. Financially, for instance, it's a totally different ballgame for the two of us—for me it's a truly foolish if not insane hobby to have, the money I've poured into *Allegro*. I've racked up so much debt I don't know how I'll ever climb out from under it, good thing Lydia has always stuck her head in the sand when it comes to our finances . . ."

Sven, like myself, had been a musician all his life, a child prodigy, he went straight into the orchestra after college but, unlike me, he was well fed up with it and made no bones about it. While music was still my great passion, Sven had lost his heart for it and sometimes (not that often) he expressed regret for the loss. For him music had become just a job, an obligation, a boring inconvenience or way to pay the bills, he'd joined the ranks of the rest of the world in loathing their work and the last few years he'd taken to spending every spare minute between rehearsals and gigs sailing or working on his boat, he hardly practiced anymore. Once he'd been a great violinist but now he showed up at world-class venues in Salzburg, Berlin, Paris and tried to slide by under the conductor's radar. The thing was I didn't think he was sliding by, I'd heard through the grapevine he was sliding down and maybe even out. I hoped it didn't come to that, he needed the income.

". . . Sure, Dean complained about the expense too, in fact that's mostly what our conversation was about, it's a tactic rich men use to relate to the peasants, commiserating about money as if you're all in the same boat, pun intended. So I didn't put a lot of stock in what he was saying but I did enjoy the conversation, in the music world you don't meet many people into sailing. And we both agreed the outrageous cost of the hobby is worth it—though we reserve the right to moan about it, ha ha—Dean was lamenting the 20K he'd just dropped on these carbon laminate sails from Auckland, very nice sails, racing sails. He said he was getting into racing, which I have no interest in myself, what's always appealed to me about sailing is the chance to move more slowly in the world rather than faster. The pace of our lives is already fast enough, it's insanity. But out on the water, with the blue sky, the salt air—"

I didn't point out the ironic name of his boat, I didn't want to encourage him on the subject, once he got started he could go on and on about sailing.

"I know. No wonder everybody's screwed-up, on anti-depressants, committing suicide. It's too much. Everybody's looking for an out. Maybe Nicola's the lucky one."

"Yeah, it's pretty fucking intense out there. Of course, you can't expect rich men to get that. Sure, some of them are workaholics and thrive on pressure, but they get to *choose* if they want to live that way or not. They don't have to rush around like everybody else, killing themselves to get ahead. As my grandfather always said, the luxury of money is time."

I finished off my raspberry martini, the waiter still hadn't brought the next one. He seemed to have disappeared on us, I didn't blame him.

"Right. So true. So anyway—your theory is . . ."

"My theory is this: so in the middle of this perfectly benign conversation we were having about sailing, a waiter came up to him, see—I should say a servant since this was at a party at his townhouse, that one they threw last winter after our *Requiem* run. You were there, you wore that orange sequined dress, sort of African style."

"You remember that?"

"It looked fantastic on you."

"Really?"

"Really. So anyway, it was winter and that's how we got onto sailing because Dean was heading down to the Bahamas the following week for a yacht race—well, right in the middle of our conversation a servant came up to him, a fifty-something Latino guy, obviously upset. The poor guy was shaking, something had happened in the kitchen. I couldn't hear everything but it did not seem to be an emergency, something like they'd run out of appetizers or broken the coffeemaker or something. The guy wasn't handling it well, barging in on us like that but Dean—and I remember being startled by this because it was not the impression he typically gave off with his jerky executive persona, you know, not to mention he didn't seem to give a damn about music, did you ever notice that? I don't think he ever brought it up with me, he showed zero curiosity in what I do. Which I always wondered how Nicola stood for that but I guess we'll never know. But this—this Dean handled with true graciousness. He listened patiently, he calmed the guy down, he even put his arm around his shoulders. And unless his hidden motive was simply to keep his party going smoothly—which I really don't think it was, it wasn't the feeling I got—he came off as a truly compassionate human being. And that," Sven raised a finger instructively, "is why I say the man is incapable of murder."

I slammed my hands on the table. "Oh my god. Sven—Dean was gay! He was gay and he wanted out of his marriage. He was secretly having an affair with that servant. Now that's motive."

"Nah. Don't you remember the way he touched Nicola? Hell, the way he looked at her. I'm a straight man, I know gay when I see it. There was nothing gay about that exchange. It was mere kindness."

"So he was bi."

He shrugged. "Meh."

The waiter arrived with Sven's fries and fresh porter. They weren't exactly fries, they were giant geometrical shapes, it looked like the kitchen had roughly quartered a couple of potatoes, and they were gleaming with grease. Sven went right at them—after dousing them with a miniature bottle of vinegar he withdrew from his suitcoat pocket. Did he always carry it? How had I never noticed it before?

"Well, I hope you're right."

He gulped his beer, wiped his mouth, and smiled at me. "I guess we'll never know."

"I guess not."

The waiter had left our table before I realized. "Where's my drink? He brought yours, but where's mine?"

"How would I know? Did you order another one?"

I didn't bother reminding him that he himself had ordered it, or rather, re-ordered it for me, I didn't bother mentioning I wouldn't have ordered another one at all if he hadn't insisted on getting sloshed even though I'd told him I had a matinee tomorrow, I'd be home in my pajamas by now, riveted by *The Seventh Seal*. It was too late, there was no turning back now. I made eye contact with the waiter, he was at another table but he caught my meaning.

"I don't know why I care," I said. "If he did do it, they'll never catch him anyway, not with his money."

Sven was ravaging his hard-won fries like they were the last scraps of food on the planet and didn't look up. I returned my gaze to the pianist, who was back at it after a break. She rocked back and forth on the bench over a Coltrane number like an epileptic, her feather boa flying all over the place. Her Coltrane I didn't mind, Satie she should leave alone.

New Year's Eve

"I don't even know you," my husband said to me on the night before New Year's Eve, holding my gaze with his own intense one. "Why won't you let me know you?"

I looked away into the fire. When my husband looks at me like this, it's all I can do to hold his gaze and at last I have to look away, to hide. It's his eerily penetrating silver eyes that unnerve me, my husband has eyes the color of mica, people call them gray but they're silver, they're very unusual, really, and very beautiful, even if he weren't my husband I'd say that.

"What do you mean? You've been married to me for seven years."

His finger trailed between my bare breasts and he whispered, "You know what I mean."

I faked ignorance. "I'm sorry, I don't. You've seen me naked how many thousand times, you've seen me piss, you've seen me cry, you've seen me puking and giving birth. What could there possibly be left to know?"

His finger detoured from its downward descent to make thoughtful circles around my navel. His lips moved softly in the dim light. "That's all outside, I'm talking about what's inside. I'm talking about who you are."

I knew what he was talking about, I'm not stupid even if I'm not Oxford-educated like him nor his equal in any other way, except perhaps in the looks department. He doesn't seem to mind. We're too happy together, too happy for a marriage and I keep waiting for it all to fall apart.

It was the eve of New Year's Eve. We lay wrapped up in the hand-dyed rug from Afghanistan he'd gotten on his trip there last month to make up for missing Thanksgiving with me and our young daughter. He'd given it to me wrapped up as a Christmas gift a few days before (even though we barely celebrate Christmas, we only make a show of it for our daughter) and now we lay naked on it, the coarse edges pulled around us, it wasn't soft but it was very beautiful, woven in the old way by women in burqas squatting on dirt floors, or that's what the picture on the tag had promised. I felt guilty walking on it, making love on it, having a husband who could pay thousands for a five by eight rug. Those women could have been my own grandmothers, I'm not Afghani, I'm Hungarian but I come from a line of women who made their living in similarly laborious ways. No doubt the weavers of the rug got only a fraction of its price.

I felt guilty, too, for having a husband like Ben Avi, who gazed into my eyes like the world would end after making love, who's wealthy and accomplished, well-liked and well-known, serious but also funny and who looks like he does, with those strange pale eyes and thick wavy black hair that's getting more and more salt and pepper every day but I like it. It's a cliché, I know, a bad line from a Hollywood romance but when I look into his eyes I feel unsteady on my feet and kind of crazy or dizzy—it's not the dreamy sensation it sounds like, actually it's very unpleasant, like the vertigo that makes your stomach sick when the elevator drops suddenly. It's the sick sensation of fear. The truth is I'm a woman desperately in love with her husband, so desperately all I can think about is losing him.

That's all I could think about on New Year's Eve, too. We went to the party we always go to, thrown by an important man in a government position who my husband has translated for for years. Such events always bring up my insecurities, too many beautiful young women clicking around in their high heels and tight skirts and my husband draws them to him like flies. He knows everyone while I know only the few friends of his I've made over the years, he drinks moderately while I drink too much, he laughs and I titter, he converses intelligently while I dance with strangers, men a decade older than me and with millions more than my husband in an effort to make him jealous, it never works. As we stepped between the marble pillars wrapped in fresh cedar boughs and red velvet and into the magnificent, museum-sized building, I felt that crazy, wild edge that rises in me in such situations. I dug my French manicure into my husband's arm, holding tight.

It was a gorgeous party. Glittering pearls of white lights were strung everywhere, draped through the arches of the stone cathedral ceiling, wound

through the marble banister. Dozens and dozens of long-stemmed red roses stood in tall brass vases, the tiny lights swirled even among their stems,
hundreds of such vases, everywhere you looked were roses, their deep red
blackish in the soft light. And candles, of course. Slender white candles
rising ten feet tall, their flames well above peoples' heads for safety's sake,
no doubt, you wouldn't want a carousing crowd around candles and even
this sophisticated bunch would soon be descending into drunkenness, the
rich drink more than anyone, I've found.

The difference is they look good while they're doing it. And tonight everyone was making an appearance as their most gorgeous self. Even the
homely, even the overgrown artichoke noses of greedy men and the thick
ruddy necks of aging women with powder wedged in the lines of their
skin or facelifts gone wrong, nips and tucks that yanked their faces toward
their ears, even these the candlelight and roses, the glow of the holiday
of new beginnings and hope, smoothed out. Everyone looks beautiful on
New Year's Eve. On New Year's Eve we put on our rose-colored glasses
along with our black ties and black velvet and pretend the world is bright
and thrilling and all the people in it exotic and intriguing rather than
shallow and irritating, vain and stingy, with mean-spirited, small eyes and
scrunched, frightened faces that will reappear in the light of the morning
to follow.

The rich are, by rights, all attractive in one way or another. The women
wore French manicures only hours old (as was my own) and upswept hair,
the men tuxes and gleaming, slicked-back hair, there were silk gloves that
covered the elbows and pearls at the throat, clean shaves, flowery perfume,
red lipstick. Everyone stood around looking at everyone else, checking out
the other's evening dress and measuring themselves against each other or
against their own reflections in the enormous Baroque mirrors or sneaking
sly glances at their miniature faces reflected in the crystal of their champagne flutes. I stood looking around, remembering how before I met my
husband, the parties I went to served boxed wine in plastic flutes.

What you have to understand about me is this is not my world. I don't
come from money, old or new, which was what everyone there had in
common but me. When people ask me about my family—which isn't
often, but sometimes they do, probably because I don't look American—I
tell them about my great-grandmother Iva Székely who survived the ref-

ugee camps of World War I by telling fortunes for a few coins and scraps of bread, enough to feed her eight children (all but three survived, an excellent rate for the times). Apparently refugees have enough hope to want to know their futures, but I'd rather not. Half a century later, at a kitchen table on another continent, Great Grandma Ivy took my small hand in her worn, leathery one and said, "You will marry a rich man who will take you to America and give you everything you desire."

My mother smiled as she stirred a pot of boiling soup at the stove. We were already in America, Grandma had forgotten. She and my mother's mother and my mother, still a child, and her three young sisters had immigrated from Hungary when the Second World War ended and become a family of women in America. I laughed with joy over this lucky prophecy. Then Grandma Iva's drooping jowls lengthened. A shadow passed over my future. She pronged a knobby finger at my chest and added, "But you will die young of a broken heart."

My mother let out a high sharp sound. "*Nagymama!*" she scolded.

She had her moments, my mother. Although she was already descending into schizophrenia at that time and would be permanently committed by the time I was fifteen.

Grandma Iva brought her paper bag face inches from mine. "It's all right, dear," she croaked just like a witch from one of my picture books, "you'll still be pretty when they put you in the ground."

Grandma had had a hard life, my mother explained sitting on the edge of my bed that night, and old age had made her mean. She wasn't a witch and she didn't have any powers anybody else didn't have, she couldn't really tell my future. Still, I cried myself to sleep that night, in my dreams my lifeless, doll-like face at the bottom of an earthen pit.

This became a nightmare I would have for years. Then when I turned thirty I thought, I'm free of her curse. I'm too old now to die still pretty.

She had been right about part of it, though, I thought as I always did on occasions such as this one when it becomes apparent I have everything a woman should ever desire. My husband swept me on his tuxedoed arm into the ballroom. Sparkling crystal flutes passed by on silver trays, champagne quivering in them. A string quartet was tuning up on the dais at the end of the room. Everyone bustled around greeting each other, schmoozing and sucking up.

Heads turned as we crossed the room. Without turning his own head, my husband said, "Everyone's staring at us, have you noticed?"

"Everyone's staring at everyone," I said. "It's a beauty pageant."

He pressed my wrist. "And you're winning." He glanced at me, half-smiling. "You do know you're a very, *very* beautiful woman?"

I pretended to ignore this, I couldn't let him know how much it meant to me when he said such things. I waved as we approached our friends Renée and Karl, who, judging by their broad smiles and lit eyes, were already well on their way.

"What about you, do you feel like you know me, Rebeka?" my husband had said the night before. "I mean really know me."

"Not all of you if that's what you mean."

Just because you're married and you spend every day or almost every day (in our case—my husband travels three months of the year) with someone, just because you sit across from them three meals a day or even two and fall asleep next to them every night doesn't mean you know what's stirring in the deepest wells of their heart. You do discover those less desirable or less attractive traits in your spouse, although none of my husband's flaws and habits, self-delusions ("I'm going to cut back on coffee this week, I swear I am," or "I'm going to the gym every day from now on") or hostilities ("the fucking Palestinians this and the fucking Palestinians that," my husband's blind when it comes to the conflict, he is, to be honest, a little racist though he tries gallantly not to be) don't bother me in the least. They only make him human.

"I don't want to know everything," I added. "I like that you can still surprise me. Why can't you embrace the mystery?"

He was busy kissing my chest. When he finished, he said, "I can. I think there will always be mystery. We're two different people, after all. It's impossible to know what it's like within someone else's skin. But I can't shake the feeling you hide parts of yourself from me. Deliberately, I mean."

"Really? Which parts?"

He closed his arms around me. "The ones I want."

If marriage means intimacy, my husband's aunt should have had it by now, but to hear her talk, all of her marriages have been based on secrets and lies. I think she exaggerates—she's an artist after all—but according to her, they've all ended in deceptions and shocking revelations (one husband turned out to be gay—not a bad rate, though, one of seven) and yet she keeps trying, she's not giving up: tomorrow we would go to her eighth wedding. Ben's aunt has married and divorced seven times and so we weren't that surprised when we received in the mail an invitation to her eighth wedding a few weeks ago, even though we'd had no idea she was even seeing someone. It was at one tomorrow and it was going to be hard to get up for it, how arrogant, I thought, how presumptuous to have your *eighth* wedding early on New Year's Day, as if people should forego their one night a year of Dionysian revelry to see you walk down the aisle a few years older and a few pounds heavier with a man you'd met only months before and who, no doubt, would be history in a short time.

But then, his aunt is eccentric, bold, free-spirited I guess you could say. She's a portrait photographer or she used to be before she closed her business and starting taking photographs and making films only of herself. I've seen one of her films, a film of her filming herself taking photographs of mannequins she'd painted to look like herself, I find it ridiculous but it's been in the MOMA. She uses an old-fashioned camera on a tripod. She sets it all up and then dances around in front of it naked or mostly naked. Not that what she's doing is anything new. Since the sixties photographers have been cavorting bare-fleshed before their own cameras—attempting, I suppose, to capture something real and raw about themselves, to glimpse the free, the uninhibited, the mysterious or essential self within but that's something that can't be captured since the moment you glimpse it, it's caught and changed.

Renée was already drunk. She'd been drinking since two.

"I started late this year," she said, flashing a dazzling smile. She looked festive, her large brown eyes a little wild, a little loose in the sockets. She wore bronze lipstick that set off her latte skin and giant onyx and diamond earrings that dangled almost to her collarbones, showing off the clean lines of her long neck. Renée has her hair cut with a razor, close to the scalp. She's mulatto, from Montreal, her first language is French while her husband is a D.C. Jew, they make as odd a couple as my husband and I, an American-born Israeli and a Hungarian-Romanian immigrant. She said, "I hate New Year's Eve."

"You look like you're in the spirit," I said.

She lifted her glass. "Martinis."

My husband put his arm around her bare shoulders. "There's nothing wrong with New Year's Eve, Renée. It's a measuring stick. A night out of time when we look back on our lives to see how we're doing. If you've had a good year, it can only be a good night."

She rolled her eyes. Renée is my only friend who's immune to his charms but then, she hates poetry and sentimentality in all its forms and my husband is a man of words, a man of romance. He speaks five languages and he writes in all of them, not only is he an interpreter for the government, he also does translations—classical Hebrew texts, political or historical stuff that's not that interesting, honestly, at least to me. Renée looked around. "It's just another fucking business meeting." She turned to me. "But *you* love these parties, don't you?"

"It's the only chance I get all year to flirt with FBI agents." I laughed and lifted a champagne off the waiter's tray. I won't drink too much tonight, I vowed silently, while a secret voice countered, oh yes you will. I knew I would but I'd rather not, liquor makes me clumsy and that was something I couldn't afford in my high, high heels and skin-tight evening gown and all those marble steps bridging the several floors of the party. I'm tall, I'm "leggy," as people like to say of supermodels, but I feel awkward and too-big in my body and when I drink the feeling's even worse, I'm like a puppet at the mercy of some alien master hand cruelly yanking the strings.

Last year I fell down, believe it or not, but that was on the ice out on the balcony upstairs and thankfully, no one saw me. I'd gone off on my own, which is something that inevitably happens at my husband's parties. I end up alone.

"Ouch," Karl said, looking sideways at Ben.

"Well, you can't make simple conversation with the paranoid bastards," he said, deftly bypassing my tease.

Karl laughed. "It's true. You can't ask about their wife and kids without them thinking you're up to something. They give you that stare."

He mocked it, narrowing his eyes to slits. I smiled coyly. "Agents don't mind talking to me, though not about their wives."

My husband smiled back. "*Men* don't mind talking to you."

See, my husband is always kind and never cutting to me, even when I try to provoke him, even in front of other people when he's at risk of appearing to be a smitten man, a man who lets his wife wear the pants in the relationship. He doesn't care, he's never been concerned with what others think. While for me—I know I should be above it but I'm not—it's everything.

For instance I'm obsessed with my nose. Not only do I feel too big in my body, too tall, too long, too much too much too much, I've always thought, too, my nose was enormous. There's nothing pert or delicate about my nose as there is most American women's noses, I have the nose of a racehorse and the face of a racehorse (and, according to my husband, the legs of a racehorse), a moody Eastern European face, or that's what I see when I look in the mirror even though I know, objectively, my nose, while on the large side, is not offensive or abhorrent. I know because people are always telling me what a beautiful woman I am and that I should model (they don't know I used to) and they never add, "if only for the nose . . .," no, they never mention my nose but I know for a fact (because I have eyes to see with) it has a tendency to dominate the rest of my, on the whole, pleasing features. I used to try to mask it with the jungle of wiry amber hair I wear in a shoulder-length triangular mass of coils and springs but lately I've been realizing the geometrical shape actually *accentuates* my nose rather than downplays it—of course, it's nothing next to the size of Ben Avi's nose as well as the snout of everyone in his family but I'm not Jewish and so the rules are completely different.

Everyone seemed to be waiting for me to say something so I said something. "I like talking to agents. It's exciting knowing at any moment they could pull out a pen knife from the heel of their shoe and stab you with it." They were all looking at me. "Isn't that what James Bond did?"

Renée and Karl laughed accommodatingly even though it wasn't that funny (Ben didn't). "Not at parties, one would hope," Renée said. She showed her empty glass to a passing Sri Lankan waiter. "Can't they hire white boys? Ever?"

She was looking at something across the room. She leaned into me, wobbly, touching her bare shoulder to mine in an almost erotic way. Renée was wearing a sequined strapless black gown, her dark arms softly glowing, she looked lovely—the dimmed chandeliers and candlelight toned down her too-wide (while mine is too long and large) nose, making her too-round chocolate eyes look just right and the gap between her front teeth interesting (why would such a rich woman leave such a gap?). She put her hand on my arm and spoke in my ear, apart from the men. "See that woman in the archway?" My eyes followed the line of her gaze. "She's just coming in. In the obnoxious copper silk?"

The woman had paused to stand at the top of the stairs leading down into the ballroom. She cast an imperious gaze over the room as if she were appraising it, judging whether it was worthy of her presence.

"Do you know who she is?"

I shook my head.

"She's an interpreter, too. Lithuanian-American, I think. She worked with Karl in the Ukraine. Avi must know her."

We turned in unison to consult my husband but he had already drifted away, he always does that at parties, he knows everyone and loves playing the social butterfly. That's how I gained my skill of pulling conversation out of FBI agents (who honestly are terrible bores and *never* pull pen knives out of their shoes or do anything interesting), I had to find someone to talk to. I let him go. I even avoid him, it's my policy as a wife, my strategy to keep him by letting him go.

We looked at Karl, who shrugged.

"You look guilty," Renée said to him.

"Jesus, it's New Year's Eve." He headed for the bar.

"Are you guys okay?" I asked her.

She waved her hand, the one with the humongous diamond ring on it. "Oh, he doesn't like it when I drink. He doesn't like it when I have *any* fun."

My eyes searched the room for my husband, darting like pinballs. It's an automatic reflex with me, something I do instinctively whenever he leaves my side. Before I could find him, Renée tugged my arm. "I met her in Kiev when I was visiting Karl over Thanksgiving. It's crazy how much she looks like you." Her words slurred. "Do you see it? Maybe she's your long lost twin."

We'd all like to know what we look like to other people since we never can know, not truly. It's impossible since even what we see in the mirror is filtered through our own eyes—as my husband had pointed out the night before. That's why catching your profile in a three-way mirror in a boutique, seeing yourself on video (as my husband's aunt loves to do) or on a security camera at the museum, even hearing your voice on the voicemail is so startling and for some people disturbing though for me it's the opposite—for me catching a glimpse of myself unexpectedly is a welcome reprieve, a sliver of joy (my doubts about my nose aside), since I'm always shocked to discover I'm more beautiful than I ever think of myself as. I had such a moment now—the woman Renée was comparing me to was stunning.

"You're flattering me, Renée," I said because it was the right thing to say.

110

"I can't be that gorgeous."

She rolled her eyes. "Have you seen yourself?"

"Well, I'd never stand there like that. What's she waiting for?"

The woman hadn't moved. For a few minutes she'd been standing there in her movie star stance, a marble statue, a goddess, giving every man—and woman—below a good look at her.

"Mmh. But don't you think she looks like you?"

"I must have something," I said, thinking aloud in spite of myself, the champagne had already loosened me up, "to get a man like Avi." I used his other name, the one his friends call him by. The one he introduced himself by when we met on the metro eight years ago. He sat down beside me, I was on my way to a modeling job—a lingerie ad—I had a brief career but modeling wasn't for me nor was I very good at it, being photographed in my underwear isn't my idea of a career. Six months later he married me and I was able to quit working.

Renée is probably my closest friend but she has a vicious side, a side I've always feared. Now she turned to me. "A man like Avi? What's that supposed to mean? What's so great about Avi? You don't think you're his match in every way?"

"Well, I—he's my husband, but—"

"But?" Her eyes expanded, waiting.

"But it's more than that—it's that, you know, he's an amazing man. Everyone admires him. He's so self-confident, he knows who he is, and he's far more intelligent than I am, not to mention better educated. Anything he wants to do, he can."

"And you can't?

"I'm not talking about me. I'm talking about him. The way I see him—"

Lifting her glass as if to make a flamboyant toast, she nearly shouted—she was even drunker than I'd thought: "That's it! The way you see him! The way you see him is the *problem*, Rebeka."

Anger flared in me. "What's wrong with loving my husband? With thinking he's the best man I—"

She cut me off. "You don't love your husband," she spat, her face contorted, almost cruel. I stepped back, my champagne swinging. "You worship him."

"Renée. You're drunk. You're being obnoxious."

She pronged a finger at me, its manicured tangerine nail half an inch long, a veritable spear. "Love and worship, Rebeka. Two different things." She gripped my arm. "Come on. I have to pee."

"And you? What do you hide from me?" I'd said back to him last night, really, just to even the score or counterbalance his attempt to pry inside my skin, he'd asked for my secrets, now I had to ask for his or I'd appear aloof, uninterested, though no part of me, hidden or not, wanted to know. I could live my entire life without knowing about his affair with a Foreign Service girl or his infatuation with a diplomat—that one he'd worked for in Paris and that he'd made so much fun of though perhaps it was simply a cover, perhaps truly he'd fallen in love with her—I didn't want to know.

Really I don't have any reason to think my husband is anything but totally devoted to me. He's always telling me how much he loves me, every day or almost every day he says so, not that I'm counting or maybe I am, maybe on the days he doesn't (he's concentrating on a particularly rough passage for a translation, or he's preoccupied with the situation in Israel) I take it personally, I get a twinge of panic in my gut and I want to run, to pack up Aliah and run for the hills, or rather, for the shore, for a boat back to that older, humbler country where I belong. On such days I think, peering into the mirror, examining new lines around my eyes, it will happen for sure when my looks have gone or it could happen before. It'll start in the usual way—a subtle pulling away, less sex and fewer calls when he's away, and finally another woman, someone who can challenge him more than me. It could happen at any time and that's what makes my happy marriage hell.

But most days he does tell me. After showering, while clipping his toenails on the end of the bed, he'll look up and say, "I'm so lucky to have found you." Over the phone from the condo in Tehran once, he said, "I never imagined I could love a woman as much as I love you."

"What?" I said, feigning a bad connection, just so I could hear it again. Last summer when we went away to the mountains, on the sleeping roof of our cabin under a sea of stars, he said, holding my face close in both his hands, "I'll never leave you. I promise. Never." This time I considered believing him, but it must have been the spell cast by all those stars, because in the morning the fear was back. I know: there's something wrong with me.

Last night he'd answered me in his earnest way: "I try not to hide anything from you, though I'm only human, of course. Naturally there are things." My heart clenched. I'd been lying with my head on his chest, I rolled onto my back and tried to breathe. *Don't tell me. I don't want to know.* "Oh, the usual fears and vulnerabilities, I suppose I conceal those despite my best efforts not to—everyone does, unconsciously or consciously, no matter how much we trust another, it's a reflexive function of the ego, which is terrified of being seen as ignorant or weak or, God forbid, needy in any way." He grinned. "I'm a man, after all. We're conditioned to be tough in all weather, confident and in control at all times. But every morning for months after Mother died, I used to go into my office after breakfast and weep, just *weep*. You never knew, did you? I could hear you moving around in the kitchen and as soon as your steps would approach my door—bringing me a coffee or something, I'd put on my glasses and bury my head in a book. I didn't want you to see. Vain of me, I know."

I wanted to burst into laughter, I was so relieved. I rolled back on top of him and breathed into his neck, "Oh my darling, you're such a good man. You're such a *good* man."

Most of the time our lives are so busy I can keep the demons at bay. It helps that he travels so I don't have to see him every day. Some women would be eaten alive by jealousy and insecurity having a husband who travels for weeks at time, working with important and powerful people (among them, women) all over the world. My husband works mostly in the Middle East but he's had assignments in Paris, Berlin, Lisbon, and other of the world's most romantic cities but the war zones where he spends most of his time could be even more dangerous for our marriage if you think about it (which I try not to), the pressure and desperation of those environments driving him into bed with one of those important and powerful women he works with, women like the tall Lithuanian I was supposed to resemble. Some wives would worry about the strain on their marriage from all those weeks apart but it's not this that worries me, in fact, when he's gone I feel more at ease, when he's gone I can stay in house slippers and a robe all day, eating pastries, wasting time on the internet, or lately I've been in this phase of reading Romanian folk tales for hours on the couch until Aliah comes home from school, they're surprisingly violent, we're a dark-minded people, it seems. I feel guilty admitting it but I enjoy the weeks he's away, when it's just my daughter and I and I can let my guard down and be myself.

We don't get that much time alone these days, but last night he'd insisted we have an evening to ourselves. He'd just returned from Afghanistan in time to spend the week doing Christmas activities with our six-year-old daughter, and last night he said let's take a night off and send her to the movies with Carolyn—a sixty-something widowed millionaire whose grandchildren are across the country and who's the closest thing to a grandmother Aliah will ever know. My mother admitted herself to an asylum when I was fifteen—depression and schizophrenia—and she's still there, though her mind is far away, long ago and far away, while my one remaining grandmother is dying of bone cancer in a nursing home, and Great-Grandma Iva with her reckless soothsaying is long gone. Ben's family moved back to Israel and we visit every two or three years but they never visit us, his father doesn't have much use for me (I'm not Jewish). I have half a dozen aunts and uncles floating around the United States but I was never close to them or their teeming masses of offspring—the only one I loved was Aunt Sophie, my mother's youngest sister, who killed herself at thirty over a man who wouldn't leave his wife. Ben Avi and I and Aliah are a family without a family, marooned in our city apartment in this country that feels so far away from home for both of us. It's better this way, I tell myself. It makes us need each other.

Last night he opened a bottle of wine and we cooked a curry together. We talked about Aliah, about how she prefers Christmas to Hanukkah, no doubt because of the surrounding consumer culture and what we could do about that, to even it out, to give Hanukkah a fair shot, and we talked about his upcoming trip to Egypt and he asked if we wanted to go with him. We almost never do, we wouldn't this time either, we agreed it was best for Aliah not to miss that much school, and after the meal, we sat close on the couch with full stomachs, holding our glasses of merlot until we sat them down and kissed, slowly, slowly, the taste of red wine on our tongues. We kissed for several minutes like teenagers. We were in no hurry, Carolyn had strict instructions not to bring Aliah home until we turned on the little bronze lantern outside our door, she lives in the apartment next door and it's no trouble for her to put Aliah to bed there if it's gets very late and the lantern stays dark. At last he pulled me down beside him onto the beautiful but rough new rug and we made love, woozy with wine, the firelight on each other's faces, jazz playing softly on the turntable, and I thought, whose life is this I'm living? Not mine, surely, not mine.

Afterward we lay on the floor talking, naked, warmed by the fake fire in the hearth, the little fiberglass logs, our building won't allow a real fire. My husband fell into a serious mood, he wanted to talk about our future, about moving out of the city and buying a bigger house in the mountains, and he brought up having another child again—a subject I avoided. How can I tell him I don't want to have another child because I'm afraid I'll end up like my mother, my grandmother, my aunts, a woman burdened with children and no man to help care for them?

That's when he pushed my rampant curls back from my eyes and said, "It's like pushing a veil back from a cave." He stroked my face. "I'll see you from across the room—not always in public, sometimes just across the living room or while we're having coffee on the terrace and think, I have no idea who this woman is."

"I'm your wife, darling."

"You're so much more than that."

"I know. I didn't mean it that way," I said, although, I realized, I probably did.

The record we'd been listening to came to an end and spun a soft hiss in the silence. The antique clock on the mantelpiece ticked in its place. My husband clung to me like an infant.

He pulled back suddenly and said, "Tell me you love me."

I did but inside, I was thinking, I'll say the words but I'll never let you know how much I mean them, that's a risk I'm simply not willing to take, I can never let you see how much I need you and how terrified I am of not being loved back by you because if I let you see that it's sure to drive you away and I wouldn't blame you and so I'm forced to monitor every word I utter and every gesture I make so I don't give myself away, even while making love there's a part of me that remains vigilant, overseeing the convulsions and tremors of my body like a distant commander so you never see how much I need you, after all, everyone knows there's nothing more repulsive than a needy woman.

I wandered alone through the interlinked ballrooms. Renée was stuck in an interminable line for the powder room, that's one thing even these rich guys haven't figured out, they pride themselves on throwing the most lavish parties with world-class food and music and drink and every luxury and comfort you can imagine but they can't figure out how to shorten the ladies' room line (install more toilets!). The music was beginning and people were moving onto the dance floor, a few couples already waltzing around the room like professionals, perhaps they were hired dancers meant to get people out on the floor. Black and red and silver and gold gowns billowed, the men guiding them with straight postures and clean necks over their black bow ties, the women within them craning their necks to glimpse their own faces, to examine their own hair to make sure a strand hadn't slipped out of place as they swept past the mirrors on the walls. Men walked by, their eyes traveling over me like I was a territory to be colonized. The party was swinging into high gear, it was past ten o'clock, everyone who was coming would have arrived by now and those who had arrived early were well-lubricated by the ubiquitous Italian champagne, myself included. At the other end of the room my gaze caught on a woman in the mirror, at first I thought it was the Lithuanian, the woman Renée had compared me to, and I thought, of course she's standing there alone, no one will approach her because she's so beautiful, it's intimidating—then, I saw with a shock, the woman was me.

Renée was crossing the room toward me. I met her under yet another giant chandelier and took her wrist. "I want to meet that woman."

A blank look. She was pretty far gone, her lipstick cracked and eyes glassy.

"My twin."

"Ooh. That sounds like fun."

She thought she'd seen her go upstairs. In the foyer a broad marble staircase, its railing garnished by poinsettias, curved to the upper floors, at the top of which an Indian boy stood giving out directions, dispensing a steadying elbow to drunk old ladies, tidying the stems of roses in their vases. We started the climb in our heels. Renée's dress was so tight around her legs it was difficult for her to take the stairs without ripping it. I didn't have that problem since mine, though equally tight, had some give due to its high, high slit—"scandalously high," as my husband, trailing his fingers up it, put it before we left home. I wasn't wearing black or silver or gold or red like most of the women, I was wearing a pale blue designer gown I'd found in one of the ritzy shops downtown this week, a milky, ethereal blue like snow under a full moon with angel hair straps that showed a lot of my bare shoulders and chest. Okay, I looked pretty good.

A man coming down as I was going up—good-looking in an all-American way, perhaps a young senator, or a doctor or lawyer for one of the older, more established men there who had been invited as a favor, a Christmas bonus—brushed his arm against mine as we passed and murmured, "Happy New Year, Lovely."

It was sexy, I guess, not that I felt the slightest temptation, I couldn't care less about other men even if it is comforting to be admired by them. On New Year's Eve people like to flirt, to ditch their spouses and pretend they're young and single again, to throw the inhibitions and restraints they carry with them through the work-a-day year out the window on this one night.

Renée stopped at the top of the stairs to take a breath and straighten her dress. She inspected it—no rips. She looked up and put her hand on my wrist. "There."

She was standing inside the first room. The library. She stood before a wall of books, all leather-bound, probably first editions. Every wall in the room was floor-to-ceiling books, the titles on their spines dimly glowing in the lights from the lanterns affixed to the teak walls. The crowd didn't match the scholarly setting, though—the general mood in the room was hedonistic, even slightly out-of-control.

Her copper dress reached to her ankles, but it clung so tightly to her curves it didn't matter that it was so long, what I mean is it left nothing to the imagination as to what was underneath it, all the peaks and valleys of her body, even the disks of her nipples were raised outlines on the fabric. It was, I thought, even tighter than mine and Renée's. I inspected her. We were about ten feet away now, people milling between us. Her face was wide-set, large gray-green eyes and a straight, perfectly-proportioned nose, red, peaked lips, all this along with some abstract quality that is impossible to describe and that is what makes a woman beautiful, she had this, I don't know just what it is, some exotic or haunted aura, a smoky quality in her gaze as if danger hovered around her. Did I have that?

Yet, her hair was nothing like mine and my hair is my most distinct feature or that's what my husband says. She wore hers up and I wore mine down, I usually do, I encourage my piles and piles of red-gold curls to spring from my head like a living thing and the effect, I know because it's inevitably what people say to me upon greeting, was striking. "Your *hair!*" people say, and I sink down inside with a warm, if small, satisfaction. The Lithuanian's upswept style, too, made an impression, or not so much her hair as the stretch of silken neck it left exposed to plain view, the tenderness, the vulnerability of which you couldn't help but want to reach out and touch, even I could see that.

Renée was saying something—now she stopped short.

"What?" I followed the line of her gaze. It ended at my husband. My husband was standing next to the woman.

He wasn't talking to her. Worse—he was watching her. Watching her lips move as she spoke. Watching her eyes flit to the mahogany-paneled ceiling as she searched her mind for a lost word or thought. Or perhaps, I thought, he's hoping to catch a glimpse of her tongue, so he can imagine what that tongue might do in another situation, or remember what it's already done in another time. Or to catch and hold her gaze as he'd held mine the night before, except in this case he would hold it only for an instant too long, a single loaded moment that held a promise, a contract that couldn't be spoken aloud.

Not that I saw my husband and my look-alike hold such a gaze—I didn't, but not because they hadn't—rather because at that moment two men cut between them and my own gaze, they were searching for a book on the shelves and blocking my view while they did so.

Renée pressed my arm in a maternal way and said, "Of course he's talking to her. She looks just like you."

"Or I look just like her."

The Lithuanian or Lithuanian-American, rather, I'm terrible at political-correctness, turned to help or perhaps to flirt with the men looking for the book, showing my husband an extraordinary expanse of bare skin. Her dress dipped down to her waistline in the back, and it must have taken all that was in him to keep his fingers from trailing down that back, from tracing those shoulder blades, from running over the bumps of beaded vertebrae.

I asked Renée, "Do you think he loves me?"

"Oh, sweetheart, how could he not?"

"He's fucking someone in Egypt."

She did not blink. That's what scared me. I expected her to at least blink but instead she said, "When did you find out?"

"What? *Is he?*"

"I don't know, honey. You said he was."

"He doesn't want us to go to Egypt with him. He's leaving next week."

"I thought you said he asked you."

"He *mentioned* it. I got the feeling he was just saying it, hoping I'd say no."

She was looking at them thoughtfully, they were standing next to each other in a little circle of people. "I've seen him look that way at you."

"So you do see the way he's looking at her?"

She tilted her head. "Mmm. It's probably transference. The man is so in love with his wife he only wants women who look just like her."

"Thanks for being no comfort at all, Renée."

But she had my arm and was pulling me behind her, toward them. I hissed her name, shaking my head when she looked back. She hissed back, "Come *on*."

"No, no—I don't want to be rude."

"He's your fucking husband. Anyway, I'm black. People have to be nice to me."

Renée introduced herself, hardly slurring her words at all (impressive). She held her hand out and the woman shook it awkwardly with her left hand. "We met in Kiev. You were working with my husband. Karl Rathjen?"

"Of course," she said. "Karl's a wonderful interpreter." Her voice had a sexy smoky timbre, not unlike the general look of smokiness about her, starting with her gray eyes. Along with a light accent. She shifted her champagne glass to her other hand and extended her right hand to me, Renée's blunt intrusion had caught her off guard. She wore ivory velvet gloves studded with diamonds (rhinestones?) that reached all the way up to her elbows, old-fashioned and elegant, I hadn't noticed them earlier or perhaps she'd just slipped them on, she must have been carrying them in her little pearled handbag. She spoke her name—only the first—"Vilma"—as she pressed her long covered fingers in mine. I too spoke only my first name back, saying nothing more, leaving in the air the implication, I hoped, that that single name was enough and that, like her, I needed no title or occupation or nationality or husband to explain who I was.

Of course, my husband was observing me closely, I caught him from the corner of my eye. Yet he made no move to touch or speak to me nor to claim me, to reveal what existed between us—the years we'd spent together, the child we'd created by fucking hundreds (thousands?) of times, the hundreds or thousands of meals, some thrilling and others boring, the long looks and deep talks and mundane ones and sleepless or sleep-filled nights curled around each other.

I was standing next to Vilma, with Renée between Ben and I. We stood shoulder-to-shoulder, nearly identical heights. It was true, we were practically the same size, both of us taller and larger than most American women, and our skin and hair the same hue. Though beyond that I didn't see that much resemblance.

"We were just exchanging horror stories," she said, looking conspiratorially at my husband.

"Horror stories?" Renée raised her brows.

My husband said, "Stories of botched translations. There's nothing worse, when you have entire foreign policies hanging on a single word, and it's up to you to decide what word that is."

She actually put her hand on his shoulder. And let it linger. Smiling, she said, "*Nothing*. Particularly when the language is not your native tongue. It's nerve-racking, but then that's why I love this work."

"Vilma speaks eight languages," Ben said.

She ticked them off on her long fingers. "Lithuanian, which is my native tongue, Latvian, Russian—of course—Polish, Czech, and French, Italian, and English."

My husband added, apologetically, I thought, "Rebeka speaks Hungarian."

"Oh," Vilma said, "I do, too." She rattled off something I couldn't understand, I recognized it as my mother's language but I couldn't identify a word.

I smiled sheepishly. "I'm sorry, I'm out of practice."

She lifted one side of her mouth, barely making an effort. "I said this champagne tastes like horse piss. I'm going downstairs to see if they have anything decent to drink. It was a pleasure meeting you." Then, to Ben, intimately, as if he were hers already and I had to wonder if he was, she said, "Are you coming?"

Before he could answer, Renée said, "I can't help but notice how much you two resemble one another. Have you noticed?"

We appraised each other. Vilma said, almost confidentially, "Five eleven?"

A smile was so plastered on my face it felt clay-like, set. "Just. You?"

"Five eleven and one-half on the nose." It didn't look like she was half an inch taller than me, though perhaps her heels were lower than mine.

I tried to connect. "Impossible to find pants."

Renée pronged her fingers over her face like an umpire's mask. "Even the bone structure, the eyes. Maybe you were separated at birth . . ." She elbowed Ben. "You must see it. I know *you* see it."

This she said with not a hint but a heap of accusation. Vilma shifted on one heel, perhaps uncomfortably, but Ben just showed his beautiful teeth in a broad smile. The man in the iron tower, nothing rattles him. "But how do you explain the hair?" he said jovially. "No one has hair like Rebeka."

He raised his glass—brandy, he would never drink champagne—and drained it. To camouflage from the other woman's view, I thought helplessly, how he was looking at me, he didn't want her to know he desired me, too. Vilma looked back and forth between Ben and I, working it out or that's what it looked like to me. I smiled flirtatiously at my husband, to help her along.

"Well. I'm going to the bar," she said. "Does anyone need a drink?"

She said "anyone," but she looked only at my husband. Who considered his empty glass and said, "Not me."

Another beat as she took this in, no doubt a woman who looked like her wasn't used to being turned down. She turned to go, then paused uncertainly, she wouldn't let it go, she was willing to put her pride on the line. "Would you care to accompany me? They're dancing downstairs."

He smiled at her. His long black lashes over the pale, pale eyes. I couldn't blame her. Then he said, shocking me, "Thank you, but I'd better stick by my wife. The boys are circling her like wolves."

If my evil twin was shocked by this information—that I was Ben's wife—or if she felt rejected, she didn't show it. She smiled. "All right, I'll have to find my boring date then."

She turned and moved through the crowd. The three of us watched her go: those impressive shoulders, that open back with all that skin.

Ben stepped into the spot Vilma had vacated and slipped his hand around my waist, pulling me close. He leaned in and kissed my neck. "Having fun?"

"A ball."

"I've worked with her in New York a few times. She's very good."

Renée, who had been pretending to scan the room, her back to us, flipped around. "In Egypt?"

Ben looked at me—carefully, I thought, though it could have been simply a look noting how drunk Renée was. "No, in New York."

She persisted: "Doesn't she work in Egypt, too?"

I watched his face, but I couldn't pick anything up. "I don't think so. I really don't know."

A group of men was hooting in the corner, making wild toasts, their glasses clanging in the air. I said, "Why don't you join them?"

To my surprise, she walked off toward them, her smirking face saying she'd take that as a challenge. When we were alone, I said, not looking at him, "But I don't think I'm having as much fun as you are."

"What? Vilma?"

Don't say it, don't say it, don't say it, a voice inside told me. I said it. It was entirely the champagne's fault. "It must be nice to have such a gorgeous woman want you. Oh, I'm sure it happens to you all the time, it's just that usually I don't have the pleasure of witnessing it."

"Oh, dear, does Vilma want me?"

"You can't be serious."

A bemused smile flickered on his lips. "All right. What if she does?"

I ran my fingers up the back of his tux. "I'm just joking, darling. I'm just teasing you."

"No, really, what if she does?"

"Oh, let's have a drink. Forget it. The truth is I couldn't care less."

He considered me, that maddening smile still in place. "No, you haven't a jealous bone in your body, have you?"

Did he really not see that every bone that made up my skeleton was poisoned by jealousy? Or was he mocking me? I shrugged, feigning indifference. "I don't see the point. I never have. Jealousy is simply not something you feel when you trust someone like I trust you . . . Why? Do you wish I did?"

"Yes. I wish you would be a flaming bitch when I talk to another woman about work. Yes I do."

He opened some space between us so we weren't touching anymore. He set his glass on the bookshelf—too hard, I don't miss details like this when it comes to my husband and if he thinks he's hiding them from me, he's wrong. Then: "Vilma is an impressive woman."

I let a moment pass. "*Impressive?*"

"All right, she's beautiful. Intelligent. Talented."

"Why did you *say* that?"

"Maybe I wanted to see if you really are jealous. If you have it in you."

I laughed. "Well, she looks like me. I couldn't blame you."

He ignored this. "Anyway, I can observe the obvious without feeling anything about it. It doesn't mean I'm attracted to her."

"No, of course not," I said, my tone coming out colder than I'd intended. "You have eyes only for yourself."

"What's gotten into you? Are you upset at me about something?"

"Should I be?"

He made a face, looked around the room.

"No, that's right, you never do anything wrong."

"I wish you wouldn't drink. You're behaving like a child."

"While I thought you were. Excuse me, darling. They're dancing downstairs," I said, mocking Vilma's porn star voice (and giving him further evidence of my childlike behavior). "I'm going to enjoy the year while I still can."

I moved away, winding through the crowd, conscious of the sway of my hips in the tight fabric, wondering if my shoulders could possibly look as elegant, as sinewy, as strong and capable as Vilma's had passing through the library doors. My husband called after me, "What's that supposed to mean?"

I didn't answer, I didn't know myself.

The women in my family bear a curse that drives their men away. This is a long-running family joke but I can see they're not joking when they talk about the generations of desertions while sitting around the table drinking black tea and playing cards in the smoky, dark kitchen, fire flickering in the stove. Even as a child I can see the sorrow lines in their faces deepen and their eyes elongate as if the tears they'd shed for those vanished men were about to break loose from their long-held dams and spill forth again with perpetually renewing vigor. My great-grandfather deserted Great Grandma Iva when she was six months pregnant with my grandmother, which is how she ended up in the refugee camp with her eight children. My grandfather was killed in the Second World War, when he was only twenty-two, so there's no way to know if he'd have stuck around, in this way we've never really considered my grandmother an exception to the rule, just lucky, in a twisted way, that she never had to suffer the eventual betrayal. Aunt Júlia's husband immigrated to marry her, but went on a raging drunk when he hit the docks and hasn't been seen since (that was fifty years ago, so we're not expecting him any time soon). Aunt Teresa's husband ran off to Miami with another woman and poor Aunt Sophie's man was never her man. And my father? My father took his time, abandoning my mother slowly but surely over years, a desertion he seemed to delight in, making an art of it, with extravagant lies and elaborate accusations, laughing in the face of her tears, claiming—preposterously—he'd never loved her. Or that was the story I was told. By the time I was eight, he was gone for good.

On a particularly bad night some years after Grandma Iva's cruel prediction, when I was fourteen and had come home late with a red mark on my neck from making out with a boy whose name and face I can no longer remember (and would rather not), I found my mother sitting primly in the dark, upright in her lace nightgown, the black-and-white television humming dimly. It was tuned to a blank channel, the screen busy with static. She could watch static for hours. My mother was on a cocktail of medications by then so whose knows how much of it was that and how much her illness. She'd be in the asylum for good in a few months.

When I tried to tiptoe past her, her eyes flew open. She spoke in a low growl: "Everything Grandma says comes true."

Her eyes were ice blue, the TV flickering off them. She wrung her hands in the air. Her fingers were laden with jewels and her face heavily made up, she'd put every ring she owned on, she did that on bad nights, and sometimes a sexy dress—once I'd found her in her wedding dress.

"She told me he would leave and he did. He'll leave you, too." She spoke as if we shared the same man, but I didn't think it was my father she meant. "He'll leave you and put you in the grave. Isn't that what Grandma said?"

She turned back to the television, to the static, as if waiting for the story to commence.

'If he leaves me,' I thought now, wandering around that rich person's party alone for the next half an hour, searching for yet at the same time hoping to avoid anyone I knew—Renée or Karl, my husband's doctor or his wife, the parents of children from our daughter's school—'if he leaves me, I'll die. I don't believe in curses or old-woman prophecies any longer but even if I don't die physically, I'll die psychologically, I'll end up in the bed next to my mother in the sanatorium because the fact is I've sold my soul to him. Renée's right—I do worship him, he's become my god, my idol, my sun and self and without him, I'm no one. I'm a mother but not a very good one, my fears keep me too preoccupied, and I'm hardly a writer any more if I ever was. Modeling disgusts me and I'll never go back to it, so what else do I have left? Him. That's all.' I stepped through a room full of ivory candles and dancing couples, remembering his words from the night before: *I can't shake the feeling you hide parts of yourself from me.* 'He's onto me, but he doesn't know what I'm hiding, that is, the deathly fear that he'll leave me. If he died in a car accident, a plane crash, as much as he flies that's more likely, I could handle that but if he left me, I'd never get over it. He would—I know very well he'd get over me, he'd find someone else and go on traveling the world, putting the words of ambassadors and prime ministers, presidents and diplomats into his own, having his hand in history that way, without anyone realizing it, he appears the humble interpreter, the meek bystander, the harmless intellectual and yet in reality he's as egotistical and power-hungry as the rest of them—that is, men.'

I felt a rush of rage at my husband. Where was this coming from?

There was another string quartet playing in the grand ballroom upstairs, our host liked strings. It was playing, incredibly, Bartók and the couples on the dance floor jerked, trying to keep pace with the frenetic, discordant music. At least the alcohol coursing through their veins would prevent them from knowing how ridiculous they looked.

Of course, I was in the same state of mind. In an adjacent room, I stopped before a painting of a fox-hunt that covered the entire wall, complete with bloody, terrified fox (the whites of its eyes were a bright spot among dark hues) being torn to pieces by hounds in the bottom corner, the painting was sparing nothing. I saw Vilma standing a few paces away. At first I thought she'd come to speak to me, but, incredibly, she didn't seem to notice me. Or was deliberately ignoring me. I saw with relief she had a man on her arm, or she was on the arm of a man. They regarded the painting together, or perhaps they were speaking of something else, they were talking very low with their heads together, faces all but touching. His fingers lingered over her bare spine, the small of her back, as if unsure whether their touch would be welcome or not.

I drained my crystal champagne flute and said, "Happy New Year!"

She turned, flat-faced at first. Then a little smile—cruel, I thought. "Happy New Year. I see you've lost him too."

"Him?" I raised my brows, pretending not to know who she was talking about.

We'd both had enough to drink, we swayed on our long legs and spiked heels like two towers of Pisa about to topple. Her eyes were glossy, mine probably were too. Alcohol can turn even the most sophisticated people into buffoons, not that she really was acting like a buffoon, it's hard to be that gorgeous and come off as a buffoon. Actually some liquor did that crowd good, it lifted the weight of pretension and slackened the conceit they were all bloated with, swollen to the brim with the knowledge of their own good looks and fair health and extreme prosperity and general good luck, which is not really luck since when you have money you can make your luck.

"Your *husband*. How could you forget such a guy? We were having a drink at the bar downstairs and I turned around and he'd disappeared. What an elusive man!" Vilma's laughter pitched like glass breaking. Her accent was more pronounced now that she was drunk.

"He does that," I said, buoyed. Perhaps he'd left her to search for me, then again, he was probably just being a social butterfly, he loves parties. "He's a social butterfly."

"He's fantastic. One of the best in this country—professionally, I mean." The man with her was looking at me over her shoulder, unsmiling.

"I know. People are always telling me."

She flung her hand back, hitting the man's chest. They were obviously well-acquainted. "Do you think we look alike? They were saying we resemble each other but we think it's because we're both tall."

She was speaking for me now, too, her use of the plural presuming more intimacy than we in fact shared or than I felt.

He shrugged. "Maybe the eyes . . . Are you an interpreter, too?"

"No." They looked at me, waiting.

"What do you do?" he asked, more out of habit than, I felt, interest.

I smiled and gave my usual answer which, while it typically got me by, wasn't that impressive, not next to her eight languages. "I read. I do a bit of writing. We have a daughter."

It was nonetheless a crafted answer, whose success rested on a certain nonchalance meant to evoke false modesty and make me sound not like a bored and useless housewife but like one of those bluebloods who leads a life of luxury complete with dabbles in intellectual pursuits such as "a bit of writing," this was meant to sound sufficiently vague so that it could mean either several novels or a sort of Victorian puttering around in a daily diary. The latter was closer to the truth. Although I used to write— poems and folk tales for Aliah, a few memoir essays—the bit of writing I now did amounted to a frenzied scribbling down of my husband's suspected betrayals (even though I know very well he's never betrayed me, at least

I think he hasn't) and sometimes a rather neurotic mathematical charting of his comings and goings, things he's said, looks and touches he's given me, clues he's left like a trail of breadcrumbs leading to the secret hut of his heart, all put down on loose leaf paper I then crumpled and burned immediately.

Vilma put her hand on my arm. "This is Rebeka. She's married to a colleague of mine."

The man reached out his hand, still not bothering to smile. "A pleasure."

"He doesn't have a name," Vilma said.

"I don't," he said earnestly. He raised his glass—beer, it looked like—and held it out to mine, I clinked it. "Well, I have one, I just don't like to tell anyone what it is. It gets me into trouble when people know my name."

He was lean and tall though no taller than me and perhaps a bit shorter (though to be fair he didn't have heels on). He inhabited his body in a sort of rigid way beneath his probably rented tux, like a tightly coiled spring. He was young, younger than Vilma and younger than me, but you could see he'd been around, he had a rough look like the bad boys I used to love in high school. His reddish-blond hair fell in thick jagged pieces over one eye and he had shifty blue eyes and he was unshaven. That's what got my attention. You didn't come to a party like this unshaven, yet his jaw had three or four days' growth of blond stubble.

He looked at Vilma as if they were exchanging a private joke and she said, "What he means is when *women* know his name."

He grimaced and said, "I'm going to have a cigarette."

Vilma squeezed his arm. "Oh no you don't. The least you can do is dance with Rebeka. Her husband has abandoned her."

This pissed me off. "Actually, I was just going to meet him. He's downstairs."

And I walked off, hoping my bare back was as impressive as hers.

I didn't get far. In the doorway a man passed by me, staring. He turned and called, "Hey, I know you."

I hesitated. I'd never seen his balding, pudgy head before.

"We met in Cairo." My face must have been blank, he looked hurt. He insisted, "We went out for drinks, remember? We met at the embassy. You're an interpreter, right?"

He thought I was her. She *did* work in Egypt. My blood ran cold. My husband was lying to me. A more rational voice piped up: or perhaps he truly didn't know, perhaps their trips there hadn't coincided. My fear quickly squelched this notion. *My husband is lying to me.* The man was silent a moment and I thought I'd offended him. "Oh," I said. "That's right."

This pleased him. He had stepped close to me, now he leaned in, breathing liquor on my neck. "Believe me," he said, voice low, "I'm still kicking myself for that night."

I stepped back and managed a smile, twisting the stem of my glass in my fingers. "Don't do that. What's the point?"

He stepped back, too, looked at me again, this time differently. "You don't remember me, do you?"

I put my fingers on the snaps on the front of his tux. "Listen, I have a favor to ask you. This is going to sound strange, but did you ever see me with a man in Cairo? I mean—besides you. Did you ever hear any rumors about me with a man, another interpreter, maybe? There are rumors going around and I just want to know . . ."

He appeared not to have heard me at all—the music wasn't that loud, such deafness could only have been made possible by the roaring of his own monstrous ego in his ears, then again, it's something I and most women are used to, our voices go right through or never reach the ears of men we're speaking to (unless we're saying something they want to hear). We were standing in front of that fox hunt painting and now he put his hand flat on it—right on the canvas!—and crossed his ankles, striking a pose. He had a bland face, so unremarkable it was unpleasant to look at, how could he expect people to remember that boring face? He considered me like a piece of meat, eyes running up and down my body. "So what are you doing here? You're still working for the government, huh? I can't believe I ran into you. Happy New Year."

Right on cue, I saw Bad Boy approaching—the man Vilma had introduced me to. He was holding out his arm, an offer to dance.

They were playing a waltz, thank god, perhaps it had dawned on them Bartók didn't work so well for people three sheets to the wind, besides, half the crowd was over fifty, those creaky bones couldn't keep up with the modernist's rhythms, nor would have my racehorse legs, even though they were Hungarian—the rhythms and the legs, the latter of which felt rubbery and loose and disconnected from my feet, which I was having trouble feeling. Music spilled around us as Bad Boy dragged me around the dance floor.

"So what's your name?" he said in a husky way. His neck smelled like motor oil, no, it couldn't have, I was dreaming. He's a mechanic, he rides a motorcycle and shoots up, I thought, though, really, he was probably something more benign and common, like an actor who worked as a waiter.

"You have a very short memory."

"Oh, yeah. Yeah. Rebeka, right?" He was no doubt picturing it as Rebecca, he was very American.

"Very good. And yours?"

He smiled crookedly. "You're trying to trick me now, Rebeka. I'm not that drunk. I'm not even drunk."

"Why not? It's New Year's Eve."

He considered me, our eyes almost even, I was indeed taller. The candles were burning low and the lights had been gradually turned down over the course of the night, the better to conceal the streaked eyeliner, slipping bodices, and crooked ties. "You're a very beautiful woman, Rebeka. I know that sounds like a line, but it's the truth."

I hear that all the time, I wanted to say, it makes me sick to my stomach to hear it again. Instead I said, "Do you expect me to blush like a little girl?"

He laughed and put his head back, glancing momentarily at the chandelier whirling overhead. "Yeah, you hear that a lot, don't you?" He changed course. "Hey, do you want to step outside with me? I need a cigarette. I don't like this crowd. I get self-conscious around these rich fucks."

The music stopped and a gong sounded, a polite female voice with an English accent announced over the intercom it was five to midnight. The crowd shrieked. People started bustling around, frantic to find the perfect spot and perfect person to ring in the new year with as if to be in the wrong spot with the wrong person would cast a blight over the next twelve months, a curse or blight or simply leave a bad taste in the mouth for a few weeks, the memory of the wrong kiss, the wrong wish, the wrong embrace poisoning the rest of the winter. Bad Boy's blue eyes held mine, a question in them I thought was more than about stepping outside. I pictured my husband searching the building for me as the year expired, or perhaps he would be kissing my look-alike in some dark hallway.

Bad Boy grew tired of waiting. He took my hand and led me onto the balcony. I was startled to see his hands were trembling as he lit up. I wanted to reach out and still them, not for him but for me.

"I suffer from social anxiety," he said, a line off a drug commercial, and yet the sheepish way he said it made him instantly more attractive.

"Really? I couldn't tell."

"People aren't very observant, are they?"

The balcony was lantern-lit, stone, expansive, one of those castle-like balconies with a low balustrade, we stood looking over it. A few couples stood nearby, chatting or laughing or getting a head start on their midnight kisses but none of them were my husband and Vilma. Bad Boy offered me a cigarette. For some reason I nodded and let him light it (his hands only slightly stiller) and then hand it to me even though I hate it when men do that, the best drag is the first. I only smoke when I drink, a habit my husband hates. Now, it tasted good for that very reason.

We smoked in silence, staring out over the twinkling city, like two people who were comfortable with each other or had known each other a long time. There were no stars, it was cold and clouds were building up, filled with snow and sickly purple from the reflection of the city lights.

"How do you know Vilma?"

He shrugged, stroked his stubbled jaw. "It's a long story."

"I have time."

"She's not what she appears to be," he said, surprising me.

"What do you mean?"

"She's one of the most intelligent women I've ever met, for one thing. She acts like this glamorous, man-eating bitch, but really she's kind of a nerd." He grinned. "Don't tell her I said that. Obsessed with her work and all that. You know she's never been married?"

"I know nothing about her. Is she now?"

He looked at me. "I just said she's never been."

"Right. I mean—are you together?"

"We're friends. Vilma doesn't have relationships. She can't find a man who's not intimidated by her is my theory. She says she likes it that way, but I don't know. So I'm the one who gets dragged to her parties."

I tried to make this information fit with the picture the pudgy-headed man who'd had drinks with her in Cairo had painted of her—it didn't. Well, everyone is seen through someone's eyes. Anyway he was done with the subject, he flicked his cigarette into the shadows beyond the railing and turned to me. He hovered the back of his hand over my abdomen—a touch but not a touch, as if the inversion of that hand rendered its intention innocent. Still, I could feel it. "Married, huh?"

"And you're not."

He smiled and started to say—who knows what? Yes, he was married or no or none of my business, I'd never know—just then a collective roar went up inside and the gong began to chime. Someone was striking it by hand, the chimes were unevenly spaced. The clock tower a few blocks away followed suit, more precisely but a few seconds behind our gong and so the two clashed, along, no doubt, with chimes and gongs and bells we couldn't hear all over the city and all over the country. We could hear a shared roar, though, emanating from ours and from all the parties below, the time had come and everyone was in it together and in Time together.

Seven . . . six . . . five . . . gong . . . gong . . . gong . . .

He reached for me with both hands. I turned my face before he could kiss me and he brought his mouth down on my chest, hands coming up to touch my breasts, his tongue warm and wet on my bare skin. It felt good. I started to melt into it, then came to and twisted away—I wanted to kiss him but when it came down to it, I couldn't, or wouldn't. I lurched, drunk, over the balustrade and would have fallen if he hadn't caught me but he did and then held me there in front of him, for some reason in no hurry to pull me back or perhaps he was simply enjoying the weight of my body half in his arms and half suspended over the silver, buzzing air, and so I leaned out in the direction I imagined was Hungary, was home, but really I had no idea if it was, strange arms around me, as the year let go and the future arrived.

The line to the ladies' room had dwindled to nothing. It was just past midnight and everyone was celebrating, no one wanted to have a pee at the height of the party. Bad Boy said he'd wait, I think he realized how drunk I was and didn't want to leave me, he was a gentleman after all. The stalls were full, though, at least it sounded like they were by the giggles and rapid-fire snorts issuing from behind the cherry wood doors. It was an elegant place to do coke or whatever it was they were doing—probably some more sophisticated and up-to-date drug than cocaine, at thirty-eight I was behind the times, out-of-the-loop. The plushly carpeted, rose-wall-papered powder room was furnished with velvet loveseats and urns of tropical flowers—fresh, not silk, arrangements as tall as my shoulders. I glanced into the floor-length mirror, and saw not myself, but Vilma—she'd entered the powder room, she'd come to confront me, I thought with momentary panic. It was a three-way mirror and seeing my own face from an unfamiliar angle had, no doubt, prompted the hallucination but it took me a second to realize this—we *did*, after all, resemble each other, yet Vilma's nose did not appear nearly so large as mine does, day after day in my own mirror at home—indeed, before I could realize it, the girls emerged from the stalls, billionaire heiresses, probably, with striking features and red nostrils, girls no older than twenty. They weren't embarrassed when they saw me and saw in my eyes I knew what they'd been doing, they were the privileged, the elite, and they didn't have to be afraid of anyone or ashamed of anything, not their hanging down spaghetti straps or the damp locks of dark hair in their dilated eyes, their flailing too-skinny limbs, their shrill laughter. They leaned over the sinks to put their red lipstick on crookedly and meet my reflected eyes, daring me to know what they'd been up to, as Vilma retreated from the distant reaches and obtuse angles of the three-way mirror, like my long-abandoned other self, the woman I might have been.

My husband was standing at the bar. His fans circled him, listening to him expound on world politics, the conflict in Israel, the meaning of time, or all of these at once, who knew. Karl and Renée were there, and of course Vilma. Someone was standing between them, that is, between she and my husband, but she was hanging, I thought, on every word he was saying. 'He's going to look up and see me coming down the stairs with Bad Boy in tow,' I thought, reaching to take his hand, 'then he'll know how I feel, the jealousy, fear, and dread I live with every hour of every day,' but he didn't look up, he'd paused to let someone light his cigar. He resumed telling some hilarious story about a translation in Chechnya gone wrong, a story I didn't recognize, I was close enough now to hear it, one of those horror stories he and Vilma both knew so well and she was helping him out, getting the details right when he got them wrong, apparently she'd been there at the time or been told the same story before, perhaps, I thought, between Egyptian sheets.

I stopped outside the circle, waiting for him to notice me, Bad Boy at my side like a loyal dog. At last my husband's eyes met mine.

"There she is," he announced, using the third person as if I were a character in a story. "I haven't seen my wife since last year."

Everyone groaned. I gave him a tight smile. He was looking questioningly at my rough-edged companion. I said, "This is—well—I don't even know his name, honestly."

Then this came out of my mouth, surprising no one more than it did myself: "But Vilma must. I believe she's fucked him."

There was a click, as something slid into place, and everyone looked at me, then Vilma. With astonishing cool, she said, "That doesn't mean I know his name."

A nervous laugh dominoed around the group.

"But you know Avi's, don't you?" Renée addressed Vilma, words slurring wildly. "Probably in several languages, not all of them involving words."

Karl nearly choked on his drink. He grabbed her arm. "Renée!"

She shook loose. "Oh come on, can't you see Avi's fucking this woman?" She glared at Vilma, who smiled disarmingly back. "It's a new year. Let's start it with the truth."

"She does work in Egypt," I told him (as if he didn't know) as he escorted me out of the party, not hurriedly, gently, my husband maintains perfect poise at all times, he's not rattled by foreign dictators and he's not rattled by drunken insults. "Were you with her in Egypt?"

He didn't answer until we were going down the two flights of steps outside, me clinging to his arm so not to fall. Then, calmly, he said, "No. I've never seen her in Cairo."

"Then why don't you want us to come with you?"

"I do want you to. I thought you didn't want to. You said Aliah needs to be in school."

I laughed cruelly, sure he was lying. I stared up at the sky which, to my surprise, was cascading snowflakes. "Just tell me—are you in love with her?"

He stopped on the landing and looked at me. "I'm going to say it once, Rebeka, and you're going to believe me, or you're not, but I'm not going to say it again. I'm not cheating on you. I've never slept with Vilma, nor do I want to. And I'm certainly not in love with her."

A breath I felt I'd been holding for years rushed from my body. "I know you're not," I said, tears rising in me because, in fact, I did know it. "I know you wouldn't, darling."

I raised my hands to take his face in them, but he backed away. He'd never backed away from me before, and he'd never said anything to me like what he said next.

"I would think you would know that." His eyes flashed like steel. "The way I fawn over you, the way I fucking bend over backwards to prop up your fragile self-esteem. Your goddamned *infinite* insecurity. Then again, you seem to find it impossible to believe I could love you, so it's no surprise, really, you've found a way to think the worst of me." His face was full of disgust. He muttered, "No, no surprise at all."

Snow was falling down thickly, dropping a veil between us. My husband turned his back and beckoned the valet.

Ben Avi's aunt's eighth wedding was, truth be told, the loveliest one yet even though it was almost impossible to get up for it. She was becoming a master or, rather, a mistress of weddings if not marriages. Fresh cedar bows, green and gold velvet, hundreds or thousands of white candles, a sort of re-run of the night before's decor. The snow-draped cedars outside echoed those inside, as seen through the windows of the cathedral—this groom was another Catholic, a handsome Spaniard, in fact, that was a new one. It was a romantic wedding and though we'd hardly spoken and hardly touched through the hurried morning and then the grueling, ritual-laden ceremony, at the end of it my husband put his arm around my waist and whispered in my ear, let's get out of here. We slipped away before the reception, though I regretted missing out on the flan with the plastic toreador on top.

On the way home, Ben suggested we stop at a bistro we liked for a warm cup of soup so we could share a New Year's toast alone before picking up our daughter from the schoolmate's family she'd spent the day with. I was exhausted, hungover, and wired on espresso. My wool suit felt hot and prickly.

He had chowder and I butternut squash while Nina Simone sang in the background. The place was almost empty, the atmosphere sedate, subdued, in the wake of the night before.

The waiter took our bowls away and brought us each a giant glass of wine, rich and dark for the cold day, and I started to feel better. Ben looked out at the snow and said, "You think I don't see you but I do."

'Here we go,' I thought, 'he thinks you can talk everything out, for him talking is always the answer.' "I don't feel like getting in a deep talk today, Benni."

"I just want you to know I accept you."

I laughed, too quickly. "What's that supposed to mean? You sound like a greeting card."

He sighed and stroked his jaw, reminding me involuntarily of Bad Boy, who I was hoping had been only a figment of my imagination. After a minute, he said, "I'm sorry about last night. I'm sorry I spoke to you that way. I shouldn't have lost my temper."

I stared at him, the wheels turning in my head. Our fight had been entirely my fault, of course, I'd seen that as soon as I woke up though I hadn't been able to say it to him yet. He reached for my hands over the table and looked into my eyes in his intense way—which seemed, today, melodramatic. I didn't look away, I was tired of looking away. His eyes didn't look so extraordinary today anyway, they simply looked tired, a bit bloodshot, the eyes of a forty-something man who reads too much on the computer late into the night.

"What about my goddamned infinite insecurity?"

He smiled. "That was ill-put. A terrible turn of phrase, I can't believe that came out of me . . . I was too hard on you last night. Of course we're all insecure. It's part of being human."

"But in my case you think I'm *too* insecure, don't you? That's what you meant last night. You get fed up with it, don't you? Just admit it. I mean you think it's something I need to work on."

He rubbed his hands over his face, sighed. I could see him weighing his words, protecting me, as always. "I—I think that's up to you. I simply think you might be happier, if you were to, I don't know . . . pursue some of your interests. Why don't you try putting some of your writing out there? Some of the folk tales, they're good . . ." He trailed off, which wasn't like him, a man who always has the words.

"I'd never have the confidence to put my writing out there." It was probably the most honest thing I'd ever said to him.

He didn't say anything. He stared into his wineglass.

"Women are supposed to be insecure, Benni. Especially women who look like me."

He looked up, surprised.

"If I weren't insecure people would hate me—especially other women. And you know how alone I feel in this country already."

He frowned. "Maybe. Or maybe they would respect you."

I said nothing. Over his shoulder the street was quiet, not much traffic on the holiday, the snow still falling in the late afternoon lavender light. Maybe, I thought, then, a moment later, but probably they would hate me.

Across the table, my husband took his wine and leaned back in his chair, waiting for me to say something.

The Oophorectomy

'Everything is dying,' I thought, walking to work in the morning, a documentary about climate change I'd watched the night before had put me in a mood. 'And meaning is already dead. We've killed it. I finally understand what my professor in postmodern lit was talking about all those years ago.' I took in the Styrofoam cups overflowing the Hardees trash bin, the billboards advertising free minutes and free upgrades and no-cost estimates, the newscaster whining about the stock market on NPR, which was playing behind the counter of the café I stopped in for an overlarge green tea to burn off my Netflix hangover, the bright artificial colors of the culture, shiny reds and yellows and greens in all fonts on the packaged foods that weren't really food but a conglomeration of chemicals, white sugar, and bio-engineered soy and corn. 'No, nothing here is enduring or has any depth to it at all, no mystery and no essence, no wonder we're all sick and sad and searching . . . then again, the Styrofoam will be here for a while.'

At work, I watched the young writer's delicate brown fingers reach for yet another milk chocolate wafer, a plate of them sat in the middle of the particleboard table we were all trapped around. Management had called an impromptu, company-wide meeting that morning, the theme of which was turning out to be, predictably enough, "Embracing Change." The huge publishing company I'd worked for for almost ten years had lately been on a spree of cutting wages and combining departments, dissolving full-time positions and filling them with part-time ones in order to avoid having to pay benefits and decent salaries and this meeting, it appeared, would be a thinly veiled attempt to defend their actions by pointing the finger back at us, the employees, many of whom had vocally criticized the changes. Management's argument, it dawned on us after just a few PowerPoint screens, was that we opposed the changes because we were unconsciously afraid of change. Through no fault of our own! The blame was to be put on the reptilian part of our poorly evolved brains, the part of the brain responsible for instincts and the baser desires. I watched the young writer's reptilian brain tell him to reach for another wafer, the writer whose manuscript I'd begun editing over the weekend and which was—well—let's just say it was terrible in all the worst ways, and I'm being kind—but I had a feeling my boss wouldn't agree, I sat peeling my fingernails and dreading this conversation which I was scheduled to have with her as soon as the meeting was over. Now, though, I felt sorry for him, dosing himself with sugar to deal with the boring and insulting presentation, which wasn't even meant for him, he'd only come by to meet with his new editor (my boss) when we were all herded into the conference hall like cattle. I read his mind: at least there was chocolate.

In a French accent, the pony-tailed, white-haired man they must have paid thousands of dollars that could have gone toward our salaries to fly in and speak to us encouraged us to "align" and "develop" with the "natural current" of the organization as it evolved. Appearing, like any accomplished yogi, in several places at once—both behind the podium at the front of the room and on the several giant flat-screens suspended from the ceiling, he patiently explained that an organization didn't just change, it "activated" change, and to do so, it needed T.E.A.M. work, which was cleverly broken down into an acronym, Together Energetic Active Movement, or not so cleverly, since the words meant N.O.T.H.I.N.G.—they were simply more of those corporate-speak words that are meaningless enough to mean nothing and so have the ability to shapeshift into whatever fascist meaning the organization wishes them to hold. My teammates fingered their ten-ounce Styrofoam cups of chemical-smelling coffee and stared at the particleboard, as bored and repulsed by this drivel as I was. If the company was so "progressive," another word Frenchie had been flinging around this morning, couldn't they at least provide decent coffee instead of coffee from South American factory plantations that was drenched in pesticides and stored in aluminum cans for months before it reached us, when the aluminum was then released into the coffee grounds (okay, maybe my science was suspect but it was something I worried about) as they were steeped in fluoridated hot water, and then escorted into our brains, slowly but inevitably resulting in brain inflammation; i.e., Alzheimer's or Parkinson's or both, which is known as Alzheimer's Plus, as if the additional disease were a gain and not a loss? Couldn't they at least give us that in-house espresso bar we'd been clamoring for for years? Our reptiles brains were frightened, the French expert explained, by change. It's okay. Everyone's are. But fear shouldn't be trusted. It leads to irrational thinking. And therefore the company could make whatever unethical moves it wanted to, and chalk up resistance to the alligator brains of its union-less Neanderthal employees. This he left out.

The presentation dragged itself into mid-morning (like an albatross? too heavy-handed?). The challenge was how to "add value" to the "action plan," which required "thinking outside the box" and even "living on the edge of chaos." This last bit I liked the sound of, though I was sure it didn't mean to them what it meant to me: canoeing through Thailand, dancing to a punk band until you dropped even though you were in your thirties, refusing to worry about the extra ten pounds the culture claimed made you ghastly and unlovable.

There was only one word to describe my response to all this. After I had doodled it in all the different fonts (hundred fifty plus) on my tablet, I texted it—a juvenile and vulgar word I won't spell out here, I'll only say it starts with F and ends with K but I ended it with a row of exclamation points, which you can never use too many of these days but you should *never* use them in literature, as in !!!!!!!—across the table to Noel, hoping she'd silenced her phone. It made her smile.

I handed my boss the young writer's manuscript. After some warm-up small talk, in which I made every effort to compliment the manuscript but didn't, I'm afraid, succeed in doing so, I said, "Are we publishing this because he's black?"

She looked up from her iPad, open to Twitter (the manuscript she'd tossed aside), reading glasses about to slide off the end of her nose. "Yes."

"Oh, come on. Really? But there are so many amazing African American writers. We shouldn't have to stoop to this." I rattled off a list of names, black writers who truly moved and impressed me, who were taking risks, changing the language, saying important things about race or not about race but simply telling great stories, at the end of which my boss pointed out, rightly, that those authors already had publishing houses.

"I'll be embarrassed to have our name on this," I warned.

"We only have one black writer in the fall catalogue, and that's in non-fiction. Talk about embarrassing. We need a black fiction writer. This one will do."

I desperately wanted to point out her racist generalizations ("this one") but while my boss and I have a good relationship, it's not that good. I focused on the manuscript. "But this is *terrible*. It's about . . . what was it . . . people that shapeshift into fruits and vegetables, become some sort of non-GMO organic utopia and gnaw on each other as a way of lovemaking."

My boss held the pages up and read the terrible title from over the top of her reading glasses. She looked at me and narrowed her eyes, then—using terrible syntax, said: "Are you sure you don't like it because he's black?"

End of conversation. I would have another look at it, with a more open mind this time. She buzzed the young writer in, rising to greet him so warmly I thought she was going to hug him.

That afternoon, I sat in my gynecological surgeon's office waiting for him to come in—he was running late, naturally, since he's a doctor and, thanks to the greedy insurance companies and malpractice lawyers, can barely make ends meet and so has to cram his schedule to the gills, double-booking patients in the way airlines sell the same seat twice. Forty-five minutes ticked by. Finally, having exhausted my phone for entertainment, I picked up one of the shiny pamphlets I'd been eyeing in the plastic envelope on the wall and read it: "New breakthrough in contraception! Install a hormone delivery system in your uterus that lasts up to fifteen years!"

When the nurse came in, I told her, "I don't want a *system* in my uterus," holding up the pamphlet, trying to make a joke but at the same time to let her know how patients feel about being turned into cyborgs for the profit of pharmaceutical companies.

She didn't get it. "It's a good option for some women. Anyway you're not going to need birth control anymore," she said, pecking in my blood pressure and temperature on the laptop. She didn't look at me when she said it, she preferred the shield of the laptop screen: "Dr. Chan is recommending a hysterectomy for you."

I wasn't surprised. Still, the announcement sent waves of fear pumping through my body. "But I want to have babies. I mean, someday."

I knew the nurse well and she knew me, probably she didn't like me, I was always cantankerous when I came in, you would be too if you'd had your reproductive organs scraped off four times in six years and the surgeon still didn't know your name or meet your eyes, let alone show any interest in getting you healthy. She was about twenty-five, pretty. Not long ago she'd been a college sorority girl as evidenced by the tramp stamp I saw on her sacrum when she bent over to get a paper gown out for me, Greek letters in black and purple ink overseeing reproductive organs that were no doubt plump and pink with health between those hips. She handed me the gown and gave me a tight smile. "Someday was last week. You'd better think about it. He says it's your best chance at this point."

Chance at what? It was true Chan had been telling me for years if I wanted to get pregnant, I'd better do it right away, but the time had never been right. I was still getting my career off the ground, I didn't have a partner, or when I did, he didn't want kids. Six years ago, I'd been diagnosed with benign mesothelioma, a mysterious condition, rare but not that rare anymore (the rate of every mysterious disease is exploding) in which grape-sized cysts grew all over my ovaries and uterus in an out-of-control, mad-scientist, bougainvillea-on-steroids way as if trying to decorate my pelvic cavity for a gaudy party. It was a benign condition, but the surgeon had always warned the cysts could turn cancerous at any moment, like an army suddenly reversing direction. The only option was to cut them out when they got large enough they were compromising the function of my ovaries and endangering my health were they to become malignant. And so the slicing had begun: the first two laparotomies, six-inch openings on my lower abdomen, going through the same scar twice, the last two laparoscopies, laser surgeries done by a robot with the surgeon at the computer in the corner of the operating room, the horse-sized robot deep diving over my body. The laser surgeries required only five small incisions, but each time they cut in new places and so my belly was speckled with crenelated scars. Against my doctor's better judgment, I tried to get well.

I downloaded e-books with miracle cures, downed mountains of herbs and supplements, juice fasted, saunaed, coffe-enemaed, ate only brown rice and radishes for twenty-one days. I gave up alcohol, tobacco, negative thinking, toxic relationships and television and took up (albeit briefly) yoga, meditation, acupuncture, art, and affirmations and still my ovaries pumped away, stuck in the on position, popping out little clear sacs of blisters that bloomed into something I imagined resembled undersea coral but was probably closer to tapioca jello. Now it had been only nine months since my last surgery and already they were back, expanded to the collective size of an organic honeydew (but smaller than a conventional one!).

The doctor arrived at last, forgetting or not bothering to apologize. He put his latex-gloved hand inside me and palpated the clumped-together growths and then told me the same thing the nurse had. "We can't keep cutting you open," he said, feigning concern or perhaps that's my bitterness talking. "Every time we do, we create more scar tissue, which leads to adhesions, which you don't want. And your risk of cancer only increases with age."

I sat up, hugging the paper gown to my cold ribs, shaking my head as he spoke. Words had left me. All I could do was shake my head. Eventually I managed to ask him if he thought it was cancer. He didn't know. It could be, though so far every time it had not.

"At least let me take your ovaries," he said, a used car salesman striking a deal. "If you want to have children in the future, you can always use donor eggs."

I told him I'd think about it, promising myself I wouldn't.

"I hate my boyfriend," I told Noel the following Monday over our caramel frappuccinos. We had a late morning meeting and so we'd agreed to meet at Starbuck's to go over some details beforehand. We talked about everything but the meeting. I told her what the doctor had said, explained the decision I was facing and that I wasn't really facing a decision since I'd already made up my mind: I wasn't about to let a male doctor put me into menopause at thirty-four. She supported my decision. We knew doctors had been recklessly robbing women of their wombs for decades with no heed for the health consequences which were now coming to light. Plenty of recent and not so recent studies had shown that ovaries if not uteruses (uteri?) were not for baby-making alone: they were also essential to long-term health, continuing to make hormones into a woman's eighties rather than stopping cold at menopause as my doctor had told me they did. I switched the subject—or thought I was switching the subject—to my relationship.

"What?"

"I hate him. I just realized I hate him."

"You love Jason! I thought you guys were going to get married."

"I don't know. Something's wrong. It's like I can't stand being around him anymore. Thank God he's in Africa for another month. This is *really* good." I slurped the whipped cream speckled with nutmeg off the milky surface, sucking in 220% of my daily allowance of sugar, my pancreas dutifully pumping out insulin, my liver fat and storing it away in my thighs where it would be almost impossible to get rid of. I'd learned this last night from a YouTube documentary, along with the fact that the FDA deliberately leaves the daily allowances for sugar on food labels blank because the numbers would be shocking if they put them on and might lead to people making healthier choices and reversing their type two diabetes, costing the sugar industry billions.

"Oh, that's very mature of you. It *is*." She slurped hers. "Good, I mean. How could you hate Jason? He does good work. He does important work."

He did. That's what everyone said about him, as if that made him a man worth loving. He was, no doubt, a man worth loving, but I wasn't sure *I* loved him. Jason was the director of a non-profit that provided a variety of services for children in Africa, from cleft palate surgeries to vaccines and schoolbooks. We'd met when he submitted a manuscript of his book called *Lessons in Life: Educating Africa* to our press, which I edited and then re-wrote in the midst of our developing romance, changing the title to *Lessons in Hope: Educating Uganda*, a title I still found pretentious and sentimental, but at least it was better than claiming his organization was educating all of Africa. Jason had great ideas, a big heart, and a wealth of international experience but he wasn't a very good writer. In my expert hands, the book had been doing well on Amazon since it came out six months ago, and ever since, it was as if we'd run out of things to talk about. He'd become, I felt, clingy and whiny, and he pestered me relentlessly about how I needed to face my fears and write my own book, how my job was just a prop, an excuse, a smokescreen for the writer I wanted to be but was too afraid to try to be. I'd told him only the vaguest details about my cystic "condition," it wasn't something I liked to share with lovers. As far as he knew, my surgeries were over, the "health problems" in my female parts a thing of the past.

Lately he'd been really getting on my nerves in that subtle creeping way so many of my lovers had done just before I drove the final nail in the coffin of our relationship (to force a metaphor). I couldn't stand the way he clipped his fingernails instead of peeling them with his other fingernails, sure, that was a quirk of mine, I can't stand the sound of fingernail clippers and prefer hand-picked nail trimming while most people are the opposite, it sounds petty I know, but it was clearly the sign of some deeper, unconscious resentment or loathing I wasn't willing to acknowledge or was afraid to express—or perhaps the two were one and the same—and it didn't seem to be going away. Hidden away in the shadows of my mind as it was, I didn't see what I could do about it.

"I don't care. I can't help my feelings."

"Are you going to break up with him?"

"Yeah. I don't know. Maybe. We'll see."

Noel looked down at her frappuccino. She was silent, then she said, whipped cream on her top lip making the somber question less somber, "Does he want kids, Molly?"

"He's mentioned it. We haven't really talked about it." Then, under my best friend's ruthless gaze, "Probably. Yes."

"So?

"So what? I can have kids."

She just looked at me. Finally she felt the whipped cream and wiped it off with a burlap-colored eco-fiber napkin made of 25% post-consumer recycled material (not nearly enough) that was bleach-free, non-toxic, and hypo-allergenic all at the same time.

That evening, I googled *hormone delivery system uterus*, far more words than necessary, the mammoth pharmaceutical company that made the system had paid well to make sure it popped up right at the top of Google. I tend to google things that freak me out, I don't know why. In a few seconds, I'd learned that the hormone delivery system was a wireless chip that could be activated and deactivated by remote control—your doctor adjusts your dose from the clinic without you even having to go in! It worked by sending an electric current through the device that melted the tiny battery implanted in the wall of your uterus a bit every day, just enough to let a synthetic hormone that dampened down your ovaries leak into your bloodstream (while at the same time wreaking havoc on your larger endocrine system and promoting breast cancer—I'm good with subtext) so no baby could be made that month, nor one in up to fifteen years unless you changed your mind and decided you wanted one, wherein you simply asked your doctor to click the remote to the off position and were ready to breed!

Jason called from Uganda, I ignored him. A few seconds later he messaged me on Facebook: *Hi dear, what's going on? How are you? How's our kitty monsters?* My two cats which at some point now impossible to pinpoint he had begun calling *our* cats.

I googled on. Wherein I discovered that ten to ninety percent of hysterectomies (I hadn't known it was *that* high!) performed in America today are not medically necessary, an absurd statistic that according to naturopaths is due to the fact that surgeons don't know what the hell they're doing (and are out only to make money) and to surgeons, a windfall that has cut reproductive cancer rates enormously since you can't get cancer on organs you don't have. Or can you? Other websites claimed cancer simply changed locations, took up residence in the colon or cervix when it found its organ of choice missing, and also that ovaries once removed can grow back—which sounded like a science fiction novel—and when they do, they are almost always diseased. An ad at the bottom of the page boasting one weird tip to reduce belly fat forever lured me in against my better judgment, and after a brief foray into a blog by a man who was convinced his wife was a reptilian shapeshifter and one of the executive members of the Illuminati, I learned that anti-GMO activists chalk the ever-increasing hysterectomy rate up to frankenfoods and pesticide contamination, which wreak havoc on our endocrine systems. This page linked an article about BPA, the insidious chemical in cash register receipts and dollar bills, plastic coffee filters, the lining of steel food cans, and thousands of other plastic items we handle or eat and drink from every day (I put a dish towel over my computer mouse at this point), which does the same and also finds time to kill or maim sperm. I learned about endocrine disruptors: chameleon-like chemicals that disguise themselves as estrogen molecules when they're really poison by-products of a post-industrial consumer capitalist system and confuse your organs, causing them to grow tumors, fibroids, and, yes—my heart stopped—cysts. Studies had shown a thousand percent increase in BPA blood levels after consuming one can of Campbell's Chicken Noodle Soup, the soup I lived on in graduate school, along with grilled cheese sandwiches of Kraft American slices in those little plastic wrappers, also probably BPA-soaked. One of the most romantic things about BPA, I learned, is that toddlers will often chew on cash register receipts and easily absorb BPA into their bloodstreams, high levels of which could be a key factor in the autism epidemic, an epidemic predicted to reach the horrifying level of one in two children by 2032. I pictured half the population wandering around autistic on the sidewalks, the strange beauty of it, humanity finally out of its head.

Another article, written by an acupuncturist from San Francisco who, I reminded myself, trying to stay calm, had no degree in chemistry and was selling BPA-cleansing herbs at the bottom of her page, explained that the FDA can't be bothered to do anything about it because in this country chemicals are considered safe until proven dangerous (whereas everywhere else in the world it's the opposite) and because the Grocery Manufacturers' Association would rather breed autistic children than take a profit hit by having to replace or re-design the steel can. Which linked to an article on spermicidal GMO corn that sterilized the men who ate it—an article which, by that point, I couldn't bring myself to read.

It was after midnight. I didn't care. Noel picked up on the second ring. "I think it's the BPA."

"What?"

"That's causing my cysts."

She yawned. "Sorry. I thought you cut that out a few years ago."

"You're thinking of PVCs. When I had my pipes inspected?"

"Oh. Right."

"Noel—am I overreacting or is this world just fucked? Our mothers never had to worry about BPA in their dollar bills. Did you know one in two women will get breast cancer? That's you or me. Did you know they now think mammograms are *causing*, not preventing, breast cancer? It's something about how they compress the breast, the concentrated dose of radiation they shoot in there."

When she recovered from her own alarm at this news, she talked me down and then told me I should go see this German energy healer named Birgit. "My friend Natasha goes to her every week, she says she couldn't function without her. I went to her once. Remember, I told you, it was last year when I was going through a rough time with Sean."

"Oh, yeah, you said it was weird."

"I said it was weird but I also said I thought it really helped me. She pulls out all the anger and fear and negative emotions that aren't serving you into her own body and then directs it out into the ethers. She told me it's like draining an infected wound, you have to get the pus out before you can heal."

"Lovely."

"And once the pus is out, she reconnects you to your soul. I mean it, I felt a lot better after and things got better with Sean too." I didn't point out that Sean had been cheating on her last year, no doubt at the time of this healing, with the Malaysian pre-med student he was now engaged to. "Maybe it would help you get some clarity about your decision, too."

I bristled, thinking she meant the hysterectomy. "I've already made my decision."

"Of course. I meant about Jason."

I took down the number.

A few nights later I was moved (for some reason) to email Jason a long, philosophical missive. It started with: "Everything is dying." And went on to lament the loss of meaning in today's world, the transience, the insidious poisoning, the hatred and division. I eloquently (I thought) described the collapse of almost every institution in our country, then moved on to the vacuousness of the culture at large as evidenced by its trite, sensationalistic, and soulless television shows ("when the stories implode, the culture implodes," I wrote, imagining someone quoting me in some post-apocalyptic blog). I hadn't written anything in years unless you counted re-writing the grammatically crippled sentences and stagnant plot lines of our authors, it felt great to fling my own words around, fueled by anger and despair. I plunged on to describe how hot spots and wi-fi zones were pumping out electromagnetic waves at rates we've never been exposed to before and really have no idea how this could affect us, not to mention the snapchats, instagrams, tweets, and texts zipping through the air at every millisecond like microscopic hypodermics. I didn't mention the terrible morphing fruits and vegetables utopian novel, my boss's accusation of racism, the energy healer nor the approaching surgery. We'd only been together a year, the man didn't need to know everything about me.

The next morning there was a message from him pointing out the excellent HBO shows of recent seasons and reminding me of several we'd watched together and which I had loved and critiquing, predictably, my faulty science, setting right my understanding of the risks of wi-fi and cell phone radiation, my lovers have always criticized my scientific understanding. He went on to argue, even more predictably, that the work he does is meaningful and will have lasting effects on Africans for generations to come (Ugandans, I mutely corrected from the other side of the globe, why does he *do* that?). Jason's very proud of his work, he loves the phrase "global non-profit" and he loves to fling it around—"I direct a global non-profit"—at dinner parties, art openings, soccer games, anywhere and everywhere he gets the chance to, I can see why, it gets him googly gazes of admiration. They'd vaccinated four hundred twenty-three babies just this week, babies that would grow up to be free of malaria and a host of other vicious diseases. I wrote back in my mind that indeed that was a wonderful thing, meaning it. I didn't bring up, not even to myself, since I didn't want to be a science-hating wacko (which Jason already thought I was, maybe he was right), the suspected link between aluminum in vaccines and autism, nor the fact that most vaccines contain a malicious soup of chemicals, metals, synthetic proteins, antibiotics, and aborted fetal DNA and that not all children are able to excrete these toxins from their skin and hair follicles and urine at the same rates as other children and it's impossible to know which ones are and which aren't and so those that aren't are effectively poisoned upon vaccination, according to the documentary I'd come across on YouTube over the weekend.

At the end of his email, as a sort of afterthought, I thought, he pointed out that my work, too, was meaningful. Disseminating important ideas into the culture via literature was crucial work in a democracy. And as for nothing lasting, well, he concluded, waxing poetic, even this very message will be stored in a Google cloud in perpetuity. He meant the image as encouraging, even awesome, but I found it depressing—I recalled the article I'd read on the internet or program I'd heard on NPR or YouTube documentary I'd watched that explained how clouds use hundreds of thousands of gallons of water *a second* in order to cool the extreme heat (climate change, anyone?) given off by the back-up generators they must keep running to prevent a server shutdown in case the grid were to falter for even a hundredth of a second. Every mundane email ever undeleted would be stored in perpetuity at the price of California's drinking water (the cloud in question was in some secret location outside Los Angeles). As California shriveled into a desert, I wondered if people would prefer being thirsty to losing emails—I wasn't sure. I wrote back several irritated replies, though only in my mind, I didn't want to add to the burden of the cloud.

My surgery was scheduled for the following Tuesday. I'd be out of work a week. I'd put in that I had to attend the funeral of a relative in another state, and so only Noel, who would drive me home from the hospital, would have to know. On Friday, I took the thirty-minute Uber to the sprawling university medical center for my pre-op. It was 8:00 a.m., and I was ten minutes late for my 7:50 appointment. The receptionist informed me she couldn't register me without the slip of paper the nurse had given me at my previous appointment, a slip of paper about four inches by four inches and which I had never been told was as valuable as gold and so, I was sure, I'd tossed it in the trash when I did my once-weekly purse-cleaning out. It was possibly in my kitchen trash, but that was half an hour away and my pre-op had to be done today, or no surgery on Tuesday.

The receptionist frowned, cow-like, resentful, as I pleaded to be let through without the paper. She was in her fifties, bi-focaled, permed graying hair, overweight. I recalled what Hannah Arendt had said, that the greatest evils are done by persons who refuse to think for themselves and who pass off all their decisions to whatever law they're operating under, however absurd or depraved that law might be. Arendt was shocked into this insight when she was covering the war trials in Jerusalem in the early sixties, where she observed what she called the "mediocrity" of high-ranking SS officer Albert Eichmann, who was no demon, no beast, only a balding, bland, personality-less bureaucrat who blithely defended himself: "I was only following orders." Many or perhaps most of the tried SS officers used the same defense for their acts of staggering evil—"I was only following orders when I tortured, starved and murdered millions of helpless people, little boys, little girls, old women, when I tossed babies into the incinerator without a second thought. I wasn't thinking, I didn't have to, I was only following orders." I knew this from the documentary about Hannah Arendt I'd streamed last night while tucked snugly in bed with my laptop, the only place I felt safe these days. "I'm only following orders," the stodgy receptionist might have said as she turned back to her computer, leaving me in tears I managed to stuff down until I was in the hospital lobby, where I let them out in a torrent, drawing the eyes of the hurrying-by. The analogy was unjust—the inconvenience was hardly akin to a concentration camp victim's suffering, I reprimanded myself, which only made me feel worse.

In the end I had to trek half a mile through the hospital halls to my doctor's office, where the young nurse who I thought didn't like me but perhaps I was wrong sneered at the pre-op office's petty rule and scribbled up another paper, forging the doctor's signature. I went back to the crabby receptionist, who didn't appear pleased for me but who did let me through and I was primed for surgery, blood drawn, list of medications recorded (fish oil, Vitamin C, wheat grass, melatonin, an herb for depression and one to boost the adrenals, all of them had to go, I got the feeling they'd rather I weren't taking them at all, supplements were very dangerous), informed consent and advance directive signed in the event something happened on the table, which is how they put it, meaning, in the event I died on the table.

That night the Grim Reaper appeared in my dreams. It morphed into Dr. Chan, who slid the Reaper's archetypal scythe across my belly, opening it bloodlessly and exposing my heart, strangely lodged in my pelvis, to the poison world where it underwent anaphylactic shock and died, resulting in the cancellation of my health insurance. The notice came to me in the mail, minus the refund I was due, and along with a dead baby. I lifted the baby out and held it in my arms, more tenderly than I had ever held anything.

Birgit the energy healer healed out of her home. On the phone she'd said—in a thick accent—she could see me on Saturday, she didn't have anything else going on this weekend. The sky was gray and white flecks of toxic ice clumps were descending from it. I checked the weather on my phone before leaving for Birgit's, I'd planned to walk the thirty-five blocks or so, a meditative walk, preparing for the healing and then on the way home, processing her insights, mulling over my life, releasing regrets and forgiving old hurts in case something happened on the table on Tuesday. The Minute-Cast weather app predicted with irritating arrogance that at 1:41 p.m. .025 percent precipitation would descend upon my neighborhood, extending just to the edge of Birgit's where only .010 would be falling. While at 1:42, it would taper off to .015, and by 1:45, to .000, in other words, the snow would not last long. I left my heavy hooded coat and umbrella behind, trusting in technology. At 2:09, the mid-November snow was assaulting me in thick, determined flakes, and I still had several blocks to go.

Birgit was a typically built German woman, or how I thought of one, tall and large-boned, blond with a broad reddish face and bright blue eyes, a warm smile. She was sixty or perhaps seventy but looked very healthy, probably she was a yoga or qi gong instructor, probably she was a vegetarian and juiced her breakfast every morning, probably she had avoided BPA for decades. Though she was, no doubt about it, plump. Her mid-section had a few rolls under that filmy purple tunic. She wore a hunk of amethyst on a silver chain, a jagged crystal that looked part weapon, part talisman. She greeted me enthusiastically and gave me a towel and I went into the bathroom to dry my wet hair, where seashells and geodes abounded.

The energy healer had, herself, a strong energy, which I took as a good sign. She radiated a sort of vitality that was obvious, and unusual, in a woman her age, as in, her voice was strong and clear and her posture not stooped at all and she moved with certainty through the elegant, well-ordered apartment with indigenous pottery placed carefully on glass tables, throw pillows in rust and gold silk arranged neatly on a red leather couch and not a speck of dust or pet hair to be seen, not like my place, where cats were in charge. I felt damp and surly, my jeans still wet. 'Fucking Minute-Cast,' I was thinking, in no mood to be healed, staring at her large shoulder blades as she led me through a maze of hallways to the healing room—the apartment was huge, and strangely complex among twenty-first century condominiums which are as a rule boxy and uninteresting. I felt as if she were leading me into the underground although our steps weren't descending. I worried vaguely that I would never find my way out, that she was going to do something irreversible to me, whether literally or metaphorically. 'Then again,' I thought, 'that's just what's needed.'

The healing room was painted a burnt orange and was warm and calming. In the background soft flute music trilled along with the artificial trickle of water either on a cd or from one of those fountains you plug in and which my mother, when she was alive, loved, I couldn't tell which. Birgit patted the massage table and I climbed onto it. She faced me and said, "You're under some pressure. You have an important choice to make, yes?"

Wow! How did she know? I stared at the dark ceiling and decided to be honest with myself. "I've already made it, but I'm not sure I made the right one."

I told her about the surgeon I'd never cared for, who had the bedside manner of an ox, and that he wanted me—no, was *pressuring* me because that was the truth—to have a hysterectomy, that there was a chance of the cysts having turned cancerous, they could do so at any moment, I'd been warned all along of this possibility and, according to the surgeon, I'd pushed my luck long enough. I paused. Also, I wanted children and I was unhappy in my relationship.

She crossed her arms and said, "I can't tell you what to do, but I can tell you I don't feel any cancer."

I felt a rush of fear leave my body.

"There. Did you feel that?"

"But you haven't even started. How can you tell? Are you sure?"

She drew a light blanket over my body. "I'm pretty sure. I feel your energy in my body. Every lightworker works differently, but that's what I do. Ever since your phone call, I've been feeling you, and I don't feel the energy of cancer. Cancer has a very fast energy, very urgent. It is blind, greedy."

In fact, I thought, it was a good description of what cancer must be. "What if you tell someone this and you're wrong and it puts their life in danger?"

She took a breath, thought. "Is there any way to tell once they get in there?"

"Possibly, and I've told them they can do it if I'm full of cancer and I'm obviously going to die if they don't give me a hysterectomy but probably they won't be able to tell until the lab does the biopsy days later. It would mean opening me back up and I'd rather avoid that."

She pressed my arm in a maternal way. "Of course. I'm not telling you what to do. You have to make your own decision. But you've come to me for my opinion, yes? I trust what I'm receiving. Now, let's see about your relationship."

"I'd rather not."

She laughed a hearty German laugh. "You don't have to do anything. I'll just take a look."

She went to the head of the table and put her hands on my head, cradling it. There was something in her fingers, a charge, like magnets, I thought, though it was probably my imagination. I closed my eyes, the trickling and fluting overtaking me. She made some sweeping movements in the air over me for a while—she was cleaning my energy body, she explained, and it needed it indeed, my chakras were clogged with fear, rage, and sadness but mostly fear, a giant globule of which was stuck on the underside of my heart and which, honestly, didn't want to go. She asked me a few questions about Jason and how I felt about him and then about being a mother and how I felt about being a mother, she asked some things I'd rather not share, let's just say they were pertinent, startlingly so, she seemed to know things I couldn't imagine how she did. She ended with a few recommendations on how I could release my fears and connect to my soul with love, one being by paying more attention to synchronicities, which Birgit wanted to know if I believed in. I said I thought so. She suggested I keep my eyes open for them, because synchronicities were guideposts from the soul.

I cried on the table for a while after she left, curled up like an infant. I felt immensely, incredibly, fundamentally better.

When I came out there were the branching hallways, leading to closed doors or open ones with empty bedrooms and offices, a laundry room, a solarium. I guess it was because I had just had my energy field hoovered, but I felt a little woozy, light in the head, and also a magnanimous warmth, an effusive gratitude, toward Birgit. I wanted to hug her, and I will, I thought, and kiss her on each cheek as the Europeans do on my way out. The walls were lined with old photographs, black and white mostly, and when I finally found the living room, there were more. Birgit was there with a large glass of water. I drank it, staring at one of the photographs on an end table: a very tall man in military uniform standing before a monument.

"My father," she said.

I picked up the silver frame—simply out of politeness, you know how you do. Then I saw it. The swastika armband.

I stared at her, waiting for a qualifier, an explanation, an apology, a defense. It came: "He was only following orders."

I nearly gasped. A synchronicity. A guidepost from my soul. But what did it mean? The water glass was empty. Birgit held her hand out for it, I wasn't thinking, she had to reach in and take it. She said, "It's three hundred."

Now I did gasp, maybe audibly. We'd never discussed the price on the phone, foolish of me. I fumblingly wrote out a check. She took it and held out her hand. "Best of luck on Tuesday. I'll be praying for you."

I took her hand, though her touch felt different to me now, repulsive, even. I murmured a thank you and hurried out.

Moments before I was to be wheeled in and put under, the surgeon appeared bedside. Looking glamorous in a *Grey's Anatomy* way in his blue latex gloves and matching cotton scrubs, he gave me one last chance to submit to a hysterectomy, which he promised would guarantee we'd never have to do this again, as if cutting me open every eleven months and making tens of thousands of dollars for it was getting to be a real nuisance for him (even though the robot, it seemed to me, would be doing most of the work). After the synchronicity with the energy healer, which I interpreted to mean she should not be trusted, and the weekend spent haunted by the Grim Reaper, who floated through all my dreams, I was pretty sure I had cancer. I told him I wished to keep my organs but if he deemed it absolutely necessary to take one or more of them out once he got in there, he had my permission to do so. I signed the paper saying this and he grunted, pleased or not, I couldn't tell, and walked out.

The surgery went without a hitch. Dr. Chan, appearing over me as I drowsily woke from the anesthesia, pain surging beneath the surface, said my body responded "marvelously," referring to my excellent hemostasis and the integrity of my uterine wall as he sliced cysts free from it. He gave me a several pages long surgical report, which against my better judgment and with a perverse cringing curiosity, I read that night under the starched and bleached covers. I had been draped in a dorsal lithotomy position with my legs in Allen stirrups, a Foley placed in my bladder and a RUMI uterine manipulator in my uterus that was then attached to the uterine positioning system in the robot, which was docked and put to work dispatching its various tools—Veress needles, trocars, monopolar scissors, PK forceps, and a single lonely tenaculum—to squeeze my organs and veins aside so the robot could hoover up a massive unwieldy glob of mesotheliomal cystic matter. A piece of Interceed was pasted on my uterus and left behind—I wondered what Interceed was made of, probably BPA—and the robot undocked, my abdomen desufflated, my uterus set free.

Of course, Dr. Chan explained while I was still barely awake and feeling like a train had run over my abdomen, the cysts would grow back and we'd have to do this again next year, but there was no cancer, not yet—Birgit had been right, though it could have been a lucky guess. "All benign," he said happily, the two words that have become the heartsong of millions of Americans, the anthem, the mantra, the plea recited in how many millions of prayers across the country.

"We did have to take the left ovary," he added almost enthusiastically, blinking behind his spectacles. Was he lying? Did they *have* to, or did they—he—choose to?

He went back to staring at his laptop on the rolling table, befuddled over something the computer was doing, the screen he wanted wasn't popping up or something.

I swallowed hard. "Will it affect my fertility?"

"Oh, no. The other ovary kicks in and takes over. There have been studies. It's called an oophorectomy. Google it."

At home in organic cotton pajamas (pesticide-free), I did google it, heart pounding with hope and dread of what I was about to find out. *Oophorectomy: Surgical removal of the ovaries.* I read some terrifying statistics about oophorectomy and its effects on long-term health such as outrageous increases in the risks of heart disease, cancer, osteoporosis, Parkinson's and so on, as well as a 170% increased early mortality rate before I realized these didn't follow, at least not entirely, for *uni-lateral* oophorectomy; i.e., the removal of only one ovary. A distinction the doctor hadn't bothered to make. I skimmed down Wikipedia, cursing myself for not doing this before the surgery, probably I hadn't wanted to know. My eye scanned the blue-highlighted sections, wherein I learned that when only one ovary is removed, the other amps up hormonal production so that hormone levels remain the same and fertility and long-term health are uncompromised. I sighed and took a sip of hot chocolate, chased by a Percocet, so relieved I wanted to cry.

Then scrolled down to see the caveat *in most cases*. I took another Percocet. Against my better judgment, I went on, pressing into the dense forests of the web. Whereupon I shortly came across a site that claimed that this other-ovary-amping-up-thing was a lie. According to the site hosted by a feminist organization, perhaps a radical one, the evil medical establishment routinely excises ovaries when there is no need to—sixty-three percent of oophorectomies are done with no identified medical problem—and, in fact, no studies have been done that show the remaining ovary always "kicks in and takes over"—in fact, it often doesn't. (Here I clicked back to the Wikipedia page but, lo and behold, it did not cite any studies to support its claims that the opposite was true. My heart beat faster.) This information was accompanied by story after story of women, young and old, written in first person and bolstered by pictures of their faces (smiling, strangely), whose other ovary did *not* rise to the occasion, take up the reins, show up at the job site, fill the bigger shoes, disgruntled and introverted ovaries who never showed their faces again, launching young women into surgical menopause which is far more intense than natural menopause and sterilizing them for life—the site used the word "castrating." All of which was conveniently increasing the rates of donor egg IVF treatments, which was a great financial boon for reproductive doctors, who no doubt were in cahoots with gynecological surgeons and Big Pharma. The organization invited women who had been victims of ignorant, butchering doctors to file a lawsuit with their team of lawyers or just sign up for a free consultation. I filled out half the form and logged off, shaking with fear and anger. I called Noel.

"They've castrated me! I'm in menopause at thirty-four!" I cried, not realizing I'd gotten her voicemail.

It would be months before I would know whether the surgery had sterilized me or not. The doctor had said it could take that long for my remaining ovary to get the memo and start working double-time. I would know when I got my first period—if I got it. The suspense was killing me.

The weekend after the surgery, I hobbled out for a walk. The Minute-Cast said it was sixty degrees out at nightfall, skyrocketed up from twenty-two the day before in the seesaw dance of climate change. I passed a bar I'd been to once or twice and, on a whim, went inside to the warm dark where red lanterns were lit, velvet drapes drawn, 80s music playing loud and glasses clinking. I'd taken my last painkiller that morning. I ordered a glass of red wine and sat down at the bar.

At the bottom of this glass, I decided to get drunk. I was in a self-destructive mood, I guess. I leaned to order another but the man next to me said he'd get it if I'd let him.

I let him—that way I wouldn't have to wait, men get served before women at a bar, that's just the way it is—the way it *still* is—and the bar was getting crowded. He was in his forties, probably, and unfit in that way most American men of his age are, potbelly camouflaged beneath a plaid shirt and sort of cool black leather biker jacket, bad skin, bags beneath his eyes and a diamond stud in his brown earlobe though beneath all this or perhaps beneath the swim of wine and opiate in my brain, he was not bad-looking. Dark hair that was thick enough, kind eyes, a crooked smile. Hispanic, which made him cuter. Women of my generation want nothing more than to be equitable in our desires when it comes to race.

He wanted to know what I was doing out alone on a Saturday night.

I lifted my wine. I felt like putty, my muscles soft and viscous under my skin. When I spoke my tongue didn't want to follow orders. I said something that didn't come out right.

An excuse to lean in—he did, cologne on leather collar. "What?"

I tried again. "I'm getting drunk."

This made him grin and he ordered another glass for me right away, men are so predictable. By the time it came I was regretting it—the walk, the wine, the fact he had started talking about his passion for hair bands (Poison was on repeat in the bar), the fact I wasn't home in my pajamas, swabbing shea butter on my incisions and searching Netflix. I asked him for a cigarette but he shook his head, that was for the best. I left him asking—practically begging—for my number.

In the Uber home I stared at the lights blurring by, the advertisements flashing, the relentless assault of manufactured desire and the frenzied people scurrying by, smiles fueled by drink or drugs or anti-depressants or denial or all of the above, and felt as desperate and ruined and done, just *done*, as I had ever felt in my life. I put my hand over my uterus, which was still there, at least according to the paperwork it was, and with it an organic system of tubes and ducts and cavities and veins, a system gone awry like a tangle of freeways snarled by a traffic accident. It was malfunctioning yet, no doubt, the cells ballooning into cysts between my hips, thriving in the newly scraped-out space, encouraged by pesticides and BPA, GMOs, EMFs, PFOAs, pollution, vaccines, negative emotions and stress. 'Maybe it's the BPA,' I thought, 'if I just get rid of the BPA . . one more liver cleanse. I could try a 40-day fast . . .' But it wasn't just the BPA, I knew. It was everything. How do we live in a world where everything is dying? I wrapped my arms around my belly and held on to what was left.

All the Lonely People

I A Forgotten Face

" . . . 'How can he not know her face,' I thought, watching the two of them contort beneath the strobe lights, 'I can't believe how incredibly arrogant and self-absorbed he is not to know his old college girlfriend. He must have known that face well enough back when he saw it every day, and up-close, too, with his lips glued to its and his eyes to its eyes—then again, who knows if they even made eye contact when he groped her in the damp sheets of his fraternity bunk bed, who knows how closely he looked at it then, knowing him hers was just another female face passing through his field of influence. And now it is no more memorable to him than the faces of the thousands of strangers we rush past every day on the streets on our way to work, their shoulders slumped and overcoats flapping, collars turned up and eyes averted. What we don't want to know or don't want to admit is to those strangers we're strangers, too—we're no more to them than they are to us: a smudge of movement barely registered, a figment, an hallucination at the edge of the eye . . . yes, to you I'm just a phantom rushing past in the rain as if I had somewhere to go, as if my beloved were awaiting me on the next corner, her umbrella open and the shadow of her hat covering her face, saving it for my eyes only . . .

'Then again, why should I be surprised he doesn't know her, it's in perfect keeping with his character,' I thought. 'Banyan has never paid any attention to anyone but himself and it's something I've known about him all along. While I on the other hand recognized her right away and *I* never professed to love her, I never even made a move on her, not even before she was his girl, though I thought about it plenty of times and I had plenty of chances to.'

I lowered myself back down into the squat chair at the too-short table where we'd been having a few drinks before Banyan got the bright idea to ask her to dance and I had to half-stand in the chair in order to see them. I couldn't do so without drawing attention to myself and openly appearing as if I were spying on someone out on the dance floor like a jealous lover or neglected sidekick, the latter of which, I suppose, I was, but everyone in the club didn't need to know it. Banyan is his surname, not his first name, I don't know the origins of that name nor do I know what the tree that shares it looks like, I haven't been near a tree in ages but as far as I know he doesn't have anything in common with it, unless that species of tree has a pathologically inflated ego. Banyan has been my best friend since college, we met freshman year. But we've never called each other by our first names, that habit from our fraternity days has stuck, anyway most men don't call any of their (men) friends by their first names. Most men are so homophobic (Banyan and I included) they're afraid if they do people will think they're lovers. Banyan has always been self-absorbed, or maybe he developed it in college and before college he was a perfectly nice, humble kid, but as long as I've known him he's had that irritating and yet somehow admirable, somehow enviable full-blown narcissism. Enviable, I suppose, because it allows him to have no conscience whatsoever, he doesn't know the meaning of the word guilt and he truly believes he has no obligation to anyone but himself, even if people—most often, myself and his wife—are constantly telling him he does have, should have, must have. Nor does he make any effort to conceal his narcissism as most of us do. Most of us are well aware how offensive it is to flaunt our vanities and so we keep them to ourselves, we stroke our egos in the dark and murmur into our mirrors before hitting the clubs, 'how good I look tonight, who could resist this face, these eyes, and I'll look even better in the darkness of the smoky club.'

But Banyan really has been blessed with good looks and he's well aware of it. He stands six-four and is as built and broad-chested as he was in college (but not obnoxiously so like a meathead bouncer). He has thick wavy black hair he wears close-cropped except for a long bang over one eye and his face is conventionally handsome, striking and strong-featured, almost Italian—though Banyan is not an Italian name, he comes straight out of the Midwest—with its full lips and straight nose, even at thirty-five his big face radiates a childlike (or childish) enthusiasm for life or perhaps those glistening, lit eyes are the effect of the scotch he drinks constantly. In college girls went crazy for Banyan, he was the star of the rugby team and could outdrink anybody in the fraternity. He was famous for setting the record of drinking for three days straight without passing out, although that was on the cheap beer or Jack and Coke we drank then and not the high-dollar scotch and water he drinks now, and no matter what he says, I know he can't hold his liquor as well now. He was never president of our fraternity nor did he date the hottest girls in the best sororities or anything, Banyan wasn't popular like that, if he had been he wouldn't have picked me as his best friend. He was more the black sheep life-of-the-party or beloved rebel, and he shunned the sorority Barbie dolls to date wild girls who smoked pot and lived off campus in dingy, black-light-lit apartments with the poster of that painting *The Kiss* (I've had so many discussions with girls about that painting it's nauseating) or Pink Floyd's *The Wall* on their walls.

Partying was Banyan's chief priority then and it still is now that we're in our thirties and have already made it in the world. Banyan and I have done well for ourselves, we've become who we said we would—'corporate dicks' (as an artsy girlfriend of mine once called us), white collar MBAs with plenty of money to throw around. We even work for the same company and have for years, we've both moved steadily up the corporate ladder and steadily up to the upper floors of the four floors our company occupies in the fifty-four story building downtown. If Banyan's always one rung ahead of me, I don't mind. I've never been as ambitious as he is and as long as I've got plenty of money to throw around and plenty of women to impress with it, I'm not that interested in scaling that slippery ladder. Banyan was the one who put it in my head to be a corporate dick in the first place. Back in college when I had no clue what I wanted to do with my life Banyan used to talk about the sports cars he'd drive and the suits that would hang in his closet once he got his business degree, black silk designer suits with mother-of-pearl buttons and chambray pinstripes, this was back when we still dressed in tee-shirts and jeans and he made it sound so glamorous to be a corporate dick. Now we wear those suits every day and it's just like wearing anything else, of course, nothing is ever as glamorous as we think it will be, nothing lives up to the longed-for and dreamed-of and I get sick of having to dry-clean those suits. In fact the one I was wearing last night is in need of it now, the designer suit is still crumpled on the floor where I left it when I crawled into bed this morning as dawn was breaking, our co-ed reunion lasted longer than expected, it was a really depressing night too and it's driven me to drinking again tonight . . .

Banyan and I have gotten everything we said we would and done every-thing we intended to with our lives, while Anna—that's what I'll call her, I've always liked that classic name, it sounds exotic, like a Russian queen, I don't want to use her real name, I can't take the chance you'd know her and I don't want to do anything to mar her reputation any more than she's already marred it herself—whereas I don't mind using Banyan's real name, his reputation can stand some marring, and besides, he deserves it—Anna had obviously gotten nothing and done nothing with hers. Who knows what she'd wanted to do with her life—I think she was a philosophy major and what did you do with that, sit around thinking?—but it couldn't have been this, what she was doing now before my very eyes, and I couldn't believe this was what she *had* done with it. I couldn't believe it. Perhaps in college my boyish or admiring eyes had missed some quality that portend-ed her trashy destiny, but I remembered Anna as a sweet (but not naïve) country girl. She was from a small town in the rural wastelands of the southern part of the state. She was pretty, smart, sporty, even half-hearted-ly Christian though that was something she'd grown out of by mid-term. I met her on her first day at college, she was just moving in to the dorm and I was dejectedly embarking on my sophomore year in that same dorm a few floors up, I'd pledged the fraternity already but couldn't afford to move in to the house—unlike Banyan, whose parents were loaded and who had been comfortably snoozing till noon in its cool dark bunks since mid-July, having somehow gotten permission to move in early. He got things like that, things no one else could.

I got to know Anna through casual exchanges in the hallway, the elevator, the cafeteria, she was one of those girls who unluckily befriends you before anything happens and so you can't get away with making a move on her ever after. Anna had her shit together, she didn't have time for jokers like me (or that's what I told myself). She was on the cross-country team and an A student, she even got an A for me, I paid her to write my Intro to Philosophy—a bastard of a course thanks to its bastard of a prof—mid-term paper, something about Socrates or Sophocles. Yet she could put the beer down with the best of them, she had a fierce wild streak and one time she came back from a weekend at home with paper bags full of ditch weed from her father's land, she passed it out covertly in the dorms (that's when I knew she was over her Christian thing). Anna wasn't a sorority girl and she wasn't a slut (not that the two were mutually exclusive by any means), nor had she ever struck me as particularly neurotic or emotionally unstable—we all had a wild streak at that age, it was *college*. Not until, that is, the night she fake tried to kill herself over my best friend. After that she dropped off my radar, and I no longer saw her in the dorms or on my way to class, she was either skipping or avoiding me or both. At some point she just disappeared. The rumors were she never came back after Thanksgiving break, didn't even finish out the semester. And I hadn't seen her since, not until last night, that is. Even so, of course I recognized her right away. Who forgets a face once gazed into, laughed with, cared for?

'But perhaps Banyan doesn't recognize her,' I thought as I watched them writhe and twist and flirt like two strangers—which is what they were in his mind—out on the packed dance floor, 'not because of some failure of his memory or eclipse of his blimpish ego, but because he doesn't want to: "this is just one more in a long parade of female faces that bat their eyes and pucker their lips at me and there's nothing special about this one, this face has meant nothing to me until it caught my eye in this moment and it need mean nothing beyond it, not unless I want it to, and that's up to me, not her."' We're always trying to hide the truth from everyone else but we're most interested in hiding it from ourselves, it's our own eyes we most avoid looking into and our own opinion we most fear. Perhaps Banyan didn't recognize Anna (or pretended not to) because he didn't want to think what he'd done to her all those years ago or that because of him she'd dropped out of school and ended up singing old-timey war tunes in lingerie before a roomful of panting strangers. 'Not that it's really his fault,' I thought, 'she's made her own choices, but *still*.' Banyan had dicked around so many women I suppose I thought at least one of them should get her payback, this one woman standing up and standing in for all the rest and demanding some slight justice, some retribution not just for the jilted women but also for those of us who did treat women well—at least, back then I did, I was never anything but a gentleman when it came to the girls I dated in college although according to Banyan it had nothing to do with my honorable character, I just didn't have the self-confidence to be a dick, and maybe he had a point.

He didn't know her but she knew him, then again she'd been expecting him—Anna and I set it up the night before last when I ran across her in the hole-in-the-wall strip joint/dance club (the place did double duty, and thus drew a really weird mix of clientele) on the waterside whose only redeeming feature was the wall of paned windows behind the stage where you could watch the blackish water in the canal lap at the glass in sync with the women writhing around on stage or with your own distorted dance movements. It was late, past midnight. I'd never been to that bar before, amazingly, I don't know how I missed it as much as I go out. I don't have a wife (and never have) and so I lead the single life of a corporate dick, going out three or four nights a week and staying up late, having coffee in the middle of the night or watching old black-and-white movies all night long if I feel like it and dating lots of women. It sounds glamorous but it gets old. The first ten years it was fun rolling over to feel the shape of a stranger's body under my hands and see a stranger's face in the dawn light but lately my footloose and fancy free lifestyle is getting more and more boring. I still date lots of women, I have plenty of money to take them out to nice restaurants and a pricey sportscar to impress them with and I'm not bad-looking if I don't have the dashing good looks Banyan does, the problem is they're all starting to look alike, those bodies and faces are all beginning to blur together. Not to mention the girls I bring home are getting younger and younger, or rather, they're staying the same age while I'm getting older. I'm getting sick of sleeping around, it's too depressing to have to tiptoe around a stranger's gaze in the knife blade morning light, nor can I bring myself to ask them to get dressed and leave right after we're done—of course, some girls leave on their own but you can never tell which ones will and which will stay for coffee nor how they'll look to you sitting at your kitchen table picking at the fresh baguette that you and your hangover have gone out and gotten for them *just because they asked you to,* their bony legs pulled up inside one of your old State U tee-shirts, what the knife blade morning light will do to girls who were beautiful the night before. Or if there will ever be one, that one who looks *good* sitting at your kitchen table in the morning, who looks right, who looks like she was made to be yours."

"It was well past midnight, a drizzly Thursday night in November when I ran into Anna again. It was only a few days after Halloween and they still hadn't cleaned up the smashed pumpkins in the streets, the streets stank even worse than usual, it was disgusting and I was in a terrible mood. I'd been out with the most obnoxious guys from the office, a mix of the young guys straight out of college and the horny middle-aged divorcées. I'd finally ditched that crowd and was stumbling home, on an impulse I decided to have one more drink before going home to my dark apartment, I didn't want to see those dark windows as I approached from the street but I didn't feel like picking up a girl either, I was in a really foul mood and so when I stepped in the club I didn't pay any attention to the long-legged, athletic-looking woman swaying on stage, a stripper in the guise of a night-club singer, in a tight black satin dress with a slit up the side almost to the hip (these details my masculine eye did catch) and a red belt type thing at the waist she toyed with, snapping and unsnapping it as she mouthed old-fashioned songs into the microphone over recorded music. It wasn't until I sat down and had my drink in front of me that I turned my eyes on her. I didn't recognize her body but I knew her face immediately, even though she had a lot of makeup on—heavy eyeshadow and mascara, rouged cheeks and bright lipstick, she was going for that forties movie star look—and looked nothing like she had in college, in college she wore her chestnut brown hair long and straight, this woman's hair was red (obviously dyed but not too tacky) and hot-rolled into a style like Barbara Stanwyck or Marlene Dietrich in one of those old World War II movies, a style such as my mother achieved on those bristly nylon curlers she used to walk around in in her bathrobe though I didn't know if Anna used the same tools, probably not, you probably couldn't even buy those old curlers any more.

'Too bad, now I can't enjoy the stripper's act,' I thought, not that I enjoy strippers that much, I can't get past the fact they're just pretending to be turned on when really they're working and most likely bored and tired, what gets me excited is when a woman is turned on and lets me know it, when she makes me feel like she wants me—that's delicate information and I'd appreciate you not sharing it with anybody and everybody . . . Anyway it turned out she didn't take much off, just a few odds and ends like the red belt and the corny feather boa, both of which she flung onto the empty chairs below the stage. When her act was over she stepped down and stooped to pick up the belt (but not the boa) and re-fastened it around her waist, it didn't seem to serve any purpose other than to be something to take off, it didn't conceal any bare skin or interesting parts. She walked past my table and I grabbed her wrist. She knew me right away, she seemed happy to see me. I stood and she kissed me on both cheeks, French style, I wondered where she picked that up, not likely on the farm or in the strip joint.

'The money isn't that great,' she said, shrugging, once she'd sat down and the bartender had brought a glass of whiskey (it appeared out of nowhere, such is the meager measure of a stripper's influence). As if I thought it was. 'It's not that glamorous either,' she continued. 'Most people think night club singers'—'so that's what she calls herself,' I thought, 'well, if it makes her feel better'—'lead this wild and crazy life, but it's not all it's cracked up to be, I gotta tell you. Late nights, a weird schedule, it can be exhausting. I'm only doing it to get my foot in the door, I mean, the music business is so competitive these days, with the internet it's actually worse, now everybody thinks they can sing even if they have no talent at all.' 'Like strippers,' the thought flashed, 'strippers who call themselves singers.' 'But Scottie's going to put me in the studio next spring—he's paying for everything, he actually thinks I've got something—and we're going to cut an album, I can't believe it.'

She didn't bother explaining who Scottie was, his reputation must have preceded him but she'd forgotten I didn't run in her circles. 'I don't remember you singing in college.' She twirled a curl around her finger, the long painted nail matched the red of that weird belt. 'Oh, I didn't. It's something I've gotten into in the last few years, I didn't know I could but it turns out I can.' When I looked at her blankly, she added, 'Sing. I'm good at it.' 'Yeah, it sounded good—what I heard of it, I came in at the very end.' I didn't remember Anna having a musical bone in her body in college and frankly she didn't seem the type. She was on the cross-country team and I think she was majoring in philosophy, or perhaps it was psychology, something brainy like that. I offered a few details about my own life, the last fifteen years in a nutshell and when I hit a pause, she brought him up: 'And how did Banyan turn out?' I couldn't believe she'd waited this long. 'Oh, well, he makes a lot of money. And he has a five-year-old kid, I never thought I'd see the day.' Her pencil-darkened eyebrows arched. 'He's married?' 'I wouldn't really call it a marriage. They've been together for years. They had a ceremony about a year ago, she was putting the pressure on but I think he did it just for the party.' A little chip of white tooth emerged on her lower lip. She made an mmmm sound, I hoped that hadn't hit too close to home.

'Bring him by sometime. I'd like to see him.' I considered this. It could be interesting. 'We always go out on Friday nights . . . Maybe we'll stop by tomorrow night.' Tiny lines around her eyes tensed. 'Wow, that would be a trip. To see him again.' Our eyes locked. She was holding so still she seemed to have stopping breathing. An understanding passed between us, though I wasn't sure what it was. 'I'll make sure it happens,' I said. She put her drink down carefully, precisely over the wet ring it had left on the table. 'Okay. But don't tell him it's me. I want to surprise him.'

I always liked Anna. We were friends before she and Banyan were a thing, in fact I could be said to be responsible for them getting together. They met when I took Anna as my date (just friends, she laid it out that way and I agreed) to the fall pledge party but I had nothing to do with it, I never introduced them and never would have introduced them. Maybe I intended to make my move on Anna that night, I don't remember but knowing myself at that age I wasn't likely to take any girl to a fraternity party who I *didn't* intend to make a move on (despite our agreement, which liquor would have washed away). But Anna never made it home with me that night so I could make one, she disappeared before midnight and after several shots of raspberry Everclear punch (house-made: Everclear and red food coloring) and I didn't see her again until the next night, when I went over for Sunday night study hours and found her sprawled in Banyan's top bunk writing his Comp paper for him, her bra swinging from the door knob. And I knew it was hers because she giggled and asked me to toss it to her as I closed the door, I remember how embarassed I was. Banyan wasn't even there, he'd left shortly after noon to play frisbee golf. Given this auspicious beginning, she shouldn't have been so shocked when he dumped her only a few months later and a few days after saying the magic words—according to Anna he had said them, Banyan didn't remember it—those words that hold so much weight for young lovers, that are the Holy Grail of youthful romance but mean virtually nothing once we become adults, we fling them around like holey underwear once we have a few broken hearts or broken marriages under our belts—that is, the words, 'I love you.'

I don't know if it was out of loyalty to Banyan or my own insecurity that I never made a move on Anna on those nights we'd sit up talking about him, sitting close together on the twin mattress of my bed, our elbows touching accidentally from time to time. We became a lot closer after they started going out, I spent more time with her than he did. Now and then she'd get off the subject of my best friend and we'd play video games or watch old *Star Trek* re-runs and drink cheap beer in cans.

That semester I still lived in the dorms while Banyan had already moved into the fraternity house and I always thought Anna should have fallen for me instead of him. Not that I sank into despair over it, it really didn't bother me that much, it was just an observation of the obvious—obviously I would have made a better boyfriend than Banyan but it wasn't like I was smitten with her or thought she was the only girl in the world. I dated plenty of girls in college, pretty girls but there was always something about Anna I liked, her narrow gray eyes and her sarcastic wit. She stood out from the other girls, too, she came from a different world and I liked to hear about her fruit farmer father and his Civil War gun collection or her Confederate flag-waving brothers (one even had a lazy eye, I met him on Parents' Weekend, when the whole family showed up in a long silver Cadillac). Anna was from the rural southern part of the state, which was mountainous and hillybilly, while Banyan and I grew up in the urban north. We met at the state university in between, to Banyan and I it was the middle of nowhere, to Anna, the bright lights, big city. Now we've all ended up where most of the graduating population of that college ends up, back in the city in the north, that's where the work is, our kind and Anna's kind, which doesn't require a degree.

As far as what kind of relationship they had—for him, it must have been the usual short-term fuck, for her, it was true love. Like every girl he dated, she was obsessed with him, she pined for him lying across my bed in her cross-country shorts, I remember those strong tanned legs like it was yesterday, they're the same legs she showed off last night, only those were paler. Twirling her hair and dreaming about their wedding in one sentence and grilling me on his previous girlfriends or his whereabouts the night before in the next, she analyzed every detail of their relationship, she ran it all through me as if through a Scantron machine. Not that she was interested in hearing what I had to say. I tried to caution her, I did. I tried to warn her of the train wreck she was heading for. Of course, it did no good—the heart, as they say, is deaf and blind. Don't they say that, hasn't someone?"

"'I want to surprise him,' she'd said the night before. Banyan didn't look too surprised out on the dance floor, writhing and twisting his huge torso and swiveling his square hips in his office slacks.

She must have expected him to know her at first glance and I didn't blame her—who forgets a face? a face once kissed if not cared for? I'd felt a twinge of impending doom when Banyan elbowed me as we hung our overcoats over the backs of our chairs and sat down at the squatty plastic table barely big enough to hold an overflowing ashtray and our two glasses of mediocre scotch (the place didn't serve our high-dollar brand) and said, 'That stripper wants me, man, she's been eyeing me ever since we set foot in here.' I didn't know if that was true, Banyan had slipped into the club without me because the meathead bouncer at the door was bullying me. He grabbed my sleeve and grumbled something about my type—'we don't like long overcoats in here,' something like that, the music was so loud I could barely hear him, at that point Anna was between sets and the speakers were pumping out techno. He had bugged-out black eyes and a shaved head, tattoos wrapping his bull neck. I couldn't believe the place would hire such a cliché, then again that place wasn't too concerned with appearances, its only charm was the window-paned wall that backed the stage where you could see the black water tirelessly lapping at the fogged-up glass, its sharp shiny crests reminded me of crumpled trash bags, I'd found it strangely calming to zone out on the night before. Otherwise the place was a dive, Banyan and I frequented places with more class when we went out and I'd had to twist his arm to get him here, now the bouncer didn't want to let me in. Apparently he thought I might be concealing a weapon in the folds of my incredibly typical corporate overcoat, you see thousands of them on the streets every day as their hunched-over occupants rush by, eyes on the pavement and ears stuck to their cell phones, in fact there were several other men in the club sitting at their tables or on barstools wearing overcoats exactly like mine and some had draped them over the backs of their chairs (carelessly, the chairs were so short the coats were getting trampled underfoot). I opened my coatflaps and showed him I was harboring neither a gun nor switchblade, not even a personal flask, I even turned the inside pockets out to show I wasn't sheltering a baggie of cocaine as, no doubt, most of the other patrons were. Finally the bouncer nodded, we'd reached some understanding. I leaned up and shouted in his ear, 'What about that guy?' I pointed at Banyan, who had walked right by him in his identical overcoat, except in black—I always wore khaki and he always wore black—and was making his way to the bar. The goon shrugged. That's how Banyan is, he gets away with shit.

So I missed the moment Anna first or, rather, once more laid eyes on the face of her long-lost love or rather, the asshole who broke her heart. Their relationship ended abruptly when Anna caught him with another girl. But my sympathies were with him, I believed him (and still do) when he told me the next day he hadn't planned on cheating on her, really he hadn't had any choice—what would I have done if a freshman with a body like that threw herself at me? I saw his point, I didn't hold it against him, back then I was wholeheartedly devoted to Banyan, I worshipped the ground he walked on. He told me the whole story the next day in the basement of the frat house while we were doing laundry and nursing our hangovers after the Halloween party the night before. How this Gamma Phi or Chi Omega or Tri Delt (we could never keep them straight, or didn't bother to) pledge, one of those California brand Barbie dolls with long blond hair and a coffee-color tanning booth tan basically *attacked* him out on the lawn where he'd been taking a piss, wrestling him to the ground in the attempt to kiss him and spilling her orange Everclear punch all over his Julius Caesar costume, a white bedsheet fashioned into a toga–see? He fished it out of his laundry basket to prove it. All while Anna in her Cleoptra costume (dates were supposed to go in paired costumes, so you knew who was with who and you didn't end up hitting on a brother's girl-friend or at least you knew which brother to avoid if you did it anyway) was inside hanging around me and my date for someone to talk to and getting drunk on orange Everclear herself so she wouldn't feel so self-con-scious, not being in a house she hardly knew anyone. Banyan was famous around campus, his giant ego combined with his natural good looks and athletic ability as well as the stupid drinking stunts he was always pulling made him famous and it wasn't hard to believe his story, it wasn't hard to believe this pledge was so overcome with lust for him she *would not let go* of his neck, her teeth sunk into it like a vampire's—see? he showed me the blueblack mark she'd left to prove it. They were rolling around on the lawn when Anna found them.

'Really? I didn't even see her there,' Banyan said when I told him my side of the story, or rather, Anna's. 'Well, she saw you.' We were lying on the big couches in the basement waiting for our laundry to dry and nursing our hangovers with cold pizza and sips of Jack Daniels. It was around mid-night when she showed up at my room, I told him, which in college wasn't that late, sometimes we didn't even hit the bars until one or two. I remem-bered the time because I was watching *Star Trek, Star Trek* ran from 11:30 to 12:30 and I'd just turned it on for a minute, I was stopping by my room to get my ID before I went back out to The Home. That's what I told Banyan, that's what I told everybody at the house when I left the party early and alone—the truth was my date had dissed me, she'd gone off to The Home with a group of girls, she hadn't even hooked up with another guy, that would have been less insulting. I blamed it on our costumes, which she'd never been in favor of, we'd gone as Captain Kirk (me) and Spock (she, she looked nothing like him, she was blond and had pudgy, rounded ears), it was a stupid idea but I was a huge *Star Trek* fan and I insisted on it. Our costumes would have been a total failure were it not for the tasers we made out of those miniature cereal boxes and which were a big hit at the party due to their ability to disintegrate the clothing off anyone just by aiming them and making a noise. The truth was I was just settling down in my boxers to watch the whole episode, this was before you could rent them on DVD and so you had to catch every one you could on TV and the truth was I was more interested in the adventures of the Enterprise in outer space than I was in going to The Home and dancing under a disco ball with a pledge who would later puke in my sheets or, worse, on me as I was struggling to put on the condom . . . Even then, it seems, I found it depressing, lonely and depressing, that party lifestyle Banyan loves and lives for and which I've continued to live right alongside him to this day.

When Anna came pounding on my door that night, I almost didn't open it. Later I wished I hadn't. It was at the height of the plot, that famous episode (but then they're all famous, I'm still a huge fan though I can't get into *The Next Generation* no matter how hard I try, anyway it's best to keep it in check, it's not something I want the guys in the company knowing, the nerdy way I spend my nights at home) where Captain Kirk and the crew are held hostage on a barren planet by a mysterious shimmering flourescent pink energy cloud which turns out to be a female energy cloud who turns out to be, rather than truly evil, simply desperate for love. Anna was my friend—not to mention my best friend's girlfriend—but I found it annoying, I told Banyan, annoying if not downright rude when she showed up at my dorm room and threatened to kill herself over him right in the middle of one of my favorite *Star Trek* episodes, she knew how much I loved that show and besides, I was getting ready to leave for The Home. Of course, the sight startled me at first, it's not every day you see a hot girl holding a gun to her head and there was something sexy about it, if you overlooked her red, puffy face and the tears mingled with mascara mingled with gold glitter (part of her Cleopatra look) running down her cheeks. Her toga (obviously one of the thin, overstarched sheets from our dorm beds) was grass-stained and torn, the gold leaves glued on as decoration were peeling off and the green plastic vines in her hair sticking out every which way and yet there was something really sexy about it all. About a pretty girl threatening to kill herself, or wielding a gun in any way, or perhaps that's just what men are trained to find sexy from TV and movies and video games and I felt vaguely ashamed for finding it so. She was sobbing, 'He told me he loved me! He told me he loved me!' She held the gun to her temple. 'I'll do it,' she threatened, 'I'll blow my brains out over that fucking asshole!'

But I wasn't that freaked out because I knew the gun was only a plastic toy. (Besides, in the dorms you got used to people threatening to kill themselves, you learned to take it with a grain of salt.) I could have pointed that out but I didn't want to humiliate her even more, I played along, doing my best to comfort her: 'Don't take it personally, that's the way he is, I did warn you.' I offered her a beer but she wouldn't take it, she called me an insensitive bastard or something like it and ran out waving the gun and snagging her toga on the doorjamb, ripping it even more, she must have had to replace that sheet, the RAs were real sticklers about stuff like that.

'She was just putting on a show,' I assured Banyan the next day, 'of course she knew I'd tell you all about it.' I told him how I figured out the gun was fake (because it looked just like a real one) by putting two-and-two together like Spock would have, or Columbo (I'm also or I used to be a big fan of that '70s detective show *Columbo*), when I saw my roommate's costume crumpled on his bed behind her. I hadn't seen O'Donnell dressed up but I knew he was going as Charles Manson, he must have come back early from his party and changed to go back out to The Home, a black turtleneck and ski mask and shaggy dark wig as well as a vintage LP of the *White* album and a battered acoustic guitar lay discarded on his bed. 'The gun must be part of O'Donnell's costume and therefore only a toy,' I reasoned. 'Anna must have picked it up when I wasn't looking and is now using it as a ploy to get my attention,' since I was obviously less interested in her nervous breakdown than in the female energy cloud who had transformed herself into that actress who played the eldest daughter in *Father Knows Best* and was still young and lovely when *Star Trek* was being made. Which is almost half a century ago now but in a sixth of a century it never occurred to me that Charlie Manson wouldn't have carried a gun. Because Manson never killed anyone, he only gave the orders and watched his devotees carry them out. And as meticulous as O'Donnell was about the details of his costume—he'd even inked a swastika tattoo between his eyes, he was determined to win the costume contest, he didn't, I remember him complaining about it, his frat had awarded the prize to a Used Condom instead—he would never have had such a historically inaccurate prop.

But in fifteen years this didn't dawn on me. 'Shit, what if she tries to kill me?' Banyan said. 'With a toy gun? I'd like to see her try.' 'I was making out with that chic *under a ladder* last night,' he said wide-eyed. 'Some idiot pledge left it there when he was painting the letters on the side of the house and we rolled under it.' He was shaken. 'You know how superstitious I am, Madsen.' It was true, I did, I may have been the only brother in the house Banyan let in on his superstitious tendencies, it wasn't very manly to be afraid of breaking mirrors and crossing black cats but Banyan was. 'Superstitious? Try paranoid. Where would she get a real gun? Besides, Anna hasn't got it in her.'

Indeed she never did a thing. She never called and pestered him for a confession or apology, not even an explanation, nor did she press to get back together, at least that much we expected and we were a little hurt she didn't even try. In fact the two of them never spoke again. Nor did I see much of her after that—she was probably too humiliated to show her face around me—and a few weeks later, Anna had dropped out of school and disappeared altogether. She never even said goodbye."

"To see her like this, so many years later, it was sad, to see her up there writhing around, she'd gone on stage shortly after we came in and was now well into her act, her red nails gripping the mic stand like claws, her skin glistening in the bluish spotlight. She seemed paler tonight, she should have put on more blush or sprayed some of that fake tan stuff on her white legs. Her eyes followed Banyan as he crossed the room to our table. Of course she'd been watching the door all night waiting for him to walk in, we never stop looking for the beloved or longed-for or obsessed-over to emerge from the mist of the long-lost past or long-awaited future or in this case the cigarette smoke and shadows. No doubt all those painful and perhaps a few tender memories were flooding back and yet her red-lipsticked lips kept opening and closing, opening, closing, her song kept flooding out while her eyes were watching Banyan struggle to fit himself into the white plastic chair that looked like it was made for a school child. She was singing a cheesy, patriotic song and sliding up and down the mic stand as if she were about to make love to it, she wrapped a thigh around it and slid it between her breasts, it was unbearable and she hadn't even taken anything off. 'Perhaps this is one of those clubs that keeps its clients coming back by teasing them,' I thought. 'Those clubs where the women tear off their skimpy lingerie the second they get on stage aren't nearly as exciting as those where they only reveal something on the rare occasion and you never know when that occasion's going to arise, it's anticipation that's the real turn-on . . . But perhaps my hopes that it won't be tonight are in vain—the way she's toying with the top of her dress—she doesn't have the red belt on tonight, perhaps it's still wrinkled from last night's performance—the way she's fiddling with that button or snap or zipper at her cleavage, it looks like she's definitely going to reveal something, that is, her breasts, any moment now, perhaps Fridays are her on-nights or, rather, off-nights, the night her boss has made clear she'd better show something or get the axe. Or perhaps she's giving a peep show for Banyan's eyes only, if so I hope she doesn't get fired for giving it away for free.' I hoped, too, she kept that zipper or snap or button fastened, I'd never seen Anna's breasts and never made a move to try to see them and I didn't want my eyes to land on them now, not at the same moment a hundred other men's eyes were landing on them.

I shut my eyes. It occurred to me she didn't have a bad voice—it was high and clear but it wasn't a "night-club singer's," it was more like Julie Andrews' voice in *The Sound of Music*, Julie Andrews or Judy Garland singing "Over the Rainbow" in *The Wizard of Oz* . . . don't ask me how I know these things, my mother loved musicals and forced me to watch them with her when I was growing up. It was the wrong fit for the sexy tunes she was singing but it fit her former self, that is, the innocent country girl I'd known and couldn't help continuing to see her as, once we get into our heads an idea about who someone is we don't want to give it up. We latch onto a face or voice or a certain expression or quirky gesture someone makes and which we consider not only charming but indispensable to their personality, that personality we think we know so well and have excavated so entirely simply by our laser insight. We think we know all its ins and outs and its darkest secrets and most cherished dreams and we can't let it go, we can't stand to see an alien expression or foreign mood on that conquered face: 'stay as you were, stay as you are in my memory and as you were in those days, how dare you dare to change.' She hit her final high notes and the music died down and came to a conclusion with a drum roll—a recorded drum roll, really Anna's act was just karaoke with skin. There were a few scattered claps and hoots. Next to me Banyan let out a wolf howl—*ow ow owww!*— to show his enthusiasm for whatever it was she must have revealed.

But I never found out what that was. When I opened my eyes she was toying with the snaps or buttons of her dress and all I could see for certain she'd lost was her long wrap-around skirt, on bottom she wore a lacy black lingerie but nothing was showing but a lot more leg and a little more cleavage. She stepped off the stage and stooped matter-of-factly to retrieve her skirt—apparently she'd flung it into the crowd but just as on the night before, no one was sitting at the front tables so it landed on the floor. The crowd wasn't any thicker tonight than last night and they weren't the typical strip club crowd that tries to get as close as possible to ogle the girls or steal a touch, they were the kind that hung back in the shadows, sipping their drinks quietly above their hard-ons. Even the customers wanted to keep up the pretense they weren't really seeing a stripper, they were appreciating a song and dance. Anna stooped over like an old woman picking her bathrobe off the bathroom floor, it was obviously a gesture her body was used to, she'd probably made it every night for months or perhaps years, I hoped she hadn't been doing it that long. The crowd's eyes didn't follow her as she made her way through them to the bar, they just looked around vaguely and some of them got up and walked out with their overcoats draped over their arms, they'd gotten what they came for.

The place was taking an unexpected turn—the black-painted wood floor of the stage being turned into a dance floor, which amounted to clearing the mic stand she'd been so affectionate with and turning on strobes and techno music at an ear-splitting volume. Anna leaned into the bar, her backless dressing showing her smooth pale skin and strong back. Anna wasn't that curvy of a woman, she was too long-legged and athletic, she had a nice body but it was no more a stripper's than her voice was a night club singer's. 'So she's going to wait him out,' I thought, 'she wants him to come to her, but I'm afraid she's playing a losing game. There's no way he's going to—.' Banyan pushed back his miniature chair and stretched his legs out. He had been watching her, I realized. 'I'm going to ask her to dance,' he said, and headed for the bar.

He came up behind her and touched her elbow. She jumped, turned. 'Now,' I thought, 'now the shit is going to hit the fan.' But the next thing they were heading to the dance floor, Banyan guiding her by a light touch on her bare back. I couldn't see their faces to read their expressions or their lips but it was clear they hadn't exchanged more than a few words, no more than a cursory introduction or invitation and certainly not the bitter or heartfelt or impassioned remembrances of old lovers.

Behind the stage through the wall of paned windows the wind was picking up. The water tossed in the canal, it appeared to be tossing in sync with the frenzied wheeling of the strobes and the spastic movements of the dancers but of course it wasn't, the water couldn't care less what rhythm the dancers moved at. A younger, rougher crowd had invaded the bar and now flooded the dance floor, the repressed white collars had put on their overcoats and left to make room for the skin-heads and punks in spikes and zippered leather, the girls with heavy black eyeshadow like hoods over their eyes and pierced faces, not the kind of girls Banyan took home, not the kind I took either. The dancers pumped their bodies to the pounding beat, their heads jerking side to side like epileptic puppets, some were better dancers than others. Banyan and Anna's moves weren't cutting it against the younger crowd, they were slightly out of sync and falling further behind as the pace of the music picked up. Banyan's moves were smoother than Anna's, hers were a little stiff, you'd think she'd be a great dancer with all the practice she got or maybe it was her precarious position on the great heights of her pencil-thin spike heels that was inhibiting her. They were further handicapped by their efforts to exchange the flirty banter of strangers out to get one another into bed or that's what it looked like as Banyan leaned over to shout in her ear, the red light on his face, she shouted back, the green strobes on hers, his brow creased, he didn't understand, he shouted back, what?, she laughed and shook her head never mind, that much was easy enough to read. No, they weren't waxing nostalgic or tying up the loose ends of their disastrous relationship—no, he still hadn't figured out who she was. Unbelievable.

Anna didn't look upset about it, her hands lingered on his lapels, while Banyan's hands had disappeared—a tall pimply kid with spiked green hair and his fat Goth girlfriend had writhed their way across my view—there was nowhere else for them to be but on her hips or even lower, toying with the idea of unwrapping that wrap-around skirt, it couldn't be that hard since she had unwrapped it herself with only one hand. I had to half-stand out of the squat chair at the tiny table barely big enough to hold our drinks in order to see them, the plastic chairs were more suitable for midgets or kindergartners than grown men and they weren't giving me much clearance nor were they too stable, my weight could fold them under anytime . . . then it occurred to me I really didn't care. Why should I care? I sat down and ordered another scotch.

Every now and then Banyan ends our Friday nights by going home with a stranger. Before he was married it wasn't that big of a deal since he and Monique had an open relationship or he claimed they had one: 'she really doesn't care if I sleep with other women, it's a French thing, to the French it's a sign of a healthy relationship if a couple sleeps around.' (Though I never heard anything about Monique having a lover, Banyan wouldn't have put up with it.) Monique is Quebeçoise, she has sleek black hair she wears cut in a very short bob and a sexy accent but what gets on my nerves is she's always bitching about America and Americans—fat slobs, capitalist pigs, crappy healthcare. And she smokes constantly, Banyan says she lights up before rolling out of bed, while he never smokes and in fact is a real snob about it (I smoke occasionally but never before rolling out of bed), it will probably be the thing that finally splits them up. I always thought it was a doomed match but last year Banyan married her and became a respectable father to the son they had five years ago. Monique has put up with a lot over the years and she's not putting up with it any more, once she got the ring on her finger she bolted down the hatches and now Banyan only gets to go out with me one night a week instead of three or four and on that night he has a two-thirty curfew, which I think is reasonable since the bars close at two but Banyan doesn't. Monique has had enough of him stumbling in at dawn smelling like other women. She's not putting up with it anymore and now every time we go out Banyan is constantly checking his cell phone to see if she's called, even though he never answers, he has Monique convinced the bars in this city are a Bermuda triangle for cell phone service. For some reason she believes him, perhaps it's a Canadian thing, perhaps the cell phone service up there isn't as good as it is in down here. Now on the nights Banyan picks up a girl he's terrified Monique is going to phone me up at home at the end of such nights since he always tells her he's staying with me when he misses his curfew and stays all night in a stranger's bed, he's sure she's going to ring me up at dawn on my landline or perhaps my cell phone since she knows very well my apartment is not in that Bermuda triangle and demand that he come to the phone. Then I'll have to impersonate him, he says, as if it's the most reasonable thing in the world. I'll have to pretend to be him and he even goes so far as to tell me some of their inside jokes, pet names, preferred sexual positions so I'll be convincing but it's the most idiotic plan I've ever heard. I always think if Monique does phone me up I'll tell her the truth, I'll say I haven't seen Banyan since he stumbled out of the bar with his arm draped over a girl I'd never seen before—a twenty-something in running shorts and a tee shirt, maybe one of those fake leather bomber jackets, that would really set Monique off, she hates the way American women dress. I've been lying for Banyan for twenty years and I'm sick of it. When such mornings dawn I lie in bed secretly hoping his wife will phone me up but who knows what I'd say if the call actually came.

After a few songs I saw Banyan heading toward our table. He leaned over and said something in my ear but I never found out what it was—the music was so loud I couldn't hear him and he was standing slightly behind me so I couldn't read his lips. It could just as well have been, 'I'm heading home' as, 'I'm leaving with her,' even though the two phrases sound nothing alike, the music was so loud I couldn't even distinguish the vowel sounds. If the latter was what he said no doubt he followed it with his conspiratorial wink, letting me know I'd better tell Monique anything but the truth if she phoned me up in the morning and that he was trusting his marriage to our friendship and he knew I wouldn't disappoint him. Or perhaps not, perhaps he never gave that loaded wink because he wasn't planning on sleeping with the woman who was still, in his mind, a sleezy stripper (he didn't want to pick up a disease, after all—the girls he usually went home with were white-collars like ourselves, young lawyers or MBA students who didn't carry diseases, not generally, though some were wilder than others or had a wild past behind them and removed their silk blouses to reveal faded tattoos or the holes of abandoned piercings). Or maybe he was planning on it being a quickie: 'A roll in the hay won't take long, I'll be back on the street in twenty minutes and home in my wife's bed before curfew, there will be no need for Madsen to lie for me tonight, good thing, I don't know how much I trust him these days anyway, he's been lying for me for years and even the most devoted get sick of covering someone else's ass after a while.' Whatever Banyan said, I never figured it out—as my ear was still puzzling over his muddled words, he was striding out the door, his overcoat slung over his shoulder. He was in a hurry and couldn't take the time to put it on.

I scanned the room for Anna, I didn't see her anywhere. Apparently she wasn't coming back to say goodnight to me or thank me for re-uniting her with her old flame, Anna hadn't met my eyes all night though she'd found them fit enough to gaze into the night before. I left a tip on the table and slung my coat over my shoulder. As I was slipping out the door, the bouncer sprang from the shadows—'Hey!' His meaty hand grasped at my private parts, I twisted to the side and his hand just grazed my hip but it was enough to make me shudder, he was probably secretly queer, macho-men like that often are.

The street was oddly deserted for outside a club on a Friday night. I didn't see Banyan, I couldn't believe he'd gotten away that fast. Black clouds were roiling overhead, a storm was coming in, the wind picking up. Suddenly Anna darted from the alley. She trotted across the bricked street, her heels clicking, taking mincy little steps so as not to slit the slit in her cheap satin dress even higher. She ran toward the streetlight, it looked like she was going to ram her head right into it, but as she approached the post moved and Banyan stepped out, he'd been standing there all the time and my eyes had missed his tall figure blended with the post.

It was a romantic scene, the two of them meeting in the gathering storm, their silhouettes lit by the circle of the streetlight. She put her arm through his and they walked off leaning into each other, like a jealous lover or hired private eye (or unwanted third wheel, which was no doubt what I was) I crept along behind them. 'Really I could care less what the two of them do,' I told myself. 'I'm only following them because there's nothing else to do but hit another bar or an all-night café or, worse, go home and slump in front of the TV and that's too depressing, only infomercials and *Planet of the Apes* will be on and I've already seen every *Planet of the Apes* ever made, I rented the box set last winter on DVD.' So I kept to the shadows alongside buildings, hopping alleyways when I came to them in case they glanced back, my overcoat was coming in handy, I pulled its thick collar up just like The Shadow or The Fugitive in those old movies that were even more popular as television series. Their steps echoed on the cobbled walkway that borders the filthy trickle of a canal that runs through this city, the city put it in in a pathetic attempt to imitate Venice or St. Petersburg but this city has nothing in common with those great ones.

Banyan thrust his hips out and clicked his heels sideways in the air, a Fred Astaire move I'd never seen him do before not that it was out of character, he's a real charmer when he's seducing a woman. Anna's laugh rang out, they were having a good time, though no doubt for different reasons. They stopped on the arched bridge and looked over the railing. They were talking softly, their voices came and went on the wind. The tails of Banyan's black overcoat flapped wildly, Banyan wore his overcoat extra-long, too long, so long it dragged the ground and made him look like a gangster and yet its hem was never ragged. I don't know how he managed that, perhaps he had the Chinese tailor around the corner repair it every morning on his way to the office, I wouldn't put it past him.

His gold cufflinks or Gucci watch (or perhaps both) flashed as he brought his arm up to touch Anna's outdated and now wind-tangled curls, he was making his move—no, he wasn't—he was just picking something out of her hair, a leaf or lint or something, he flicked it into the water. They were peering into the canal. They'd fallen silent, perhaps they were mesmerized by the lap of the water as I had been or perhaps its foul stench had jolted them out of their romantic mood. Or perhaps there was a dead body floating in the canal, that would take your breath away, every now and then you read about one drifting through the city and frightening people out of their wits before the police can snag it. 'But she would've screamed,' I thought . . . just then, she moved toward him, she touched his arm. 'Now,' I thought, 'now she's going to reveal herself, with the whisper of a single word only the two of them once knew, or a pet name or maybe she's just going to kiss him, wiping away the years with a single poison kiss though why she wants to kiss someone who was such a dick to her is beyond me . . . or maybe she's not kissing for revenge but because she *wants* to, a kiss not of vengeance but of pleasure"—she tilted her face to his, their profiles were backlit by the haze of the streetlight like in those old black-and-white movies I've passed so many dismal hours watching—

'Hey!' I stepped out of the shadows. 'Hey, how's it going?' That was the idiotic thing it occurred to me to call out as I stepped into the street, something any stranger stumbling by at that hour might say. Banyan's big face flipped in my direction as if the dark back of his head had been a mask he'd ripped off, Anna saw me, too, she hesitated, then pulled away from him. 'You guys want to have a drink?' I said. 'Let's go have a drink.' Over her shoulder Banyan was shaking his head at me. Anna glanced back. 'Well . . . '

Thunder crashed, lightning flickered behind the clouds as Anna stepped off the curb toward me. She cried out and reached for her foot, her high heel had stuck between the bricks. The rain broke open and started pouring down, it was one of those sudden downpours that soaks you instantly. Banyan stooped to help her and they both went at the shoe. They were getting in each other's way and they were going to break the spike trying to wriggle it free like that although it was, no doubt, a cheap shoe not worth the price of dry-cleaning our designer silk suits, which was definitely going to have to be done now that we'd gotten caught in the rain—not that I've done it yet, I get sick of the thousand mundane obligations required to keep up my appearance as a corporate dick and leave my silk suits crumpled on the floor where I've stepped out of them for days, it's a bad habit but it's my one way of resisting a life I never wanted to lead.

'Aah!' Anna cried triumphantly as Banyan held up the shoe, I couldn't tell in the downpour if he'd broken the heel or not. She grabbed my arm and said, 'We're going to my place,' and we ran for shelter, helter-skelter down the sidewalk sticking close to the buildings where every now and then there was an awning that blocked the rain, Anna hopping along lop-sided with the one shoe dangling from her fingers. 'It's just like old times,' I thought sentimentally as we ran, our overcoats flapping against each other's legs, 'the three of us racing home after a night of drinking and dancing to continue the party at the frat house'—not that we had ever done so, we never spent much time together as a threesome, when they were going out they never invited me along and I couldn't have stomached it anyway. Now I see that wasn't an invitation last night, either, she never meant for me to come along and was merely informing me of their plans. I might have gotten the hint had it not been pouring down rain and all of us in a hurry to get out of it. That's typical, the rain is to blame for countless misunderstandings, miscommunications, and muddled exchanges, not to mention terrible moods and even worse choices."

II You're the One

'"He doesn't even fucking know who I am,' Anna hissed. Banyan had gone into the bathroom. Probably just to look at himself in the mirror even though he'd already spent five minutes smoothing his wet hair and polishing his teeth with the back of a finger in the reflection of his (dead) cell phone while we waited in the smelly foyer of Anna's run-down building, she'd insisted she go up first to 'pick the place up.' I shook my head. 'I know, it's unbelievable. What an asshole.'

But when she had followed suit, slamming the bathroom door behind her—apparently she hadn't taken the time to go while we were waiting downstairs, she must have been frantically shoving clutter under the couch or into the coat closet, wiping off the bathroom counter or covering up the used tampons in the trash or perhaps it was syringes and spoons, baggies and burners she was covering up, I hoped not, I really did—Banyan countered in a hushed voice, leaning into my ear, a heavy paw on my shoulder, 'Of course I fucking know who she is, I went out with her all junior year.' 'Oh yeah?' I whispered back. 'More like a few months sophomore year.' 'Whatever. You were always better at remembering stuff like that than me.' 'Well, shit, why didn't you tell her?' 'And get raked over the coals for being a dick ten years ago? You know how women are, man—they can't *let things go*.' 'Well, you shouldn't fuck with her. She knows who you are.' He went into the kitchen, it stank there too, it must have been coming from the trash since the dishes were all done and in the rack. He started rummaging around in the cabinets. 'Hey, she still looks pretty good.' He wolf-whistled. 'That thing on stage, that thing with the mic stand.' He flashed his Cheshire cat grin over his shoulder, baring his big wide perfect white teeth, what an idiot. But his face was dazzling, it could have been on the cover of *GQ*. 'Leave her the fuck alone, Banyan. And it was *fifteen* years ago. You're older than you think. Why don't you start acting like it?' I turned away, disgusted. I reached for a cigarette from the half-empty pack of Camels lying on the scratched synthetic wood coffee table. 'Jesus, Maddy, what's up your butt? You need a drink.' I blew a big puff of smoke in his face, he waved at it frantically (Banyan will put the most lethal combinations of liquor and drugs into his body but he has a phobia about breathing cigarette smoke, he thinks it's going to give him instant cancer). He found three glasses. 'Now let's have some fun. Let bygones be bygones, the past is past . . . What're you drinking?'

Anna's place wasn't too nice, nothing like mine and Banyan's upscale downtown apartments, his with the two-story wall of windows in the living room and the stainless steel spiral banister, mine the built-into-the-wall big screen TV and stereo system, the remote control mood lighting. It was one room with a little kitchen with an old-style black-and-white checkered linoleum floor and a hallway leading to the bed and bath. The thin flesh-color carpet had seen better days, it showed shiny threadbare paths over the most traversed routes in the house, the walls were bare and the only furniture was the coffee table, a black vinyl couch with a rip across one arm where the stuffing squirmed out and an equally ratty upholstered chair. A TV and stereo with hundreds of cds stacked neatly in their cases and a very healthy viney plant hanging in the window, in fact it was so healthy it was crawling over the wall like it was trying to take over the apartment. No personal touches, no family pictures or memorabilia, not even stuck up by magnets on the refrigerator. There was one magnet on the fridge—it advertised a plumbing business, that must be a service she used a lot in that crusty building—and under it was a photograph ripped from a magazine of a guy with tattoos covering his back, arms, neck and face, which was half-turned to the camera and smiling, even his bald scalp and ears were tattooed, every inch of skin was covered, impressive, no doubt, if you're into that kind of thing, personally I found it unappealing nor could I see Anna being into that kind of guy. Then again I hardly knew her anymore, so much time had passed.

'Jack and Coke. Lots of ice,' she said behind us. She was standing in the doorway. One high heel swung from her fingers, sure enough, the goon had broken it off. Her red hair appeared darker now that it was damp, it curled around her face in a sexy way, making her gray eyes look paler. She'd refreshed her lipstick, it was bright red and there was a wild look in those eyes I didn't know about.

'You look good.' Banyan's eyes followed the lines of her body in the close-fitting black satin. 'So—this is my buddy Nick . . . ' She slipped the ruined shoe on before putting her hand out, I took it, it was soft and warm and still slightly damp, she must have dried it hurriedly in the bathroom, she wouldn't want to leave us alone in her apartment too long. Smirking, she spoke her real name (I've changed it to protect the innocent), and I smirked back.

He dropped the cubes in, not taking the bait, whiskey and Coke was what we drank all the time in college and she must have known it. There was a brand new bottle of Jack Daniels on the counter, of course she'd gone out and bought it just for tonight. There were two lamps on, she crossed the room in her bare feet following one of those threadbare paths in the disgusting carpet and switched one off. It dawned on me perhaps she didn't *want* him to remember her. Perhaps she wanted a second chance at the heartbreaker who got away: 'I'll turn the lights down so he won't remember the face he didn't want.' As she leaned into the circle of lamplight I saw her strong shoulders, I didn't remember Anna's shoulders being that strong—her backless dress afforded a good view of them, the dress tied or snapped around her neck to hold it on or rather, allow it to slip off more easily—I was sure those shoulders were skinnier in college and her biceps less muscled, too, 'she's a different woman now,' I thought. 'She's an entirely different woman, as are Banyan and I different people even if we think and act exactly the same. Maybe he's right and we should let the past lie, let bygones be bygones and all . . .'

He brought our drinks in and stood in the middle of the room looking around. 'Nice place,' he must have meant it ironically but he didn't make it obvious, at least he was being polite. Anna shrugged. 'It's not really my style, but thanks.' She hung her stole and our overcoats on the back of the door, they were both wet but you can't ruin fake fur or waterproof overcoats, our expensive silk suits, on the other hand, would fare worse. My pantlegs and socks were soaked, it was a miserable feeling. I asked for a towel and she brought two from the bathroom but Banyan declined his. 'What for?' he grinned. 'I won't melt.' He shook himself all over like a dog and Anna laughed a screechy laugh, a laugh like a tightly coiled spring.

'Where can I plug in my phone? The fucker won't hold a charge to save its life, I've gotta order a new battery, it lost me a sale the other day, did I tell you that, Madsen?' he rattled on. She showed him an outlet and he fiddled with the phone, when it finally came on it made a series of annoying beeps. He stared at it with some alarm. 'Um, pardon me,' he mumbled and rushed into the hall with the cord dangling.

Anna and I stood uncertainly holding our drinks. 'His wife is a French bitch,' I said, I was a little drunk and it was making me blunt, anyway it's true, I don't like Monique, I never have. 'Is she?' she said, too eagerly. 'Like how?' 'Like this kind of shit, he can't even go out anymore without her all over him, she monitors everything we do, she's like the party police.' 'Ha ha, that's just what he deserves.' 'For sure.'

I pulled a chair in from the kitchen and she sat down in the rocker. She crossed her legs, the slit in her dress riding up the thigh, the seam looked like it was strained to the breaking point, I hoped it didn't burst open, I didn't want to see any more of those thighs than I'd already seen on stage. She had nice legs, she'd always had them, in college she was on the cross country team and there's nothing like running to keep your calves in shape, I should do more of it myself, I should spend my lunch hours in the company's basement gym instead of with bloody marys or Guinness pints at the restaurants across the street. Her legs were bare—women don't wear panty hose any more like they did back in college, you hardly even see hookers in fishnets these days, it's disappointing—and bone-white, they shone translucently like the legs of a wax mannequin, truth be told it wasn't that attractive.

We could hear Banyan talking in the hallway though not clearly enough to make out his words. She drained her glass and stared into it. 'I don't even care. I know I never meant anything to him, I see that now. Not even enough that his memory bothered to keep a file on me. I guess we only remember what we want to, and black out what we'd rather forget.'

I was debating whether to blow his cover and tell her the truth—it wasn't right, he was hurting her all over again, *the nerve*—when Banyan came in. 'I gotta go. She's called *thirteen* times. That's not a good sign.' I rolled my eyes. 'Well what did she say?' 'She said to get my ass home, what she always says.' 'Did you tell her you were with me?' Monique seems to think I'm harmless, not that she likes me but she thinks I'm harmless, probably she thinks I have more trouble getting women than in actuality I do, I'm not as good-looking as Banyan but I've never had any trouble getting girls even if some of them it takes a few drinks. 'What? I didn't talk to her.' 'I thought you just talked to her.' 'No! Why would I do that? I was calling a cab but the bastards hung up on me.' He went to the door, wriggled into his damp overcoat. 'I hope nothing's happened,' he said, meaning, I hope she hasn't found out how I really spend my nights out, I hope one of the head cases I've slept with hasn't spray-painted some vile insult across the garage door or something (like they do in the movies, sometimes real life isn't that far off). 'I'm supposed to care,' I thought, 'but the truth is I don't, I don't give a damn if Monique keeps calling, in fact I hope she calls *me*, I can't *wait* until Monique calls me so I can tell her everything, everything she ought to know,' but all I said was, 'You'd better get going then.'

Anna had gone into the kitchen, I guessed she didn't want to hear about his wife. Now she reappeared in the doorway, she was holding something behind her back and she wasn't doing a very good job of concealing the fact if she was trying to conceal it, I thought it was the whiskey bottle.

'I'm gonna head out,' said Banyan. 'It was nice to meet you.' He stepped in and kissed her on the cheek. 'This was fun, I had a great time, you're beautiful.' A string of pointless phrases came out of his mouth, the Turret's syndrome of the playboy.

'Oh, don't,' she said. 'Don't go yet. We were just getting started. ' He took this as an innuendo, he stepped in again and trailed his fingers down her ribs. 'Oh, baby, if you only knew, how I wish I could stay. But—' he reached for the doorknob, giving a back-handed wave—'duty calls—'

That's when she brought the gun out. It looked just like the guns you see on TV in crime dramas or detective shows, I've watched enough to know. She pointed it at Banyan's back.

'*Tyler*,' she said. It was strange to hear his first name, I almost never heard it, not even the guys at work used it, even the company CEO called him Banyan as if they were old frat brothers (though he called me Nick). 'Okay,' he said, like a kid caught in the cookie jar. He turned, grinning.

'It's you,' she said. Her words swerved but the gun she held steady. 'You're the one.' We waited for her to say more—'you're the one who fucked me over,' 'you're the one who ruined my life'—but she didn't. She didn't say another word, she just cocked the trigger.

I have to say I enjoyed watching his smart-ass grin vanish and all the blood drain from his face. His fat lips tremble and his legs shake in his loafers. I barely recognized him, it was fantastic."

III I'm Not the One

"The trigger when she cocked it made that sinister clicking sound exactly like it does on TV or in the movies—*click,* a single sharp *click,* eerily familiar—'it's like we're in one of those detective shows,' I thought, 'only I don't want to know what happens next, because in those shows someone always ends up dead on the floor, and it's usually not the good-looking villain but the minor character or sidekick, which would be me.'

Banyan was standing there shaking, his palms in the air like he was being arrested. 'Don't shoot! Don't shoot! I didn't do anything, I'm sorry. I'm sorry, I didn't do anything.' That must have got her, his sheer cowardice, because Anna started laughing. She let the trigger down and the gun clicked but nothing happened. 'I'm *kidding,*' she said, barely controlling her urge for the giggles. 'Relax.' He lowered his hands warily. 'Oh Jesus oh Jesus oh Jesus. You got me. You really got me.' 'But . . . I do believe you're staying.'

He looked at me. 'It's empty,' I said expositorily. 'It's not loaded.' Anna frowned. 'Well, that chamber's empty. This is a .45 Automatic and if you know anything about guns at all—' she chuckled—'and I'm sure you guys don't, you city boys have probably never even seen one up close'—but I *have,* I wanted to correct her, I've seen hundreds zoomed in on and in black and white and color both—'this particular one holds seven rounds. The other chambers we'll have to see about. Now *sit down,* Tyler.' She waved the gun at the couch. 'Let's have a drink together, for old times' sake. Now that the charades are over.'

Banyan perched on the edge of the couch, I was on the other end and I could see his hands still trembling in the cuffs of his overcoat as he picked up his whiskey, I couldn't help taking some satisfaction in that. The huge wet coat bunched up under him but he didn't seem to notice or care. He started tapping his foot frenetically on the floor, a thing he does when he's wound up and it drives me nuts. Anna set the gun on the arm of the chair and sat down too, crossing her legs in the tight dress, the pointed toes of her shoes pointing at us, better them than the gun. The two of them looked at each other, silent . . .

At last she raised her glass, a sliver of amber liquid swinging in the bottom, she'd made a good dent in it already. 'To the good old days,' she said. 'To the old days,' I said, raising mine. 'Were they really that good, or do they just seem that way now?' 'They just seem that way,' Anna said. Banyan snorted. 'They were better.' She arched a single pencil-darkened eyebrow. 'Oh really? Nicky says you've done pretty well for yourself. Money, a beautiful wife, a fabulous apartment . . . ' He shrugged, he was pouting, he didn't like being pushed around. 'I've done all right.' She leaned up, giving us a free glance at her cleavage, took a cigarette from the pack I'd already helped myself to and lit it. She blew the smoke at Banyan. 'You didn't even fucking know me.' 'I knew you. I just didn't want to embarrass you. I was trying to be *nice*.' That surprised her, she hadn't seen that coming, nor had I, it was a genius move I have to admit. She considered it, pursing her lips, circling her fingers on her thigh. Finally she said simply, 'Nice?' 'Well, I mean, you've changed a little . . .' She turned to me. 'Do you think I've changed, Nicky?' I shifted in my damp trousers, crossed my legs. 'Umm . . . well the gun seems a little—I was wondering what you're doing with a gun.' 'I had one back in college, too. Or don't you remember?'

The memory of her standing on my desk chair holding a gun to her head flickered in my head. Mascara was streaking down her cheeks, her hair all over the place, her toga had slipped to show a yellow bikini swimsuit top beneath. 'Well,' I said, re-crossing my legs the other way, 'if you're talking about a certain night—' She cut me off. 'Yes, asshole. I'm talking about a certain night.' She stood up, I'd gotten under her skin, she circled the room, taking the gun with her not that she was pointing it at anything, she carried it down at her side more like a high heel than a lethal weapon, then again, high heels can be lethal weapons, especially spikes like hers and I'm sure they've been used successfully by many a woman in dire straits. She touched the ambitious plant at the window. 'The night I almost killed myself over this bastard.'

Her cigarette was burning in the ashtray, she didn't care, she had something to say. 'I was upset because he'd cheated on me. I saw him making out with another girl, some sorority slut, one of those Barbie dolls, a blond with a fake tan, that was the kind he went for, he and every other guy, stupid girls like that, I hated girls like that in college which made it even worse, nobody likes to be cheated on and then with somebody like that. I freaked out, I know I overreacted but I was nineteen, you know. I liked him but we weren't that serious'—she continued to use the third person for a person who was sitting right in front of her, perhaps she was trying to appear as if she was telling the story for my sake though we all knew whose she was telling it for—she waved her hand, 'it's not like I was in love with him or anything.' 'That's not how I remember it,' I thought.

She went on, contradicting herself but she didn't seem to notice, 'Even though we were getting kind of serious. I mean, he was, he'd started talking about bringing me home to meet his parents on Christmas break, he even told me he loved me. So when I saw them of course I was like, what the fuck? And you know how much we drank back then, I was totally wasted, I ran all the way across campus barefoot in my toga. I had this bright idea I was going to get my revolver and go back to the party and scare the wits out of him with it, luckily I sobered up enough not to, I'd have been the laughing stock of the whole campus if I'd done that. Not that I was planning on using it, I just wanted to get him back, freak him out a little . . . My dad gave me this revolver to take with me to school and I've had it ever since, I even take it to work these days, it's a rough business as you can imagine. My family's a bunch of hicks, we all "pack," ha. My dad thinks everybody should in the city, he thinks all cities are like . . . what's that place in the Bible?' 'Babylon?' I ventured. 'Sodom and Gomorrah, that's it. I've known how to shoot'—she looked at the pistol like it was a beloved pet—'since I was a little girl, I'm not afraid of guns but the girls in the dorms thought I was nuts for having it, they were all scared of me, ha, I had fun with that. But Dad thought I needed a firearm to protect me from all the robbers and rapists and thugs at school, he never guessed I'd turn out to be the one myself, the one I needed protecting from although that's not exactly the whole truth because'—she hadn't looked at Banyan all this time, now she did, she aimed her gaze and switched to the second person—'the truth is it was *you,* you're the one.'

Banyan looked back at her boredly. I knew he was on edge, though, his foot crossed on his knee was vibrating a million miles an hour. Once again he didn't take the bait so I did, 'let's get on with this,' I thought, 'I haven't got all night,' although, of course, I did, I had that night and every other one thereafter as far into the future as I could see. 'He's the one what?'

'The one to blame for what I did that night. Oh, I didn't hurt myself. Obviously I didn't kill myself even though I went with that idea for a while, thank god, he's not worth it. But I did kill something and I'll never forgive myself for it.'

We waited to hear what she had killed but she paused—I took the opportunity to lean forward and stub out her cigarette, moving very slowly, you always want to move at a turtle's pace when in the presence of someone wielding a gun, especially when that someone is unstable, which most gun wielders are. That reminded her, she left the gun on the sill and came to the coffee table, she took another one from the pack and lit it, rocking on her compromised heels, for an instant I thought she was going to topple over but she recovered. I could feel Banyan looking at me to do something, he was too far away to and she was right there by me, right there, I could have grabbed her wrist and it would have all been over. But then we may have never known the rest of the story.

She backed away to the window, smoking. She raised the window a few inches and bent to exhale out it, keeping us in the corner of her eye, I could see that. She straightened and crossed her arms over her chest, took a breath. 'After stopping by Nicky's room and getting nothing, no sympathy at all, he couldn't even look up from his precious *Star Trek* to see me blow my brains out—' 'I thought it was a toy!' I protested, she didn't care, too many years had gone by when I'd never mattered to her in the first place, it was all about Banyan, he was the locus of her world, and her life, she was gradually revealing whether she wanted to or not, had orbited around him like a moon around a planet. 'I quickly gave up that idea, I figured if I couldn't even get a rise out of Nicky it wouldn't have much impact on you. Somehow I ended up driving—bright idea wasted as I was but you know how you are in college, and that's how I always calmed myself down, I went for a drive. I don't remember even where it happened, I know I went west on the freeway a long ways but after that it's all hazy, I have a flash of driving like a maniac down some hilly dirt roads, going like a hundred, it's a wonder I didn't crash and paralyze myself or something. At some point I pulled off the road. I had the gun in the seat next to me and it was begging to be used. I was so fucking *mad*, see, and once you get a gun out you're going to use it sooner or later.' Banyan and I exchanged looks. 'For some reason I pulled off by some horses in a pasture. I've always loved horses, I grew up riding, I bet you didn't know that about me, I rode all over the mountains bareback, it was beautiful, some of my favorite childhood memories are with horses—or they used to be. Now I can't even think about them.' She shuddered. 'Yeah, that's right, I shot a horse. I stopped the car, went over to the fence and like I was possessed or something, like there was someone else inside me, someone I didn't even know because I would have never done that myself but then I did do it, I took aim through the boards, it was one of those nice white-railed fences, a fancy horse farm, breeders or racehorses, expensive horses. I aimed at this little brown horse—a baby, who knows how old but not that old—and pulled the trigger and it went over like a piece of cardboard. God, it was terrible.'

She took a last drag, let it out and flicked the butt out the screenless window. The rain was coming down hard outside. We could hear it drumming the streets and the side of the building, I looked out the window at it pouring down in silver streaks or bullets, Anna did too, or perhaps she wasn't looking at the rain at all, perhaps she was seeing her reflection in the glass instead. I could see her face there, elongated in the murky, fogged-up pane, the eyes dark holes, the mouth distorted, it reminded me of that creepy painting *The Scream* which along with *The Kiss* was popular on dorm room walls back then. Banyan uncrossed his legs, cleared his throat. 'You dropped out of school because of a horse?'

She covered her face with her hands and spoke through them. 'You don't understand. *You* wouldn't understand because you've probably never been near a horse or an animal of any kind. It doesn't matter. That's not why I told you. I didn't even plan on telling you any of this . . . I just wanted you to *know*. What you did, the consequences of what you did to me.'

'Hey, I'm not the one. You're the one who pulled the trigger. Sorry, lady, but that's how it is.' For a second I thought she was going to grab the gun and blow a hole in him, the sheer hatred in her eyes. Then it was gone and she was sobbing into her hands, 'I'm a stripper, I'm a fucking stripper,' and I could see what it was all about.

'You're a singer really,' I said gently. 'A damn good one, too. I think you've got a great voice.' *Snort!* Banyan made a pig-like noise through his nose. 'Ah, Nicky, always the gentleman. Yeah right, she's good at something—.' There were footsteps on the landing, the thunks of heavy boots. A key clicked in the lock—needlessly, no one had bothered to lock it when we came in—and the knob turned. A twin or clone of the meathead bouncer that had tried to molest me earlier in the night stepped into the room—it wasn't the same guy but at first I thought it was, it gave me a jolt. He was a skinhead with a broad chest and formidable biceps in his white muscle shirt. Tattooes covered his bare arms that were glistening with rainwater, that explained the picture on the fridge, that must have represented his tattoo aspirations, it was something to shoot for but he had a long ways to go. His zippered leather jacket was slung over his shoulder, he didn't need a jacket in the rain and no doubt wouldn't have been caught dead in an overcoat. He grunted acknowledgement, he hardly looked surprised to see us, perhaps Anna had men like us over all the time or at least on her work nights. He stumbled down the hall and slammed the bedroom door, he was done partying for the night or had no interest in partying with our types. 'It's actually Scottie's place,' Anna said, wiping her mascara-smudged eyes. 'I'm staying with him for a few weeks. I had to move out of my old place for a while. I was . . . ' She sighed. 'Well . . . I was in rehab.'

'Rehab? You've been drinking all night,' I pointed out. 'It was for other stuff. Alcohol doesn't bother me, alcohol I'm fine with.' Anna left the window and came back and sat down in her chair, this time putting the gun on the coffee table between us, though nearer her than us. Banyan ran his cool black eyes over her body as if seeing her anew in light of this information. He'd been sitting with his legs open slouched down in the squishy couch, jiggling the ice in his sweating drink with his mouth half-open, now he sat up and sat his drink down, adjusted the coat he'd never taken off. He leaned up and looked Anna in the eyes. In a low voice—a voice he must have preferred I didn't hear—he said, 'You are one wild lady. Why did I ever let you go?'

Anna leaned up to meet him. Her face showed nothing, I was watching it carefully but it showed no sign of being moved by those words she must have longed to hear for so many years, instead her hand reached out, I thought she was going for the gun but instead she touched Banyan's hand. She trailed her fingertips in a single stroke, almost a claw, over the back of his huge hand, I could almost feel them on my own skin, those long red nails, their tender bite and the softness of the fingers beneath. I thought Banyan was going for the gun too but he went for her knee, he put his big hand over her bare knee, cupping it, he made little circles with his fingers on the knee. 'So he still has his priorities straight,' I thought, 'sex before life-or-death.' He gave it a moment, he let it take effect, he was a "sexpert" after all or that's what he liked to call himself, a term that made me cringe.

Anna's eyelids lowered. With his other hand he snatched up the gun. She didn't even jump, she was done with it. He tossed it to me, scaring the daylights out of me.

I caught it like a hot potato. 'What do you want me to do with it?' 'I don't know, get rid of the bullets or whatever.' I fumbled with the gun, feeling like Colombo or rather, Colombo's apprentice, Peter Falk would never have been so clumsy with a firearm. 'Here. Give it to me,' Anna said calmly. 'I can do it, I've seen this done before,' I lied. I managed to get what I thought was the cartridge or magazine, the thing in the handle that held the bullets, dislodged. It was empty. I thunked the gun on the table. 'It's empty,' I said. Banyan threw up his arms. 'Oh for chrissake!' Anna looked surprised but she could have been faking it. 'Is it? I wasn't sure . . . ' she murmured.

'I'm outta here,' Banyan said though he didn't stand up. 'I've had enough of this . . . *horse*shit.' Anna blew two jets of smoke out her nose. 'Oh, that was a low blow. That was really—was that necessary? Anyway chill out'— her words slurred, she really had drank a lot, we all had by that time—'I didn't give you a scare back then, maybe I wanted to give you one now. It was all in fun. So maybe my life hasn't turned out like I wanted and I blame you. So what. Whose life has turned out like they wanted it to?' I hoisted my glass in the air. 'That's it,' I said. 'That's the thing we have to face at this point—that our lives look nothing like what we hoped or dreamed they would when we were in college and even less so when we were kids. We have to face the fact that what we did with them looks nothing like what we wanted to do.' 'Shit,' Anna said almost happily, 'that's what it comes down to.' We clinked empty glasses. 'Speak for yourselves, you miserable shits,' Banyan said. 'I've done exactly what I wanted to with my life and everything I said I would in college. I make a lot of money, I have a great family, I still go out and have fun. I love my job. I drive a Jaguar. I hate to rain on your parade, but I have no regrets.' I set my glass down on the table, hard. I said, 'No, you wouldn't.'

He met my eyes and laughed, he didn't get it. 'Our eyes have met thousands of times,' I was thinking, 'thousands or tens of thousands of times in our fifteen-year friendship but we've never really seen each other, we've never really looked because neither one of us wanted to admit if we did, we couldn't stand what we'd see.'

We all sat there for a little while after that. A weird mood had come over us, even Banyan seemed contemplative, sunk back in the couch with his legs stretched out. Anna finally slipped off those wrecked high heels, they must have been uncomfortable, some women hate high heels but she'd been sitting there with her feet stuffed in them as if they were house slippers. She set the broken one up on the table with the gun, it teetered and fell over. She gripped her glass to her chest, her eyes went stony and faraway. The rain had stopped. I could hear its drip drip drip off the eaves in the cracked window. I could hear, too, footsteps click by on the sidewalk below, perhaps it was some depressed bachelor heading back to his dark apartment after another night out drinking, where no lights would be waiting for him in the windows and no body would turn over in the bed when it heard his key in the lock, no breath would catch and no heart skip in anticipation of his hands on its body. There are plenty of people like that out there, people who have no one, people all alone in the world. It reminded me of that Beatles song, I just heard it the other day when I was out somewhere, at the grocery store or picking up the dry-cleaning—you know, the sad one, how does it go . . . *A-a-ah, look at all the lonely people . . . where do-o-o they all come from? . . . . A-a-ah, look at all the lonely people . . . where do-o-o they all belong? . . .* "

IV Here Comes the Rain

"When we got up to leave I told Banyan to go on down. 'No. Why?' 'Because I want to talk to Anna. Go on, I'm right behind you.' He gave me a look, he didn't like it but he went, shutting the door hard, Banyan is like a five-year-old sometimes, him and his kid must get along great. I waited for his steps to fade before turning to her, we were standing face to face and close, so close I could smell her breath and her skin, whiskey and rain. I met her gray eyes, the same ones I'd known so long ago. 'Look, can I call you?' She seemed surprised. 'Why?' 'You know, to talk. If you ever want to.' 'I guess.' 'What's your cell number?' 'I don't have a cell.' She reached behind me and flipped the light switch on, the light harsh on our faces. 'Never mind,' I mumbled. I went out the door and closed it, she didn't bother to stop me, not that I expected she would.

Downstairs Banyan was waiting in the foul-smelling foyer. He made a circle by his ear with his finger, the universal sign for loonie, crazy, nutso, bonkers and rolled his eyes, I knew how I was to take that, I was to take it as 'what a crazy bitch, I expect you'll not be holding any of this against me or mentioning it to anyone who doesn't need to know about it.' I laughed to show I wouldn't and he laughed too and clapped me on the back, said something about Monday morning coming too soon.

When we stepped into the street we went our separate ways. Banyan was heading downtown to grab a cab, he was in a bigger hurry than I to get home, his wife would be up soon and standing in the window smoking cigarettes and staring down at the street watching for him. He'd barely have time to catch a few winks before she'd have him up, she expected him to spend every second of his Saturdays with his young son. It was still dark but the dawn was coming on, light was showing over the tops of the buildings and a cold November wind was blowing, it wasn't going to be any more pleasant of a day than the stormy night before. Banyan invited me to share his cab but I declined, it was probably only a half hour walk to my place and I thought I'd stop and get a cup of coffee and maybe something to eat, I didn't know this part of the city that well but there would be something on the way.

I watched him stride off across the street, waving back once without turning around, the too-long tails of his overcoat flapping like black fingers, he seemed to have regained his usual jolly mood. I walked on in the near-dark. The shopkeepers were sliding their metal doors up and lights were coming on in windows. A few strangers appeared in doorways or stepped from alleys, they weren't the overcoated, suit-and-tie wearing ones I saw on my morning walk to work, it was a Saturday and anyway it was the wrong part of town for corporate dicks but they were strangers all the same and they hurried past like ghosts, bent against the wind. Up ahead on the corner a figure moved but it was just an old woman struggling to open her umbrella while she waited for the bus, it wasn't my beloved, my beloved is already gone or she never existed at all. Overhead a crack of thunder, it was going to storm again. 'Of course,' I thought, 'here comes the rain, the world is out to get us, every one . . . ' I took out my cell phone. A few drops spattered on the screen as I dialed Monique, although you'll never know if I hung up before the call connected or if I went through with it, that's one thing even I'm not fool enough to tell a perfect stranger like you."

www.ingramcontent.com/pod-product-compliance
Lightning Source LLC
Chambersburg PA
CBHW050840180626
46814CB00007B/2548